REVENGE OF METALHAVEN

METAL AND BLOOD
BOOK 5

G J OGDEN

Copyright © 2024 by G J Ogden
All rights reserved.

No part of this book may be reproduced in any form or by any electronic or mechanical means, including information storage and retrieval systems, without written permission from the author, except for the use of brief quotations in a book review.

These novels are entirely works of fiction. The names, characters and incidents portrayed in it are the work of the author's imagination. Any resemblance to actual persons, living or dead, events or localities is entirely coincidental.

Illustration © Phil Dannels
www.phildannelsdesign.com

Editing by S L Ogden
Published by Ogden Media Ltd
www.ogdenmedia.net

1

DON'T EVER FORGET

THE SONOROUS BEAT of rotor blades thumped the air and Finn wheeled around, spotting three special prefect skycars hugging the electrified border fence, flying fast and low. Xia ran past him, and he caught her arm, spinning her to a stop.

"Is everyone out?" Finn asked, and the rebel shook her head.

"Not all," Xia mumbled. "Many trapped."

"Fuck, then we have to get back in there!" Finn cursed.

He turned back to the workhouse building, but for some reason the rescue trucks and evacuation teams had all left, and the flames that had almost been extinguished were taking hold once more.

"Where is everyone?" Finn wondered, turning back to Xia, but instead of the rebel commander, he found that it was Juniper Jones standing in front of him.

"You can't save them, Finn," Juniper said. She was wearing her white, satin pantsuit, instead of her commissar carapace armor, and had her hands pressed neatly together in front of her stomach. "They're already dead."

Finn reeled back then looked for Elara, but she was also gone, as were Chiefy and Scraps, and all of the rebels who'd been frantically trying to rescue children from the workhouse, after Gideon Alexander Reznikov had bombarded it from Nimbus.

"Elara!" Finn shouted, but his voice was carried away on the wind. "Scraps!" he yelled, trying to find his robot pal instead. "Scraps, I need you!"

"They're gone too," Juniper said, smiling her pleasant half-smile at him; the same smile that had tricked Finn and made him fall for her lies and deceptions. "You killed them."

"What?" Finn said, taking another step back.

"You killed them, just like you killed Owen, and all the others who were stupid enough to follow you."

"That's a lie, I've saved people," Finn hit back, stabbing a fist at Juniper. "I freed Metalhaven, and the Authority sector. I beat you!"

"And look how many have died, because of your personal vendetta," Juniper answered, coolly. She pointed at the workhouse. "The blood of those children is on your hands, Finn, not mine. You did this."

Finn looked at the enormous building, which was now fully ablaze, with flames leaping from every window. He could see shapes moving inside, shrouded by the smoke and the flames. Then he heard the terrified cries of children, begging to be saved. Begging for their lives.

"No, not again!" Finn said, as the screams continued to torture him. "I have to save them!"

Finn sprinted toward the workhouse, then out of the curtain of smoke that had enveloped the building, an army of children advanced in formation, like a cohort of Roman legionaries. Juniper Jones was leading them, but instead of her suit, she was wearing her special prefect armor and carrying a pistol.

"Juniper, get out of the way!" Finn cried, as the cohort came to a stop, blocking his path. "I have to save the children!"

"I told you, they're already dead," Juniper snarled. She was no longer smiling, and the tone of her voice matched the shadowy hue of her armor. "Sierra-seven-seven-four-two, step forward!"

A girl marched out of the formation and stopped beside Juniper. She was twelve or thirteen years old, and wearing workhouse overalls with a white patch on the shoulder.

"Zoe?" Finn said, suddenly recognizing the brave young girl who had helped to co-ordinate the rescue of her fellow orphans from the workhouse. "But you're already safe in the prosecutor barracks, in my old room. I saw you!"

"No," Juniper said, racking the slider of the pistol. "You killed her, just as you sentenced every man, woman and child in Zavetgrad to die when you defied Gideon Alexander Reznikov."

Juniper aimed the pistol at Zoe's head and pulled the trigger. The report of the weapon pierced the air so sharply it felt like Finn's heart had exploded. He tried to go to her, but his legs wouldn't move, and instead he crumpled to his knees, hands outstretched toward the dead girl.

"No, you're lying!" Finn said, pressing his fists to his eyes as tears streamed from them. "I saved her, and thousands more…"

"You haven't saved anyone, Finn," Juniper said, shaking her head. "Soon, everyone in this city will be burned to ash in a nuclear fire, and you will be the cause. You're not the Hero of Metalhaven, Finn, you're its destroyer. You're death. And if anyone deserves to die, it's you."

Finn tried to stand but he was paralyzed with guilt and fear. Then the prefect skycars turned toward the workhouse and unleashed a flurry of missiles that slammed into the building and incinerated Juniper Jones and the legion of children at her back. Finn was caught in the blast, but the fire didn't consume him instantly, and he was forced to watch as the explosion not only engulfed the workhouse, but the entire sector, and then the city itself, leaving nothing behind but ash. Then as the mushroom cloud climbed higher into the sky, obscuring Nimbus, his flesh finally melted from his bones, and he gladly welcomed the mercy of death.

Finn woke with a start, screaming and drenched in sweat, his heart racing. The room was pitch black and his skin felt ice cold. Then, suddenly, there was a hand on his chest, pressed over his palpitating heart, and its warmth filled him, and eased the tremors that were shaking his body.

"Hey, it's okay," said Elara. The light on the nightstand beside their bed was switched on, but the dim orange glow barely cut through the darkness. "You had a nightmare, but it's over now. I'm here."

"I'm okay," Finn lied, taking hold of Elara's hand, which was still clamped to his chest, like a lifeline. "I'm sorry, I didn't mean to wake you."

"You don't have to apologize," Elara said, shuffling closer and pulling the bedsheets up so that they covered them both.

"You probably did me a favor by waking me up. I don't sleep so well, either."

Finn smiled then wrapped his free arm around Elara, and hoisted the sheets up higher so that she didn't get cold, though unlike his own body, her skin was hot to the touch.

"Was it about Owen again?" Elara asked, resting her head on Finn's shoulder.

"No, not this time," Finn said. As with all of his dreams and nightmares, once he was awake, the memory of them faded quickly, and he had to concentrate to keep the experience alive in his mind. "This was about the workhouse." He laughed weakly. "I guess that's progress, of sorts."

"I know this won't help right now, but the workhouse wasn't your fault," Elara said, squeezing his chest more tightly. "You can't lose sight of that, Finn. Even if your subconscious mind won't allow you to accept it yet, it's the truth, and the truth matters."

Finn nodded and tried to smile but the muscles in his face could barely stretch to more than a resigned grimace. If it had been anyone else besides Elara with him, he'd have shrugged off his nightmare, put on a brave face, and said all the right things, but he couldn't fool her, and he didn't want to try.

"But what if the Volkovs are right, and we're only making things worse," Finn said. The version of Juniper Jones in his nightmare may not have been real, but the words she had spoken continued to plague him. "All our meddling has done is provoke Reznikov. Instead of freeing the workers of this city, we might end up being the ones who get them killed."

Elara sat up and looked at him with her fierce green eyes, and he felt suddenly intimidated by her. Despite their ever-growing closeness, Elara Cage still held a power over him that was almost supernatural in nature.

"Don't do that," Elara said, speaking now as his mentor, not his lover. "Reznikov's plan all along was to strip Zavetgrad of its resources then wipe it from the face of the Earth. The difference is that without us, everyone in Zavetgrad, whether worker or gold, would have gone on as normal, sleepwalking toward annihilation." She moved her hand from his heart and grabbed his shoulder. Her grip was so firm, it hurt. "We're all that stands between Reznikov and the end of civilization on Earth. Don't ever forget that. Don't ever forget how important you are."

Finn straightened his back. He felt suitably scolded, but more than this, Elara's pep talk had actually worked, and knocked some sense into him.

"You're important too, especially to me," Finn said, holding her gaze, despite the intensity of her stare. "We could stop Reznikov and free the city, but if I didn't have you, then none of it would matter."

Elara raised an eyebrow and the corner of her mouth turned up into a smirk.

"That's a little corny, don't you think?" Elara said, switching from mentor to partner again in a heartbeat. "I think you've spent too much time reading potboiler romance novels on your old data device."

Finn smiled then stole a kiss on her lips. "I can't help being a romantic, it's all part of the dashing 'hero' persona."

"Dashing?" Elara said, teasing him now. "I think that's a stretch. Brooding, maybe."

Finn laughed and kissed her again. "What the hell is a

potboiler romance novel, anyway?" he said, suddenly struck by something Elara had said.

"I don't really know, but I used to see the golds reading them and talking about them on trains and in cafes," Elara said. She had stopped gripping his shoulder and was now tracing a line down the center of Finn's chest with her index finger. "I got the impression that they were a bit titillating and naughty."

Finn's smile grew wider. "That's sounds like something I could get invested in," he said, sliding the bedsheet off Elara's shoulder.

"I bet you could," she whispered, then they kissed.

"Hi-hi!"

Scraps came zooming into the bedroom, waving his hands above his head. Finn jolted back and hurriedly pulled the bedsheet back over Elara's shoulders, to hide her naked body.

"Oops!" Scraps said, spinning around in mid-air and turning his back on them. "Scraps sorry!"

"It's okay, pal, we were just talking," Finn lied. His face was burning hot like the surface of the sun, and it annoyed him that Elara appeared more amused than she did embarrassed. Her unflappability was her superpower.

"Okay-kay!" Scraps said, innocently accepting Finn's excuse and spinning around again. "Scraps reminding you it trial day! Thirty-hours till Nimbus rockets launch!"

"Yes, thank you, buddy," Finn said. "We were just about to get ready."

Finn didn't need reminding that in only a few hours, he and Elara would attempt another seemingly impossible feat, and try to steal aboard a Nimbus rocket, bound for the space citadel. It had consumed his thoughts ever since the plan had been agreed, apart from during the merciful four hours of sleep he'd just woken from, and the even more precious few minutes with Elara just then, when his troubles seemed a world away.

"Are you both ready?" Chiefy said, poking his head around the door. The foreman robot then saw that they were still very much not ready, and covered his eyes. "Oh, I do apologize. I hope I wasn't interrupting anything... titillating..."

Since his reinstatement in a Gen-VII body, the robot had developed a mastery of smut and subtle innuendo, and Scraps giggled, finding Chiefy's brazenness to be highly amusing.

"You weren't interrupting anything, but you are now," Finn said, giving as good as he got. "Now, if you both don't mind getting lost so we can get out of bed, that would be great."

"No hurry," Chiefy said, still shielding his mechanical eyes. "Saving the human race can wait until you've... finished..."

"We're not doing anything!" Finn protested, but Chiefy had already slipped away, and Scraps was flying out of the door too, playing along with his robot friend by also shielding his eyes.

"Those robots are getting worse," Finn said, shaking his head. "The thing is, I don't know which one is the bad influence, Chiefy or Scraps."

"If you ask me, I blame the master programmer," Elara said, before sliding off the mattress and whipping the sheets off the bed to wrap around herself. "Now hurry up and get dressed, we have a big day ahead of us."

Elara slipped away and locked herself in the master

bathroom, leaving Finn naked and exposed, like a newborn baby. Cursing, he grabbed a pillow and used it to hide his embarrassment, before tentatively getting off the bed. He heard snickering from outside, then saw two shadows lurking near the door. One was shaped like an oil-can, and the other was seven-feet tall.

"I can hear you two out there, you know that, right?" Finn said, though the snickering continued. He looked around the bed for his base layer uniform, then remembered that he'd put it through the laundry processor before going to sleep. "How about you do something useful, and find my goddamn clothes!"

Chiefy appeared outside, with Finn's base-layer in his hands. The robot then threw the two-piece jumpsuit at Finn, and he caught it, dropping the pillow in the process, and exposing himself once again. He cursed and shook his fist at the doorway, but the robot tag-team had already snuck away, and all Finn could hear was the echo of their laughter.

2

CALM BEFORE THE STORM

Finn turned off the faucet and rested his forehead against the cool, tiled wall of the shower cubicle. The bathroom was still thick with steam, and he drew in a long breath through his nose, allowing the hot, soap-scented vapors to percolate, like tea leaves in a pot. Yet nothing could wash away the memory of the workhouse being hit by missile strikes and reduced to rubble. He'd only just started to accept that nothing would ever stop his subconscious mind from tormenting him about Owen's death, but he hadn't banked on an even more traumatic event taking its place.

"Hey, are you okay in there?" Elara said, banging gently on the bathroom door.

"Yeah, I'm almost done," Finn called back. "I'll be out in a minute."

Finn pushed himself off the wall then drew back the shower screen, allowing the cooler air in the bathroom to wash over him. Grabbing a cotton bath towel, another luxury that the golds of the Authority enjoyed, he quickly dried himself then pulled on his base-layer uniform, before staring at himself in the mirror. The glass was heated, creating a circular window in the center of the mirror that was free of steam. Finn leaned closer and stared into his own eyes, but while his face was unchanged, accounting for a few extra scars, the man in the mirror was nothing like the Finn Brasa he had once known.

The razor that Finn had used to shave off his stubble was still beside the sink, and he picked it up, before resting the blade on his chin and pressing gently. There was sting of pain, and he breathed a sigh of relief. *I can still feel...* he thought, watching a trickle of blood meander a chaotic path across his skin, before dripping into the wide basin. *I suppose that's something...*

Suddenly, Elara pulled opened the door and Finn quickly placed the razor back onto the sink, before turning to his partner and smiling at her.

"I'm surprised you haven't shriveled up like a dead leaf, given how long you spent in here," Elara said. She was smiling, but there was concern behind her placid expression.

"I was just making the most of it," Finn said, shrugging off the comment. "Who knows when we'll next get to shower?"

Elara scowled at him then wiped the blood off his chin with her thumb, her concerned expression hardening by the second.

"Are you sure you're okay?"

"Never better!" Finn said, breezing past Elara into the bedroom, with a bounce in his step. He didn't want them to get bogged down in a conversation about whether he was 'okay'. This was no time for introspection, he told himself. "Is there anything to eat in this place? I'm starving!" he added, changing the subject.

"Sure, Chiefy brought some things in a few minutes ago," Elara said, seeming to accept Finn's answers and choosing not to push him. "You'll find most of them pretty familiar."

Finn adjusted the zip on his base-layer to ensure the uniform was fitted securely, then walked into the lounge area of their adopted quarters in the prosecutor barracks. On the dining room table were a selection of breakfast items, and Finn smiled broadly, recognizing them at once, just as Elara said he would.

"It's like a mini breakfast spread from when I was training here at the barracks," Finn said, making a direct line to the plate of croissants. He picked up one of the pastries and took a hearty bite. It was just as he remembered.

"Make sure you drink some of the fruit juice too," Elara said, joining him and helping himself to scrambled eggs and bacon. "It's full of electrolytes that will help keep us hydrated and fresh."

Finn nodded then considered grabbing himself a few slices of bacon too, before he remembered the pig he'd seen floating in a jar in Laboratory Seven, back in the Metalhaven gene bank, and he lost his appetite.

"Whose place was this, anyway?" Finn said, idly looking around the palatial suite inside the prosecutor barracks that they'd temporarily adopted as their personal quarters.

"It belonged to Voss." Finn noted a touch of acid in Elara's tone as she mentioned the former Chief Prosecutor and Judge General of the Authority.

"Dante Voss..." Finn said, stepping back from the breakfast table. It was a name he'd forgotten, until then, and it stunned him, like being slapped across the face. "What happened to Apex, anyway? The last time I saw Voss, he was flying Ivan Volkov and Tonya Duke out of the test crucible, just before I…"

Finn paused, as the unhappy memory of him abandoning a badly wounded Elara during his test trial, flooded his thoughts. It was that act that had led to Elara being captured and tortured by Juniper Jones. It was far from his proudest moment; despite the fact everything had worked out well in the end.

"Before you left me and escaped to Haven?" Elara said, finishing Finn's sentence for him. Finn looked at his feet, shame coloring his cheeks, but Elara grabbed his arm and squeezed it gently. "And before you came back to rescue me, like the damned fool hero that you are," she added, stressing Finn's redeeming act with more gusto.

"You would have done the same for me," Finn said. Now it was bashfulness that was flushing his skin, instead of guilt.

"If you say so," Elara answered, shrugging.

Finn narrowed his eyes at his partner, who was trying hard to conceal a smile by stuffing her face with three slices of bacon. Scraps chortled from across the far side of the room, where he and Chiefy were plugged into a power outlet, recharging. Finn redirected his glower at the robots, who began to look around the room, acting casual, as if they hadn't been eavesdropping at all.

"Do we know what happened to Voss?" Finn said, while filling a glass with fruit juice. He'd decided to avoid anything on the table that might have originated from jar-pig.

"I asked Xia to check into it a while back, but so far, nothing," Elara replied. "I had expected Voss to show up at my trial, but there was no sign of him there, either. It's like he disappeared."

"Maybe Ivan punished Voss for insulting him, and for not preventing my escape to Haven?" Finn suggested. "Maybe he was even executed."

"Now wouldn't that be something?" Elara said, wistfully. She picked up her plate and carried it in one hand, while she began a quick tour of Voss' old quarters. "Sadly, though, I think Apex is still alive, and to be honest, it pisses me off not knowing where he is."

Finn downed his juice in one, like he was racing Elara to drink a pint of ale, then picked up his plate and followed her. Elara had stopped at a bookcase and was picking through its contents, which contained a mixture of trophies and medals, framed photographs, and other mementos of the man's illustrious career, leading up to his appointment as Chief Prosecutor.

"What are these?" Finn said, stopping at a rack of medals dangling from the wall beside the bookcase.

"Each one marks ten kills in the crucible," Elara said.

Finn frowned then counted the number of medals. There were ten in total.

"A hundred kills..." Finn said, the words escaping his mouth as a sigh.

"More than most, fewer than some," Elara commented. "He was promoted to Chief Prosecutor after his hundredth kill, otherwise he would have gone on to amass a great many more. Probably more than any other prosecutor in history."

"Even more than your old mentor, Magnus Drexler?" Finn asked.

Elara's mentor, the infamous 'Ironclaw', had carried out

one hundred and seventy kills inside the crucible, before Elara had secretly poisoned the man and murdered him.

"Apex would have surpassed even him, yes," Elara replied, without any doubt. "Voss wasn't cruel, or particularly brutal. He didn't enjoy killing, like most prosecutors did. Instead, he saw it as his vocation, and it was professional pride that compelled him to be the best. Voss killed quickly, without risking himself. That's why he was chosen to lead the prosecutor academy, because he understood the art of murder better than anyone else."

"It almost sounds like you admire him?" Finn said, recognizing the chilling undertones of The Shadow, Elara's prosecutor persona, in the tone of her responses.

"I respect his ability," Elara answered, curtly. "But I don't admire him. I loathe him, just as I loathed all of the prosecutors, myself most of all."

Finn paused, considering whether to challenge Elara over her self-condemnation, but just as he didn't want to be consoled or coddled, he sensed that Elara didn't either. *This is no time for introspection*, he reminded himself.

"Hi-hi!" Scraps said.

Finn turned from the bookcase to see Scraps hovering in the middle of the room, fully recharged. Chiefy was standing to attention behind him, his Gen-VII foreman robot body freshly oiled and tuned-up.

"Hey, pal, are you all set?" Finn asked.

"Yes-yes!" Scraps said, hovering closer. "One hour to go. Finn-Finn and Elara-good must get ready!"

"Shit, an hour until the trial?" Finn said. He checked the clock on the wall and saw that his robot buddy was correct. "We have to get suited up."

"I will assist you," Chiefy said, jumping into action.

The robot stomped over to where Finn and Elara's weapons and armor had been neatly stacked in the corner of the room. Chiefy had worked his magic on them, hammering out any dents and ensuring that the armor panels gleamed and that the weapons were charged, sharpened, and in pristine condition.

"Do you think Ivan will fall for our plan?" Finn asked.

"Whether he falls for it or not, we have to be on one of those rockets," Elara replied, as ever undeterred by their slim odds of success. "Only from on board Nimbus can we stop Reznikov from nuking the city."

Finn nodded and sighed. In truth, he didn't need to go over the plan again, because he knew it off by heart. He was just looking for something to occupy the time, while Chiefy got their equipment ready. The plan, such as it was, was simple. The Authority central square had been converted into a miniature crucible for the sole purpose of putting Maxim Volkov and Gabriel Montgomery on trial. Ivan Volkov cared nothing for the former regent of Metalhaven, but Finn's belief was that rather than witness his father be bludgeoned to death at the hands of a hundred foremen, Ivan would attempt an armed rescue. Then, when the Authority forces were distracted, General Riley would launch an attack on Spacehaven, throwing Ivan's prefects into disarray, and allowing Elara and Finn to sneak inside the sector, and board one of the last few rockets to Nimbus. Like all simple plans, it sounded easy on paper, but it ignored the fact that an army of prefects and special prefects stood in the way of achieving their goal.

"Please stand with your legs shoulder-width apart, and your arms out to your sides," Chiefy said, approaching Finn.

Finn did as he was instructed and Chiefy worked fast to attach his armor panels to his base layer uniform. Before long, only Finn's chest plate remained, but as Chiefy offered the panel up to his body, Elara stepped forward and stopped the robot from completing the action.

"Let me do this last part," she said, smiling at the robot.

"Of course," Chiefy said, handing the chest plate to her then stepping back.

"Do you remember your armoring ceremony?" Elara said, replacing Chiefy in front of Finn.

"I remember that you were pissed off at me," Finn replied. He huffed a laugh. "And for good reason, as usual."

"Then let's do it properly, this time," Elara said.

Finn nodded then stood tall as Elara raised the final section of armor and hovered it in front of his chest.

"May this armor protect you as you dispense justice in the name of Haven, and the workers of Zavetgrad," Elara said, paraphrasing the words from his original armoring ceremony. The armor panel snapped into place.

"Redeemer!" chanted Chiefy and Scraps in harmony with one another.

Elara then collected Finn's laser cannon and the modified spear that he'd taken from the custodian robot that Chiefy had defeated in the regents' sub-oceanic complex.

"These weapons are the means through which you will deliver righteous judgement to those who have been oppressed," Elara added, snapping the weapons into their places.

Chiefy and Scraps chanted, "Redeemer!"

Elara stepped back. "Together with these weapons and armor, you are more than a man and you are more than gold," she continued. "You are the Hero of Metalhaven." She turned to Chiefy and Scraps. "Say his name!"

"Redeemer!"

Elara applauded and the two robots joined in. It was a genuine moment of celebration and Finn couldn't stop himself from smiling.

"Now, for you," Finn said. he collected a couple pieces of Elara's armor and approached her, but she stepped back and waved him away.

"That's okay, I don't really feel like celebrating my prosecutor name," Elara said. "It's hardly brought me honor."

Finn thought for a moment, but it didn't feel right to let the moment pass without recognizing everything that Elara had become, since she had first adopted the name, Shadow. Then he had an idea.

"Then how about we give you a new name?" he said, armor panels still in hand.

Elara raised an eyebrow. "What did you have in mind?" she asked, intrigued.

Finn smiled then cleared his throat and adopted a ceremonial tone of voice, mimicking the booming delivery that Dante 'Apex' Voss had been renowned for, during his tenure as Chief Prosecutor.

"In sight of those assembled, namely Chiefy and Scraps," Finn began, gesturing to the two robots, who stood to attention on cue, "and with the power granted to me by..." he thought for a second then shrugged, "by, well, no-one..." he admitted, "...you will henceforward be known as, Sentinel!"

"Sentinel!" announced Chiefy and Scraps, though the smaller robot's voice was consumed by the boisterous cheer of the larger foreman.

"Sentinel?" Elara repeated, not looking entirely convinced.

"Yes, it means guardian and protector," Finn said. "I thought it was fitting."

"I know what it means, I'm a double-five too, remember?" Elara said, still appearing cynical. Then she shrugged. "I guess Sentinel has a nice ring to it."

"Then it's decided," Finn said, offering up the first piece of armor, which snapped to Elara's base layer with a satisfying clunk. "Redeemer and Sentinel will prosecute Maxim Volkov and Gabriel Montgomery for their crimes against humanity."

Chiefy helped to fit Elara's remaining panels, then attach her crossbow and axe, before stepping back, and allowing Finn and Elara to look at themselves, side-by-side, in the mirror.

"We're ready," Elara said, making minute adjustments to her vambraces. "This will be Zavetgrad's last trial."

3

LET THE TRIAL BEGIN

Chiefy drove the ground car in front of the mayor's building, which occupied a commanding position on the Authority central square, then engaged the parking brake, but left the engine running. The sound of the powerful motor was barely audible over the murmur of the crowd that had gathered outside to witness Zavetgrad's last trial. Thousands of workers from Metalhaven had assembled, while the golds remained locked inside their luxury apartments. Even so, Finn could still see hundreds of faces, pressed to windows and peeking around the sides of curtains in the prestigious condos and apartment blocks that bordered the capital city's administrative center. The golds, too, would witness the trial, but for them it wouldn't be a celebration of justice and freedom, but an act of mourning that marked the end of their privileged existences.

"We're here," Trip said, turning to Finn and Elara from the passenger seat of the armored vehicle. "Everything is in place."

Finn nodded and grabbed the lever to open the door,

before discovering that his hand was trembling, and his heart was racing. The short journey from the prosecutor barracks to the central square had provided just enough time for intrusive thoughts to poison his mind and force him to dwell on the dangers and challenges of their gambit. It wasn't as if they hadn't faced high-stakes situations in the past, but this was different. If Finn and Elara failed on this occasion, it wasn't only their lives on the line, but the fate of every man, woman and child in Zavetgrad. Worse, success was more out of their control than ever before. Success relied on an act of humanity from a man who'd proven scarcely capable of empathy or compassion. Everything hinged on one question: did Ivan Volkov love his father enough to risk attempting a rescue?

"Keep the engine running, Chiefy," Finn said, finally twisting the door handle to release the mechanism. "If this works, we'll need to get out of here in a hurry."

"Do not worry, I am ready," Chiefy answered. Scraps was sitting in the robot's lap, interfaced with the ground car's computer. "All systems are active and standing by."

Finn blew out a shaky breath then pulled open the door fully, letting in the noise of the crowd, which rose to a tumultuous roar as he stepped out in full view of the assembled workers. Elara exited next and raised a clenched fist to the crowd, causing the roar to intensify twofold.

"Show off," Finn said, turning to humor to help deal with his anxiety. Being the center of attention was not in his nature.

"This *is* a show, Finn," Elara replied, while still smiling and waving to the crowd. "You don't have to like it; you just have to play your part."

Finn sighed again for what seemed like the hundredth time since they're left the prosecutor barracks, but he knew Elara was right. Detaching his spear from his back scabbard, his raised it high above his head then electrified the blade, causing the weapon to crackle and fizz.

"Metal and Blood!" Finn shouted, waving the spear, and conducting the crowd into a frenzy. He could feel the pressure of the sound waves vibrating his chest, as if it were an antenna that was channeling the raw energy of the crowd into his bones.

Suddenly, the tremors became more violent, and Finn realized that the ground beneath his feet was shaking too. For a horrifying moment, he wondered if it was an earthquake, or that the ancient sewer system deep beneath Zavetgrad was collapsing, and about to pull them down into a rocky grave, until he saw the tip of a rocket peek above the horizon line, followed by another, and then another.

The sound of the crowd was soon drowned out by the thunderous roar of three Solaris rockets, which were blasting off from Spacehaven at the same time. All eyes turned from Finn and Elara to watch the titanic spacecraft stretch into the sky ahead of columns of flames that burned brighter than the sun and hotter than hell. Within a minute of their launch, the trio of rockets were so high as to be almost invisible.

"That makes six in the last hour alone," Trip said. Under cover of the rocket launches, the rebel had exited the ground car without being noticed. "There are still thirty-seven more rockets being fueled and prepared for launch, but after that, Reznikov has everything he needs."

"I understand," Finn said. He hadn't needed reminding of the urgency of their mission, even before the trio of rockets had stolen attention away from his and Elara's arrival. "Find Briggs and Xia. They should be on the podium with us."

"They're already up there," Trip said, pointing to the two other rebel commanders on the stage that had been erected close to the crucible. Trip then noticed that his hand was shaking, and he quickly squeezed it into a fist and pressed it to his side in an attempt to hide his nerves, though Finn and Elara had already noticed. "I haven't had a single pint yet this morning." Trip said, explaining his jitters.

"Not even one?" Elara asked, raising an inquisitorial eyebrow at the rebel commander, and Trip caved in like rotten floorboards.

"Okay, I had one pint," Trip admitted. Elara's stare remained firm. "Fine, two pints, but for me, that counts as almost nothing."

"If this works, you can celebrate with an entire keg," Finn said, giving Trip's shoulder a comforting squeeze.

"Oh, don't you worry, I intend to," the man replied. "I've already had three more barrels moved into the prosecutor barracks."

Finn idly wondered exactly how many barrels of ale in total Trip had set aside for his planned festivities, before deciding that talk of celebration was premature. He looked up, barely able to see the rockets, which were little more than twinkling specks of light, but their destination was clear. Nimbus loomed large above the city, as it always had done, and before any congratulatory pints of ale could be drunk, he and Elara had to find a way to board it.

"Are you ready?" Elara said, stealing Finn's focus back to their immediate task.

"Not at all, but let's do this anyway," he replied.

Finn moved beside Elara then together they marched to the podium. With the Nimbus Solaris rockets already out of sight, leaving only wispy smoke trails behind to remind anyone that they had launched at all, the crowd was again focused on the Hero and Iron Bitch of Metalhaven. Climbing the wooden stairs to the platform, Finn and Elara clasped their hands together and raised them in the salute of the thousands of workers who had gathered to see justice served to Zavetgrad's last two regents. A chant of "Metal and Blood" began, and quickly built, so that the words carried to every corner of the Authority sector, and beyond. If Gideon Alexander Reznikov had been listening from his space citadel, Finn imagined that the president might have even heard the chant too.

Xia nodded to Finn then moved a wooden lectern into the center of the platform. Attached to it was a plain-looking microphone, but thanks to Chiefy and Scraps, the device had been hooked into every loudspeaker in every sector. Then a dozen giant TV screens detached from their resting places on the walls of tenement buildings and took up positions, hovering around the central square. Finn could see his face on each of the screens, blown up to a freakish size so that everyone in the city could witness the trials, whether they wanted to or not. He tried to read his own expression, which was a mix of fear, confusion and consternation that blended together to make him look suitably serious. Mercifully, the bright screens washed out the colors, so that the redness of his cheeks was blanched away.

"Ready?" Xia said, her finger poised on a switch at the microphone's base.

"Are we connected to all the recovery centers in the work

sectors too?" Finn asked, and Xia nodded.

"Robots did it," Xia mumbled, gesturing toward the armored ground car, where Chiefy and Scraps remained tucked out of sight. "Everyone listens. Everyone sees."

The sudden realization that every sector in Zavetgrad was about to witness his speech made Finn doubly nervous, but it was crucial that his announcement wasn't only heard by workers who were already free. In order to distract the prefect divisions that were holed up in force inside Spacehaven, Finn had to incite a riot on a city-wide scale. Chaos was to be their disguise. Chaos would force the prefects to turn their eyes away from the gates and sentry posts that surrounded Spacehaven, long enough that Finn and Elara could get inside. It troubled him deeply to know that in the chaos, people might die, but they no longer had a choice. Once the last of the Nimbus rockets had departed Spacehaven, Reznikov would have no further need of Zavetgrad, and the city would be annihilated by a primal force of chaos that three centuries earlier had killed billions, and rendered the planet almost uninhabitable. Finn's choice was the lesser of two evils, but in their bankrupt world, there were no good choices. The good would have to come later, assuming they survived.

"I'm ready," Finn said to Xia.

The rebel commander activated the microphone, before tapping it to check it was working. The bassy thud of Xia's finger striking the foam cover sounded like a bomb exploding. At the same time, the crowd grew silent, though they remained restless with anticipation, like a dormant volcano that was threatening to erupt.

Finn approached the lectern and grabbed the sides of the wooden plinth, partly to present an appearance of strength, but mainly to ensure that no-one could see his hands trembling. Between themselves, Finn and Elara had decided that Finn, as the face of the rebellion, should be the one to address the crowd. It was a role in which he did not feel comfortable. He was a fighter, not a politician, and he had no taste for words or rhetoric, but just as the Authority's trials were theatrical events dressed up as public tribunals, he had to put on a show to get Ivan Volkov's attention.

"For over two centuries, the Regents of Zavetgrad have used the trials to keep us afraid, but that ends today," Finn began, and the crowd exploded into cheers. "Thanks to your strength, and to the determination of our allies from Haven, who have worked tirelessly to bring about this day, the Authority has crumbled, and the people are now in control."

There were more roars from the assembled masses, followed by a renewed chant of "Metal and Blood" that seemed to electrify the air around the central square, and cause Finn's hairs to stand on end.

"Today, Zavetgrad's last surviving regents, Maxim Volkov of Spacehaven and Gabriel Montgomery of Metalhaven, will face their own brand of justice." Finn pointed to the regents, boxed inside the central square by a formation of two hundred foreman robots, and the crowd hissed and booed. "Today will be Zavetgrad's last trial, and once these tyrants have faced their fates with whatever courage their festering hearts can muster, there will not be another, and this city will finally be free!"

Another roar swept across the sector and Finn allowed it and the accompanying chants of "Metal and Blood" to build and build, to the point where they were more deafening even than the rocket launches. Inside the crucible, the foreman robots tightened their formation and marched forward, closing the net around Volkov and Montgomery. The two regents were still wearing the offenders' jumpsuits that Makehaven purples had specially created for them, though while Montgomery's clothing had been laundered prior to the trial in order to remove the stench and stain of his shame, the man had already soiled himself again. The former regent of Metalhaven was cowering in the middle of the crucible, tucked into a fetal position, while gently rocking back and forth. Finn felt a twinge of compassion for the man, before he remembered that Gabriel Montgomery had personally signed the death orders of thousands of Metalhaven workers, just like him, and any sympathy he felt vanished like smoke.

Maxim Volkov, on the other hand, remained dogged and defiant. The former mayor had picked up one of the electrified riot batons that had been left in the center of the crucible so that the two regents could defend themselves, though it was a token gesture, considering the army of robots that faced them. Even so, Volkov wielded the weapon with confidence and brio, and was even waving them on, encouraging the machines to attack, with a cocky arrogance that suggested he believed he could win.

Finn continued to watch for a moment then wet his lips and leaned into the microphone to make his next announcement. Briggs, Trip and Xia stood ready to take over the formal proceedings, while Finn and Elara embarked on the next stage of their daring plan. First, however, Finn had one final duty to perform.

"People of Zavetgrad," Finn said, and his voice thundered across the sector like it had been spoken by a god. "Let the trial begin!"

4

FOR BETTER OR WORSE

A KLAXON SOUNDED that was loud enough even to cut through the roar of the crowd, then fireworks burst into the sky above the crucible, bathing the golden streets in vivid hues of red, green, blue, purple, and more. The color of each work sector was represented, even gold, in recognition of the two offenders on trial, but this would be the very last time that the Authority's color was seen above Zavetgrad.

A second klaxon sounded then the two hundred foreman robots began to slowly close in on the regents, though only Maxim Volkov was aware of their advance, since Gabriel Montgomery remained insensible. A smaller group of five broke away from the main pack and marched faster, electrified nightsticks outstretched in their hands. Maxim Volkov let out a blood-curdling war cry then charged, hacking and slashing at the closest machine before a nightstick was thrust into the man's back. Volkov screamed in agony and dropped to one knee, but the man's cry of pain was drowned out by the bloodthirsty cheer of the crowd, who were savoring every exquisite second of the regent's downfall.

Finn and Elara used this moment to slip away, nodding to Trip, Briggs and Xia as they did so. The rebel commanders replaced them on the podium. The hope was that the audience would remain too engrossed in the spectacle of the trial to notice them leave, and as they hurried back to the armored ground car, its side door swung open waiting for them, their suspicions were confirmed. Despite their celebrity status, nothing competed with watching Maxim Volkov receive a dose of righteous retribution.

"Floor it, Chiefy, we don't have a lot of time," Finn said, slamming the door shut behind him.

"I would say not, judging by Volkov's performance so far," the robot replied, accelerating away from the crucible then quickly angling the ground car down a side street and out of sight. "I doubt he will last another sixty seconds."

"The foremen in the arena are only there to stop Volkov from escaping, they won't kill him," Elara replied, anxiously tapping the crossbow on her hip. "We need that bastard to stay alive, at least until Ivan charges to his rescue."

"So, you are using Maxim Volkov as bait?" Chiefy asked. The robot had not been party to the finer details of their plan, since he'd had another task to perform, one which was soon to bear fruit.

"That's right," Finn answered. "Ivan won't stand for his father being tormented and humiliated in front of the worker class. If love for his father doesn't drive him out of hiding, pride will."

Chiefy nodded, though even with the robot's relatively limited array of facial expressions and mannerisms, it was clear that the machine considered their plan distasteful.

"You don't approve?" Elara asked, also having witnessed the robot's silent condemnation.

"It is not for me to say," Chiefy replied, flatly. "But I never fail to be surprised by humanity's capacity for cruelty. I should know, I was originally programmed to be an instrument of your malice."

"Not our malice, Chiefy, the Authority's," Elara hit back. "And you can stand in judgment all you like. This has to be done."

"I will note your comments for posterity, and allow future generations to decide if you were right or wrong," Chiefy replied. "That is, of course, assuming any of us survive."

"My point exactly," Elara said.

"We'll be on the autoway soon," Finn said, leaning forward to get a clearer view through the tinted windshield. "Shouldn't you activate your little trick?"

"Yes, stand by," Chiefy said. The robot nodded to Scraps, who was in the passenger seat, interfaced with the ground car's computer. "Engaging stealth systems... now."

The lights inside the ground car switched off, including all of the instrument lights, pitching the interior of the vehicle into almost total darkness. Energy hummed through the floor, then through their blacked-out windows, Finn saw the world shimmer, as if the car had been suddenly consumed inside a heat haze.

"Stealth systems are active," Chiefy confirmed, while moving off the slip road and onto the autoway that connected the Authority sector to Spacehaven. "We are invisible."

"Where are the skycars?" Elara said, squinting her eyes in

an effort to see through the dark tint in the glass. "Where are the prefects? Ivan must be watching. We're beaming the trial to every screen in the city."

Finn gripped the headrest in front of him and pulled himself between the driver and passenger seats. The opaque glass and shimmering distortion caused by the stealth field made it almost impossible to see the route ahead clearly. If it were not for Scraps' scanners, Chiefy would have almost certainly crashed, but Finn could still see enough to know that Ivan Volkov hadn't left his fortress. His gut began to knot painfully, and he felt sick. If their plan failed to lure Ivan Volkov out of hiding, they didn't have a backup. Their only other choice was to fight their way inside Spacehaven, but with more than half of the Authority's prefect forces stationed inside the sector's walls, it was a fight they had little chance of winning.

"Can you give us a feed from the trial?" Finn asked. "I need to see what's happening."

Chiefy looked to Scraps, and the robot scrunched up his metal eyebrows in concentration. Finn knew that tapping into the trial feed brought with it a risk of them being detected, but he had to know what was happening inside the crucible. If Maxim Volkov was already dead, then Ivan had no reason to risk his neck.

"Yes-yes," Scraps finally answered. "But only one screen. More, too risky!"

"One screen is enough, pal," Finn said.

A single computer terminal in the rear of the ground car was reactivated. The screen went white, momentarily dazzling Finn, before the brightness dimmed and the display flickered. A few moments later, Finn and Elara were watching the trial feed from the crucible; the same feed that was being forced onto every TV and computer terminal in Zavetgrad.

"He's still alive," Finn said, breathing a sigh of relief. Maxim Volkov was fighting tooth and nail, and three foremen lay crumpled at his feet, disabled by electrified strikes from the former regent's nightstick. "The bastard has guts, I'll give him that."

The camera focused in on Volkov and Finn watched as the man launched himself into another assault, landing a blow on one of three foremen that had encircled him. The machine spasmed involuntarily as current overloaded its circuits, and its arm jerked, striking Volkov across the side of the head and knocking the man down. Suddenly, all three machines were standing over the former regent, who held up his hand to cover his face. It was then that Finn realized Volkov's eyes were puffy and wet with tears. Again, he felt a stab of pity and guilt, inspired by Chiefy's valid condemnation of their macabre tactics. What they were doing was no better than what the Authority had done to them.

Elara would have argued that they had to be willing to take any action necessary to ensure Reznikov was stopped, even if those actions were morally wrong. Finn understood the point, and even agreed with it. Their goal was nothing less than the survival of the species on Earth. Weighed against the consequences of them doing nothing, there was no choice but to walk the dark path they had set down, no matter where it led, but it didn't make Finn feel any better to know this.

"Wait, something's happening..." Elara said, pulling herself between the two front seats beside Finn. "Look, in the sky, there!"

Finn was still struggling to see anything outside, and he

was about to question whether Elara had been mistaken, when he saw the skycars too. There were five of them, jet black and little more than smears on the horizon, but they were definitely heading their way.

"Get Briggs on the line, we need to let him know the Authority is coming," Finn said.

Scraps nodded and tried to open a secure connection to Briggs' C.O.N.F.I.R.M.E. computer, which the rebel was wearing for this precise purpose. In the meantime, Finn turned his attention to the gates of Spacehaven, which were barely half a mile ahead of them. Chiefy had slowed the ground car to little more than a crawl so as to maintain their distance, but unless the gates were opened, it didn't matter how close they got.

"Come on, damn it, send in the ground cars too!" Finn growled. Five special prefect skycars weren't enough to break through the defenses that Briggs and the others had painstakingly set in place to defend the city's capitol. "Send in the troops, you bastard. Show us you have a heart, after all."

"Briggs here…" the rebel's voice was barely audible over the background noise of the trial, which was still proceeding in earnest.

"Briggs, you have five skycars incoming," Elara said, leaning in close to the computer so that her voice would carry strongly across the airwaves. "They might be trying to swoop in and steal Volkov from under you noses."

"Let the fuckers try," Briggs grunted, defiantly. "What about ground cars?"

"Nothing yet," Elara said, though she remained defiant, like Briggs. "But they'll come. I know it."

The squadron of special prefect skycars roared overhead, flying so low that they were caught in their engine wake and rocked from side-to-side like a crib. A klaxon blared through the computer terminal, and suddenly the workers surrounding the crucible dissipated, running inside buildings, down alleys, and into cover wherever they could find it. The two hundred foreman robots, minus the few that Maxim Volkov had managed to subdue, remained in place.

"It's now or never," Briggs said, as the sound of rifle and laser fire replaced the tumult of the crowd. "Either he opens the gates, or we have to break them down."

Finn sighed through his teeth and rubbed his face. He knew what Briggs meant, but he was loathed to go down that road. Already, Haven's forces were hurtling across the Davis Strait, bound for Seahaven, but the plan had been for General Riley to attack once Finn and Elara were already inside Spacehaven. With the gates still holding fast, Riley's assault would need to be focused against the sector's fortifications, to punch a hole through the wall, but in doing this, Haven's limited supply of skycars would be decimated by anti-aircraft fire.

"We don't get a second chance at this," Elara said, looking Finn dead in the eye. She knew the call had to be made. "It's all or nothing."

Finn nodded. *The dark path grows darker...* he said to himself, before clearing his throat and preparing to give the order to attack.

"Wait-wait!" Scraps called out. The robot jumped onto the dashboard and pointed toward the gates of Spacehaven. "Look-look!"

"Briggs, standby!" Finn said, aware that the rebel commander was likely already in contact with General Riley. He leaned forward and squinted his eyes, then saw what Scraps' scanners had already detected. The gates to Spacehaven were opening.

"We're on," Elara said, grabbing Chiefy's shoulder. "Take us in, nice and slow!"

Chiefy picked up speed and steered the armored ground car to the far left-hand edge of the road, onto the hard shoulder that was usually reserved for Autohaven vehicles that had been pulled over by patrols for regular stop and search actions. Prefect ground cars then raced through the gates in single file, armed officers clinging to their side-sills to maximize the troop-carrying capacity of the vehicles.

"This is where we find out if Chiefy's stealth systems work on something this size," Elara said, as the first three ground cars sped past, buffeting them just as the skycars had done.

"It will work," Chiefy replied. The robot then slowly turned his head to look at them both. "Probably…"

In other circumstances, Chiefy might have been joking, but there was nothing about the robot's demeanor that suggested he was trying to play one of his pranks.

"I thought computers were binary, one or zero, yes or no?" Finn said, annoyed by the robot's uncertainty. "It either works or it doesn't, so which is it?"

Chiefy raised one of his mechanical eyebrows. "We are about to find out."

Ten ground cars raced past, then twenty, and still the convoy showed no sign of ending. After the thirtieth armored vehicle had sped past, Finn began to wonder how many prefects Ivan still had left inside Spacehaven to guard his precious rockets, then finally the last car exited through the gates, and the barrier began to close again.

"Chiefy, now!" Elara said, still gripping the robot's shoulder, urging the machine on.

Chiefy floored the accelerator, and Finn was thrown against the back seat of the armored car to the soundtrack of tires squealing on the cracked asphalt surface of the autoway. He pulled himself upright then was distracted by the computer terminal, which was still connected to the trial feed. The special prefect skycars had made it inside the sector, and a dozen officers in black carapace armor were rappelling down on lines.

"Briggs, where are you?" Finn said, but there was only static in reply. "If you can hear me, get out of there, there's an army headed your way."

The rebel commander didn't answer, nor could Finn see him or any of the other Metals and workers on the TV feed. The central square had been completely emptied, and even the foreman robots were now rushing to safety, whist being blitzed with gunfire from the column of armored vehicles that were storming the sector. A trio of special prefects unhooked themselves and rushed to Maxim Volkov, who clambered to his feet, standing as tall as his battered and fatigued body could manage. Montgomery had finally unfurled himself from the fetal position and was on his knees, hands clasped together as if in prayer.

"Hold on!" Chiefy called out.

Finn's eyes snapped from the screen to the view outside,

and every muscle in his body tensed up. Distracted by the TV feed, he hadn't seen that the gates to Spacehaven had almost closed, but Chiefy was fully committed and gunning for the opening, which was shrinking by the second. With nothing more he could do, Finn gritted his teeth and held onto the back of the passenger chair with all his strength, like it was lifebuoy, and he was stranded in the ocean. Then they were through, the car missing the gate and side wall by mere inches, and Chiefy slammed on the brakes, slamming Finn's face into the back of the headrest with such force that he thought his brain was about to push itself out through his nose. The vehicle lurched left then sped down an alley before coming to an abrupt stop. No-one spoke, or even moved, and only the ping and hiss of the ground car's labored engine punctuated the silence.

"We made it," Chiefy said, his voice quiet and calm. "We were not detected."

Finn threw himself onto the rear seat and Elara practically collapsed beside him. Then their eyes were drawn to the computer screen, which was still connected to the trial feed. Maxim Volkov and Gabriel Montgomery were being led toward a special prefect skycar that had touched down in the middle of the central square. The two regents – the two tyrants – were only seconds away from being rescued, but neither Finn nor Elara were anxious, because they knew what came next. It had been the plan all along, for better or worse, for right or wrong.

Two shots rang out across the Authority sector, crystal clear even over the computer terminal's tinny speaker, then Maxim Volkov and Gabriel Montgomery fell face first onto the golden bricks of what had once been their dominion, each shot once in the head. The snipers on the rooftop of the mayor's building had aimed true. The last two regents of Zavetgrad were dead. The trial was over, but the fight had only just begun.

5

I STILL DON'T LIKE YOU

Finn eased open the door and aimed his laser cannon through the gap. After the spectacular manner of their arrival into Spacehaven, he'd expected to find an army of prefects already racing toward them, but the side-street that Chiefy had swerved the ground car down was empty and quiet.

"Scraps, are there any prefects heading our way?" Finn asked, wanting to be doubly sure he didn't step out into an ambush.

"Nope-nope!" Scraps replied, cheerfully. "But plenty elsewhere!"

The robot's answer was both reassuring and concerning. There may not have been squads baring down on them at that moment, but Spacehaven still contained half of Zavetgrad's entire complement of prefects. The convoy of rescue vehicles that Ivan Volkov had sent in vain to rescue his father had thinned their ranks a little, but not enough to make a serious dent in the acting mayor's defenses.

"We'll just have to rely on our stealth fields to keep us hidden," Elara said. She had unhooked her crossbow from her armor, and a bolt was already loaded. "Scraps, it might be best if you take cover inside Chiefy."

The smaller robot nodded then pulled open Chiefy's chest compartment, which the robot had purpose-designed to keep his smaller friend safe, and climbed into it. The larger machine activated his stealth field and all but vanished, then Finn and Elara did the same, before stealing out onto the eerily empty street. Finn picked up the distant rattle of gunfire coming from the direction of the Authority sector, then saw a deluge of laser blasts streak across the sky. Turret gunners inside the Authority sector were taking pot shots at prefect skycars, which were growing in number by the second.

Suddenly, the beat of rotor blades sped toward them and drowned out any other sounds, then moments later three full squadrons of golden skycars raced overhead, followed by twelve heavy troop transports, laden with officers. The downdraught from their spinning blades kicked up dust into Finn's eyes, and forced him to duck and cover his head. It was like being inside a tornado, and he had to grab onto the door of the ground car to keep himself from being blown down the alley. No sooner had the skycars flown over than the gates opened again, and columns of armored cars powered through, three abreast. Finn counted forty vehicles before the gates closed, but there could have been more, not that any further reinforcements seemed necessary. All told, several hundred prefects had just been deployed, and they were all heading for the Authority sector.

"Ivan must have ordered a counterattack," Finn said, spitting dust and dirt out of his mouth. "I think we pissed him off."

"It's a retaliation, not a counterattack," Elara corrected

him, while also picking grit from her teeth. "Volkov has lost sight of his mission, which is exactly what we wanted to happen. He's lashing out at us because we executed his father."

Elara climbed onto the roof of their armored ground car and spied over the fence that surrounded Spacehaven, but instead of looking in the direction of the Authority sector, her eyes probed deeper, toward Seahaven and the Davis Strait.

"Where the fuck is General Riley?" Elara said, speaking like an angry mother waiting for a child who was out past curfew. "If the forces from Haven don't arrive soon, the rebels won't even be able to hold the central square, let alone the Authority sector."

"Let Briggs worry about that," Finn said. "We have other problems."

Finn crept to the intersection closest to where Chiefy had dumped the ground car and stole a glance toward the closest rocket launch tower, which was half a mile away. He could see searchlights probing the streets outside the barrier fence, and the silhouette of prefect guards walking the perimeter, but there weren't nearly as many as he'd feared.

"Ivan's temper tantrum might actually have helped us," Finn said, as Elara jumped down and joined him. "It's left some of the rocket launch towers almost unguarded."

Elara moved to the other side of the intersection and inspected the launch pad and the rocket that was waiting to blast off. It was a Solaris Ignition II platform, one of the smaller and older designs, but Finn noted that the crew capsule sat atop the gleaming gold rocket looked like a much newer addition. Even so, it was relatively small, and Finn had no idea whether it had the capacity to carry them into orbit, in addition to whatever cargo had already been stuffed inside.

"Do we go for the Solaris Two, or one of the bigger rockets?" Finn asked, noting that there was a titanic Solaris Ignition IV on the next pad along. "It would be easier to hide amongst the cargo in the Solaris Four."

"We go for the closest one, and hope for the best," Elara answered, without hesitation. "We have no idea what the launch schedules of these rockets are. These things could blast off at any moment."

As if to make Elara's point for her, the ground suddenly began to tremble, and a rocket rose above the horizon line, blasting off from the far corner of Spacehaven. Smoke mushroomed around the launch pad as if Reznikov had already detonated one of his nuclear warheads, then a rocket that was larger than any Finn had seen before climbed into the sky. The column of flames that propelled it was almost too bright to look at, and Finn had to squint his eyes to follow the rocket as it sped skyward, accelerating at a phenomenal rate.

"That looks like a Solaris Five," Elara said, one eye squeezed shut because of the back draught from the launch. "I thought they were still in the trial phase."

"If that's true then Volkov is getting desperate," Finn said. "He's launching everything, even if there's a chance the rockets will crash and burn."

The ground shook again and another rocket blasted off from a pad on the northeastern corner, much closer to where Finn and Elara had entered Spacehaven. It was Solaris a III, a relatively common sight in Zavetgrad, but the fact it had launched so soon after its titanic bigger brother suggested time was running out faster than Finn thought.

"You're right, we should go for that Solaris Two, while we still have a chance to catch it," Finn said.

Finn took lead, taking tentative steps down the street toward the launch platform. Their stealth fields may have hidden them from the guards, but their footprints still left marks in the snow, and they had to be careful to cover their tracks. Then a security drone swept overhead, and Finn stopped dead, pressing his body to the wall. He heard Elara's armor thud against the bricks a moment later, and though he couldn't see her clearly, he could hear her breathing.

"Chiefy, can that thing see us?" Finn whispered. The drone had stopped and appeared to be scanning.

"Unclear," Chiefy replied. The robot took another moment for its electronic brain to further assess the situation, then added. "It's possible..."

Finn cursed under his breath. The flying surveillance devices were more commonly used beyond the city's high, electrified fence, where they prowled the perimeter looking for Haven operatives, but it seemed clear that Volkov had redeployed them. The drone's scanner package was far less sophisticated than one Scraps had at his disposal, but it included infrared imaging, and even with their special base layers and stealth field, it was possible their heat would show up against the ice-cold background of Spacehaven's streets.

Suddenly, a klaxon sounded, similar to the one that Briggs had used to warn the workers in the Authority sector that prefects were coming, except this siren emanated from inside Spacehaven. Finn aimed his laser at the drone, convinced that the surveillance device had seen them, and was about to pull the trigger, when Elara warned him.

"Look, coming in from over Metalhaven," Elara said, nudging Finn with her camouflaged shoulder. "Skycars from Haven. Maybe fifty or more."

Finn turned away from the drone and looked back toward his old sector. Tracer fire was lighting up the sky from Seahaven and the surrounding sectors, but Elara was right; General Riley was on the way, and arriving in force. The klaxon continued to sound, then the thrum of skycar rotors filled every street and alley in the sector, as prefect attack craft, both gold and black, took off and raced to intercept the invading force.

"Riley was true to his word," Elara said, though Finn noted the touch of surprise in her voice.

"You doubted that he'd come?" Finn asked.

"He was Head Prefect of Stonehaven, remember?" Elara answered. "Once a gold, always a gold."

"Maybe, for once, you were wrong," Finn said, smirking at Elara, despite the fact she couldn't see anything of his face, beyond a hazy shimmer.

There was a sharp, electronic noise, like a speaker squealing with distortion, and Finn wheeled around to see the surveillance probe, hovering barely more than five meters away, its probing red eye staring directly at him. Startled, Finn jumped back and knocked into Elara and Chiefy, sending them both crashing into the snowy street. He aimed his cannon but slipped on the ice and the laser blast flew wide and high. Then he was hit in the chest by a shock dart that lodged into his armor and dumped tens of thousands of volts into his body. His stealth system was overloaded, and he materialized in full view of a prefect patrol that was marching past the end of the street. The two prefects stopped suddenly, their boots skidding and sliding in the snow, before calling out and running toward them, but they were still a hundred meters away.

Finn gritted his teeth and tried to fight the incapacitating pain, but the drone's shock dart had ensnared him like a lasso, and it wasn't letting go. Suddenly, a crossbow bolt thudded into the surveillance probe and the robot squealed like a stuck pig, before another shock dart leapt from its spherical body and struck the shimmering outline of Elara. He heard her scream, then saw her appear in the middle of the street, as her stealth field also failed. She was crouched on one knee, and paralyzed with pain, like he was.

Chiefy deactivated his stealth field and yanked the shock dart out of Elara's thigh. Incredibly, the robot managed to withstand the voltage long enough to toss the electrified weapon into the snow, where it sparked and fizzed like hot fat. His body still trembling, and heart racing, Finn fired his laser cannon at the drone, needing five shots to hit the machine before finally putting it down. Gunfire crackled ahead of them, and Finn covered his head as bullets skipped off the asphalt and walls around him. He felt three rounds punch his chest and side, then fired blind with the laser, risking hitting Chiefy and even Elara, but chance favored him, and one of the prefects went down, a deep hole burned into the man's neck. The officer's partner turned and ran, but Elara chased after the man, black roundel dagger in hand, before pouncing on the prefect and slitting his throat.

A stillness fell over the street again, and they waited, listening for the sound of more footsteps, or the blare of another alarm klaxon. Five seconds passed, then ten, and Finn started to feel hope that they'd somehow gotten away with it, before the thump of bootsteps told him otherwise.

"Fall back!" Elara called out, helping Chiefy to stand. The shock dart had stunned him, like a sharp jab to the nose. "Fall back to the ground car!"

Finn grabbed Chiefy's other arm, but the robot's circuits were still scrambled, and the machine could barely put one foot in front of the other. Throwing Chiefy's heavy arm over his shoulder, he and Elara began hauling the seven-foot robot back to their vehicle, but they'd barely made it a few meters before a squad of prefects blocked the street. Finn turned back toward the Solaris II rocket, but a second squad had arrived and cordoned off the other end of the road. They were boxed in.

"What do we do?" Finn said. He imagined that the only reason they weren't already filled with lead was because if either prefect squad had opened fire, they would end up shooting each other.

"We do the only thing we can," Elara said, letting go of Chiefy, who dropped to his knees, dazed but recovering. She slid a bolt into her crossbow and wound back the string "We stand and fight."

Finn raised his cannon and dialed the power setting to maximum. He wasn't naïve enough to believe they stood even half a chance of surviving, but he'd rather die with a laser in his hand, than become Ivan Volkov's prisoner.

"Put down your weapons!" The order was shouted by a Prefect Supervisor, a snot-nosed gold that looked barely more than nineteen years old. "Surrender, or we will kill you!"

Elara loosed her bolt and shot the prefect supervisor in

the eye, sending the man down, screaming, and with blood gushing from the wound. The familiar sound of rifles being racked and loaded reverberated off the buildings that lined the narrow street, but Finn stood tall and stood his ground, with Elara at his back. He figured he'd get off one or two shots before he was cut down in a hailstorm of bullets, and he intended to make every blast count. He fired at the prefects who were blocking access to their ground car, and the entire squad was consumed in an explosion that tore open the street as if a bomb had detonated.

Debris clattered into Finn's armor, and he ducked and covered his head until the onslaught subsided, before checking his weapon to make sure it hadn't somehow been transformed into a grenade launcher. Scowling, he aimed at the second squad, hoping for a similarly explosive outcome, but the prefects were cut to pieces by gunfire before he could squeeze the trigger. Finn looked to Chiefy, assuming that the innovative robot had built a heavy machine gun into his frame without any of them noticing, but the robot was still barely able to stand. Then rotors pounded the air and a craft dropped out of the sky like a stone, before settling into a hover barely a meter above street level. At first, Finn was still too stunned to do anything but gawp, then he saw the face of the pilot, partly obscured by a pair of aviator sunglasses, and all he could do was laugh.

"Hey there, Major," Ensign Thorne called down, tossing up a lazy salute. "How's it going?"

"Better now that you're here!" Finn called back. He pointed to the Solaris II rocket. "Can you get us to that launch pad?"

"Not my department, sir," Thorne answered, smirking.

Finn noticed that she was now wearing Lieutenant's rank tabs. A well-earned promotion. "But I think I know some folks who can help."

The door to the rear compartment was thrown open, and Haven troops wearing arctic-pattern camo fatigues piled out, led by General Riley himself.

"Dust off but stay close," Riley grunted, speaking to Thorne before even acknowledging Finn or Elara.

"You got it, boss," Thorne said, saluting again, more stiffly this time.

"And Lieutenant," Riley added, slamming the door shut behind him, "give them hell!"

"Aye, sir, gunners at the ready," Thorne answered.

Two foreman robots, also wearing arctic camo fatigues, took up positions on the skycar's side sills, manning the craft's two heavy machine guns. Thorne lifted off, and at the same time, a dozen more Haven skycars soared overhead, twisting and turning through the air as they engaged the Authority's craft in high-speed dogfights.

"Why aren't you on a rocket yet?" Riley said, turning to Finn. True to form, the general didn't bother exchanging pleasantries, and Finn preferred it that way.

"We ran into a few dozen problems," Finn said, looking at the bodies strewn across the street. He then pointed to the Nimbus II rocket. "But that's our target, assuming it doesn't blast off without us."

"The Authority forces are in retreat, but we still have time," Riley grunted. "Follow me, and stay close…"

Riley's squad had already formed up ahead of them, and the general moved out to lead the force that would fight their way to the launch pad. Finn turned back to Chiefy, and was glad to see that the robot was recovered. Through the peephole in his chest compartment, he could also see the bright eyes of Scraps peering back at him.

"Are you two ready?" Finn said, as Chiefy hauled his sizable frame back to his feet.

"We're a little scorched, but okay," Chiefy said, managing a robotic smile. "Gen seven Foreman bodies are resilient, especially those that have been modified by a certain other robot."

Chiefy tapped his chest as he said this, and Scraps giggled and waved, accepting the compliment.

"Major, we don't have all day," Riley grunted.

Feeling suitably scolded, Finn glanced at Elara, who merely raised an eyebrow.

"Okay, maybe I was wrong about him," Elara admitted. Finn was stunned into silence again, but before he could manage to get in a word in, she added, "...but gloat about it, and I'll cut off your balls."

"Major!" Riley yelled, and this time Finn moved, though it was the threat of Elara's knife, not Riley's ill-temper, that had compelled him to act.

Elara and Chiefy took up position to the right of the squad and Finn slotted in on the left. He inspected the soldier next to him – a burly man with a sizable gut, who looked like he could handle himself. He looked the soldier in the eye, intending to give the man a nod of appreciation, before his brain almost exploded.

"Soren?" Finn said, unable to believe what he was seeing.

"Yeah, who else would I be, you dumb pussy?" Soren Driscoll hit back.

"What the fuck are you doing here?" Finn said. He didn't know whether to hug the man or shoot him in the face.

"I'm being a fucking hero, what does it look like?" Soren said, before spitting a globule of phlegm into the snow. "I'm sick of you getting all the glory."

Finn laughed. It was all he could do.

"Well, thanks, I guess," Finn said, as Riley ordered the advance.

"Fuck you, Finn, I still don't like you," Soren grunted, though the man was trying to hide a smile.

Finn laughed again and shook his head. The sight of Soren Driscoll, the man he'd blamed for the death of Owen, should have filled him with rage, but instead, he felt the opposite. He felt hope, because if someone as contemptible as Soren could find the courage to fight, and to do what was right, then maybe – just maybe – they still had a chance to win.

6

FOR NOW

GENERAL RILEY'S squad charged toward the launch pad, supported by Lieutenant Mara Thorne, who was clearing a path ahead of them while the rest of her squadron engaged the Authority craft in aerial warfare. Finn dropped back, leaving Soren Driscoll to storm the prefect ranks, firing from the hip like he'd gone berserk. For all the time he'd known Soren, Finn had considered the bully to be an Authority sycophant, always sticking up for the regime, despite the atrocities they committed, but in reality, Soren was no different to any other chrome. The man despised the golds, and twenty-nine years of pent-up anger and hatred were now pouring out of Soren Driscoll through the barrel of his assault rifle.

"With any luck, he'll get himself killed," Elara said, nodding toward Soren, though her sarcastic smile suggested she didn't actually mean it.

"I almost feel sorry for the prefects who get in his way," Finn said, as Soren charged an officer then proceeded to batter the man senseless with the butt of his rifle. "Soren Driscoll may be an asshole, but the man knows how to fight, and for the first time in his life, he actually has something worthwhile to fight for."

"As do we," Elara said, turning her attention to the Solaris Ignition II rocket that was now only a few hundred meters ahead of them. Increased activity around the launch pad suggested it was undergoing final preparations to blast off. "We'll use Riley's cover for as long as we can, then break through the gates and make a run for the launch tower, before anyone sees us."

Finn nodded, then suddenly remembered their unique advantage. "Speaking of anyone seeing us, we should re-enable our stealth fields."

Finn tried to activate his camouflage, but the system didn't respond. Resetting the actuation program, he tried again, but while his armor shimmered for a brief moment as the stealth field tried to form, it rapidly fizzled to nothing.

"Shit, it's not working," Finn said, trying for a third time, without success. "How about you?"

Elara shook her head. "The system is down. It must have been overloaded when that surveillance drone hit us with shock darts."

Finn turned to Chiefy, ducking down behind the rear rank of Haven soldiers, who were mowing down the Authority forces like a combine harvester.

"Chiefy, is your stealth field still working?" Finn asked.

"Negative, the system is offline," Chiefy replied, shaking his head. "I have already conferred with Scraps, and Elara's analysis is correct."

"Can you fix it?" Finn asked. He didn't like the idea of

roaming around the Nimbus space citadel, in full view of whatever the hell Reznikov had up there.

"System kaput!" Scraps said, through his cubby. "Can't fix!"

"Shit," Finn cursed, for a second time.

"It is what it is," Elara cut in, refusing to let anything phase her. "If we can't cloak then we just fight. Besides, I'd like to see anyone try to stop us from boarding that rocket."

Riley's squad reached the end of the road and took up positions outside the fence that cordoned off the rocket launch pad. Directly above them, four aircraft, two from Haven and two from the Authority, were engaged in a furious dogfight. A golden skycar was hit by gunfire and began spiraling out of control. Finn watched, heart in his mouth, as the aircraft weaved a chaotic path across the sky, until he realized that it was ultimately headed for the launch pad and the Solaris II rocket. The once distant drone of its rotors was transformed in a piercing whine, rising in pitch and volume as the doomed skycar hurtled past the rocket, missing it by barely more than twenty meters, before crashing into the ground and smashing open a section of the border fence.

"Fuck, that was close!" cried Soren, who had paused from hammering gunfire into the prefect defenders to watch the skycar plummet to its death. Instead of looking shocked, the former Metalhaven worker looked happy and excited, as if he were watching a fireworks display that preceded a trial.

"Keep your head down, Private!" Riley grunted.

The general grabbed Soren's jacket, and shoved the man into cover, before rushing across the street toward Finn and Elara. Old Soren Driscoll would have bristled and talked shit back to Riley, but new Soren obeyed the command and returned to fighting. It blew Finn's mind.

"There's your way in," Riley continued, pointing toward the section of the fence that had been smashed by the crashing skycar. Burning debris littered the road, and the fence itself was on fire, but there was a way through. "Move out, and my squad will continue to give you cover."

"Thank you, General," Finn said, suddenly realizing how much he owed the man for his tireless efforts to get them this far. "Not just for having our backs here, but for everything. You're a good man."

"Far from it, Major, I'm just a soldier," Riley grunted, gruffly rebutting Finn's compliment. "But that's good enough for me." The general then surprised Finn with a smile before thumping him on the shoulder. "Now go, and stick a knife in Reznikov's black heart. Do it for all of us."

Riley returned to his squad, rifle tucked in his shoulder, and gave the order to cover their advance. The Haven soldiers repositioned, and the way ahead was cleared for them by a furious onslaught of automatic gunfire.

"We will have a clear route to the rocket in seven seconds," Chiefy said. The foreman's eyes had been fixed on the prefects that had a sightline to the skycar crash site. Thorne's robot door gunners were making short work of the forces inside the launch pad. "Follow me, and stay close!"

Chiefy ran ahead without another word, and Finn had to hustle to keep pace with the machine, and its long, robot strides. The area surrounding the launch pad was in disarray, and prefects were crisscrossing the streets, some running into battle as reinforcements, others fleeing. Acting as their extended eyes and ears, Chiefy called out the targets as they appeared, and between Elara's crossbow and Finn's laser, the gold-armored prefects were cut down before they could halt their advance toward the launch tower.

Jumping over burning debris, Finn braved the flames and the intense heat from the skycar wreckage, and pushed on. The Solaris II was now less than a hundred meters away, and Finn could see vapor clouding the base of rocket, as excess liquid oxygen was boiled off in preparation for launch.

"We might only have a few minutes," Finn said, recognizing the event from the many other rocket launches he'd witnessed, and remembering that it usually occurred shortly before launch.

"We're almost there," Elara said, and Finn could hear the anticipation in her voice. She remained confident, and her confidence inspired him.

Elara reached a door in the low fence that cordoned off the launch tower from the rest of the pad, and she tried the handle, but it wouldn't open. Finn looked at the top of the fence, considering simply scaling it to get inside, but it was covered in razor wire, and the prospect of becoming entangled in its lethal web didn't enthrall him.

"Chiefy, break it down," Finn said, nodding to the seven-foot robot.

"My pleasure," Chiefy replied, ever cheerful.

Elara stood aside then Chiefy drove his metal fingers through the wire links and tore open the fence as effortlessly as Finn might have ripped a piece of paper in half. Elara moved through first, switching from her crossbow to her double-headed axe in expectation of close-quarters encounters. Finn stuck to his laser cannon, though he suspected that he might need to employ the electrified spear before the assault was over.

"I don't like it, it's too quiet," Finn said. "Where are the guards?"

"I think they're too preoccupied with General Riley to care about us," Elara said, staying upbeat. She paused to point to a crude digital clock with bright red letters, which was fixed above the elevator door at the base of the launch tower. The number read 00:09:42 and it was ticking down, second by second. "Ten minutes to blast-off," Elara added, glancing back at Finn. "If you need to pee, I suggest you go now."

Chiefy chuckled at Elara's joke, and from inside the robot's chest compartment, Finn heard Scraps snickering and enjoying the much-needed break in tension. They continued unchallenged until they were almost at the foot of the launch tower. Finn looked up, but even the comparatively compact Solaris II rocket was imposingly tall. At close to fifty meters long, it was twice as tall as many of the nuclear ICMBs that had rendered cities to dust during the last war.

Then, out of the corner of his eye, Finn spotted movement near a building close to the tower. His muscles tensed as a column of eight special prefects in carapace armor marched out, followed by two figures wearing partial pressure spacesuits made from an ethereal-looking, silvery material. Both carried helmets under their arms, and Finn recognized Ivan Volkov's cocky swagger before he'd even seen the man's face. With him was Commissar Juniper Jones, her blonde hair slicked back and red lips glistening like oil on water. The pair were laughing and joking with each other, Juniper hanging off Ivan's arm like they were prom queen and king, heading to a party. Then Juniper's eagle-eyes spotted Finn, and she stopped dead, yanking Ivan to a halt beside her. The young aristocrat was confused at first, until he locked eyes with Finn across the enclosure, and the man barked orders for his guards to attack.

Finn blasted two special prefects before the officers had even managed to raise their rifles, and at the same time, Elara charged into their ranks, double-headed axe drawn back like a scorpion's stinger. Regular prefects might have broken and run at this point, but the special prefecture was comprised of zealots who would not falter, especially in the defense of a regent successor and a commissar. Rifle fire was returned at Finn, but he was safely in cover and able to laser two more prefects before any of their shots had even come close.

Elara's assault was less understated but no less effective. Moving like the wind, she cut through the remaining four special prefects like a swarm of shuriken stars, aiming the blade of her axe at exposed necks, and into armpits and the backs of knees, where the carapace armor was at its weakest. Finn hustled out of cover and looked for Ivan and Juniper, expecting to find them standing between them and the launch tower, weapons drawn and ready to fight, but the pair had vanished.

"Where did they go?" Finn said, aiming his laser into every dark corner, anticipating an ambush, but still there was no sign of them.

"I don't know, I don't see them," Elara said, blood dripping from her axe. "Scraps, run a scan. Find them, quickly!"

"No need," Chiefy said, flatly. The robot pointed to the elevator at the base of the launch tower. Ivan and Juniper were already inside, and the door was about to close.

Finn aimed his laser, but Ivan merely smiled and drew back into cover, denying him a shot. He considered making a run for the elevator, but it was twenty meters away, and he had no chance of stopping the doors before they closed. A feeling of utter desperation consumed him, but just as the doors began to slide together, another figure swept out of the shadows. Finn adjusted the aim of his weapon, expecting to see another special prefect, but the silver-haired man was not a soldier of the Authority – at least, not anymore.

General Riley thrust his arm in-between the closing doors then forced them open before standing in the threshold in full view of Ivan and Juniper. Ivan pulled a pistol and pressed it to the man's head, but didn't pull the trigger. At first, Finn couldn't understand why, until he saw that Riley was holding a grenade in his other hand, and that the weapon was primed.

"You won't do it," Ivan said, still with the gun to Riley's head.

"Son, if you shoot me, then I drop this and it blows us to pieces," Riley answered, coolly. "So, really, the question is, will *you* do it?"

Finn and Elara stalked closer, and Ivan tried to aim his pistol at them instead, but Riley continued to block the man's shot.

"Put it down," Riley said, standing tall. "Put it down or die."

"But you'd blow yourself to hell too," Ivan said, his hand trembling.

"I'm already there, son, where I belong," Riley grunted. "If you want to join me, then pull that trigger."

Ivan met Riley's stare, perhaps looking for doubt in the old soldier's eyes, but there was none. William Riley was a man burdened by unforgivable guilt and filled with a deep regret. He didn't fear death, and Ivan could see it. Cursing under his breath, the regent successor lowered his weapon and handed it to Riley, who then stepped aside, his back still holding open the door.

Finn approached the elevator, but he'd barely taken a step before Elara raced ahead of him, axe in hand. Before he knew what was happening, she'd pinned Juniper Jones to the rear wall of the elevator car, and pressed the blade of her axe to her throat.

"Stop!" Ivan yelled. He tried to grab Elara, but she elbowed him in the face, and sent the man staggering back.

Finn rushed inside and aimed his laser at the regent successor, though his attention was focused only on Elara's axe. There was a burning hatred in her eyes and murder was clearly on her mind.

"You have no idea how long I've waited for this moment," Elara hissed, cutting Juniper's perfect skin.

"Ivan... Finn... help me!" Juniper cried, but Ivan could do nothing, and Finn wasn't about to get between The Shadow and the woman who'd tortured her.

"I could do to you what you did to me," Elara continued, barely holding back. "I could humiliate you, hurt you, torment you until you begged for death. I could make your life a living hell..."

"If you want to get to Nimbus then Juniper lives," Ivan said, dabbing blood from his nose.

"He's right," Juniper whispered, almost too scared to speak. "You need us..."

"We need him, not you," Elara said, drawing more blood.

"I'll take you to Nimbus, and do whatever you want, but

Juniper comes too," Ivan said, showing the same mettle his father was famous for. "This is my personal rocket, and only I can launch it. If you want to reach the citadel, I'm you're only way in, but only so long as you don't harm a hair on her head!"

Finn wanted to tell Elara to stop and think, and to listen to reason, but he knew that nothing he or anyone else on the planet said would make a difference. If Elara wanted to kill Juniper Jones, then she was dead.

"Please..." Juniper said, tears running down her face. "Please..."

Elara drew back the axe then screamed with rage and swung it at Juniper's head. There was a sharp clash of metal striking metal as the blade sank into the wall next to Juniper's ear. Strands of her golden hair floated down and landed on the elevator floor, sticking to the blood that was dripping from the commissar's neck.

"You get to live," Elara said, stepping back, though she was still a raw nerve. "For now."

7

A FINAL ACT

General Riley finally allowed the elevator doors to close then disarmed the grenade he'd used to threaten Ivan Volkov, and slid it back into his webbing. The elevator jolted into action and began to ascend the fifty meters to the top of the Solaris Ignition II launch tower. Finn kept his laser handy, but Ivan Volkov showed no sign of resisting. Instead, he had his arms wrapped around Juniper Jones, consoling her while she buried her face into his neck. Finn snorted and shook his head. He'd seen the actress at work before, though even now he couldn't be certain that what Juniper felt for Ivan was real or a deception.

Another jolt signified that the elevator had reached its destination, and the heavy doors wound open, exposing the elevator car to the arctic wind, and the sound of battle raging outside. Dozens of skycars were still engaged in close-quarters dogfights, weaving between the plumes of smoke that were rising from craft that had been shot down in all sectors of the city. At the same time, soldiers from Haven continued to fight with prefects on the ground, and from Finn's elevated vantage, it was clear that the Authority forces were losing.

Finn stepped out onto the crew access arm that extended from the tower to the space capsule sat atop the Solaris II rocket, and looked toward the central square in the city's capitol. Buildings were on fire, and there was still heavy fighting on the ground. Had it only been Haven's troops and fighters from Metalhaven standing against the prefects, it might have been a hopeless cause, but revolution was contagious, and the rebellion had spread. From Volthaven and Seedhaven to the north, and Makehaven and Stonehaven to the south and west, workers from all sectors had risen up against their oppressive masters and joined the fight. Hundreds of thousands of people were now flooding onto the streets, torching prefect hubs, and driving back the golden-armored enforcers with makeshift weapons fashioned from the tools of their sector. Even a screwdriver or a trowel could be deadly in the hands of someone determined enough to kill.

It was an awe-inspiring sight, but Finn was keenly aware that it would all be in vain, unless they could reach Nimbus and stop Gideon Alexander Reznikov from unleashing his nuclear missiles on the city, and extinguishing the hope of a brighter future in a flash of atomic fire.

"Let me do the talking," Ivan Volkov said, moving past Finn with Juniper Jones still huddled at this side.

Finn had been too caught up in the fighting that was spilling out all around Zavetgrad that he hadn't noticed two special prefects and an evaluator robot standing guard at the far end of the crew access arm. Their black shells set against the dark sky had made them almost invisible.

"Take it slowly, and don't try anything stupid," Elara said, shoving Ivan ahead, despite the fact he was already walking toward the rocket of his own free will.

Elara had a loaded crossbow held behind her back, while General Riley had slung his rifle and pressed his hands into the pockets of his jacket, along with his sidearm. Chiefy had stayed at the rear of the group, and was acting more robotic than usual, perhaps in an effort to appear like a regular foreman, following orders. Taking his cues from them, Finn snapped his laser cannon to its magnetic holster, but flexed his fingers to keep them nimble, should he need to draw the weapon again in a hurry.

"Halt!" the evaluator robot demanded.

The machine stomped toward them, and the mass of its heavily-armored frame shook the crew access arm, making it bounce alarmingly, like a rickety rope bridge over a deep ravine. Behind the machine, the two Special Prefects remained in position, guarding the space capsule's access hatch, with their submachine guns held at low ready. Their visors were down, hiding their faces and eyes, but Finn could feel them looking in his direction, and he tucked himself in behind Ivan, his head bowed low. Because of his notoriety, it wouldn't take much for the prefects to recognize him.

"Identify yourselves, at once!" The evaluator said, blocking Ivan's path.

"Use your eyes, you stupid machine," Ivan hissed, standing tall and facing down the robot. "I am Ivan Volkov, regent successor, and acting mayor of Zavetgrad. This is my rocket. You will step aside at once and allow me to board."

The robot's eyes flashed as it scanned Ivan's face, probing

his retinal pattern and every line and contour of his face to confirm the man's identity.

"My apologies, Master Volkov," the evaluator said, bowing its head deferentially. "I have a new directive from the president himself to confirm the identify of all those attempting to leave Zavetgrad."

"Well, now that you've confirmed who I am, you are commanded to stand down and leave the tower," Ivan said.

The evaluator nodded then stepped aside, but as Ivan tried to move past, the machine pressed a hand to Juniper's shoulder.

"I must confirm the identifies of all those wishing to depart," the evaluator said, repeating the new directive it had been given.

Juniper drew away from Ivan then looked directly into the robot's probing, mechanical eyes.

"I am Commissar Juniper Jones of the Special Prefecture," Juniper began, speaking severely to the robot. The damsel in distress routine hadn't worked on the evaluator's logical machine mind, so Juniper was now working from a different playbook. "As an evaluator, you are under my Authority. Is that clear?"

"Yes, Commissar," the robot replied.

Juniper again tried to move past, but the robot kept hold of her arm and pushed her back.

"Release me at once," Juniper snarled, trying to unfurl the machine's finger. "You are programmed to obey my orders!"

"My new directive supersedes your orders," the evaluator said, still pushing Juniper back. "Acting Mayor Volkov is authorized to proceed." The machine then looked toward

Finn and the others, who continued to hide their faces as best they could. "No others will be permitted to board."

There was a finality to the robot's statement that implied it would not be swayed from its position. Finn knew this meant they'd have to fight their way on-board, but unloading a barrage of laser and gunfire at the robot and the special prefects would risk damaging the rocket, and their chances of reaching orbit intact. He glanced across to Elara and he could see that she was working on the same conundrum, but the fact she had not yet acted, suggested that his partner didn't have an answer either. Before either of them could do anything, Juniper swept the evaluator's arm aside then pointed a finger at the two special prefects standing by the hatch.

"I order you to assist me," Juniper called out to the prefects, who were also under her direct authority. She looked the robot up and down with disdain. "Get this machine out of my way."

The special prefects looked to one another, then at the evaluator, which had swiveled its body in order to keep them in its field of view.

"Now!" Juniper roared.

The command was issued with such force that the two prefects actually jumped. Shouldering their weapons, the officers advanced toward the evaluator, but the machine reacted just as swiftly. Taking a long stride toward the prefects, the evaluator swatted the first officer across the chest with its club-like forearm, sending the man screaming to the ground, fifty meters below. Finn drew his cannon and tried to get a shot, but the robot was still directly in front of the rocket, and he couldn't risk missing. The second special prefect lashed the evaluator with gunfire at close range, but the rounds rattled off its thick armor, and ricocheted harmlessly in the dark sky. The robot snatched the special prefect's rifle and bent the barrel, rendering the weapon useless, before grabbing the officer's throat and lifting the man off his feet.

Suddenly, Chiefy rushed past, barging Ivan and Juniper out of the way. The evaluator saw him coming, and dropped the prefect before blocking Chiefy's punch and retaliating with a hard left that struck the foreman cleanly across the head. The clang of metal striking metal rang out clearly and Chiefy staggered back, stunned by the blow. The evaluator pressed its advantage, and swung another hard punch, but Chiefy caught the robot's fist in his hand in a stunning display of machine reflexes. The evaluator swung again, and again Chiefy caught its fist, then gears and motors strained and labored, as the two machines wrestled with one another, testing each other's robotic might. The evaluator was bigger and on spec it was stronger too, but Chiefy was no ordinary Gen VII, and before long he had overpowered the evaluator and driven it to its knees.

"Your programming is corrupt," The evaluator said, its vocal processor distorting because of the immense power drain required to keep Chiefy at bay. "You must comply..."

"In my evaluation, you are obsolete," Chiefy replied, as motors exploded and servos ruptured, causing the evaluator's arms to become limp in the robot's hands. "I recommend... decommissioning."

Chiefy drove his knee into the evaluator's head, crushing its metal skull and destroying its logic processor in a single, brutal strike. The machine crumpled into a heap, sparks flying from its body, which fizzed and crackled like a damp firework.

"Those machines have been going crazy for days," the special prefect said. The man had picked himself up off the deck and was dusting down his armor. "Thank you, Commissar," the man added, nodding his head to Juniper. "You can board now."

Juniper returned the nod, then she and Ivan continued toward the pod, which was now unguarded. Finn slowly clipped his laser to his holster then stepped over the wreckage of the evaluator robot, keeping his head turned away from the prefect, but the officer shuffled back and drew his sidearm.

"Wait, I still need to check that these others are cleared for departure," the special prefect continued. The man cocked his head to one side, and appeared to be scrutinizing Finn far more closely than was comfortable. "Wait a second, I know you!" the man yelled, leveling his pistol at Finn.

Elara swung her crossbow out from behind her back, but before she could shoot the special prefect, Juniper Jones had swept behind the man, stolen his knife, and slit the officer's throat in a single fluid motion. The man croaked and gargled on his own blood, then Juniper pushed the officer over the railings, where he landed with a meaty thud, beside his already dead partner. Elara switched her aim to Juniper, but she held up her hands then casually tossed the blood-stained knife over the railings too.

"No need to thank me," Juniper said, shooting a condescending smile at Elara, which Finn considered extremely brave and stupid, considering she was still aiming a crossbow bolt at her throat. "Now let's get out of here, before anyone else shows up."

"I can launch manually from inside the capsule," Ivan said, spinning the wheel on the hatch then pulling open the heavy door.

"Take it slow," Elara said, grabbing Juniper's wrist and pressing the crossbow into her gut. "I wouldn't want you to leave without us."

Juniper smiled. "The thought never crossed my mind."

Ivan waited by the hatch, his eyes flicking between Elara and Juniper. Finn recognized the look on the man's face, because it was the same look he'd had when Tonya Duke had smiled at him across the breakfast table in the prosecutor barracks. The acting mayor was clearly smitten with Juniper, perhaps even in love with her, and because of this he would do nothing to jeopardize her safety. Ivan knew that Elara was capable of killing the people he cared about, and it seemed that through her careful manipulation of the man, Juniper Jones had become the last human being on Earth that fit that description.

Chiefy stepped inside the capsule first, followed by Juniper and then Elara, while General Riley stood guard on the crew access arm, rifle held ready.

"You next," Finn said, shoving Ivan into the hatchway. "I don't trust that you wouldn't slam the door shut on us, and find another rocket off this planet."

"This is the last one," Ivan said, shaking Finn's hand off his arm. "At least, it's the last one that's capable of transporting people. Everything else is cargo."

Ivan stepped over the threshold and Finn grabbed the hatch door, ready to pull himself inside the cabin and seal it, ready for launch, when he heard the tower's elevator whir into action. Stopping, he checked the far end of the crew arm and saw that the elevator was on the way up. Because of the fight with the evaluator and the special prefects, he hadn't even realized it had returned to the ground level.

"You need to go," General Riley said, pulling his rifle tightly into his shoulder.

The elevator doors swung open, and three evaluator robots piled out. They quickly surveyed their surroundings, then saw Finn standing in the hatchway and ran.

"Go, now!" Riley grunted, glancing back at Finn.

"Come with us!" Finn said, extending a hand to Riley. "We could use the extra gun."

"My place is here," Riley said, hammering shots in the lead robot and disabling it legs, but the other two machines stormed past it, shoving the damaged evaluator aside.

"But they'll kill you!" Finn called out, imploring the general to see reason, but the man was unmoved.

"I was ready to die the day I surrendered to Haven," Riley said. He slapped a fresh magazine into his weapon and fired on automatic, destroying the second evaluator with a flurry of headshots. The third continued on. "At least this way, I die for something worthy."

Suddenly, Riley kicked Finn hard in the chest, sending him barreling into the capsule, then slammed the hatch door shut and locked it. Finn got to his feet just in time to see Riley's face at the porthole window; incomprehensibly, the man was smiling. Then the evaluator robot grabbed Riley and tore the general away from the hatch, before driving its open hand into the man's gut like a knife.

"No!" Finn yelled.

Finn tried to turn the locking wheel, but the rocket was sealed for launch, and there was nothing he could do. Blood leaked from Riley's mouth as the evaluator brushed him aside, determined to stop the launch, but the general still had enough strength for one final act. He wrapped his arms around the evaluator's neck and then threw them both through the railings that ran alongside the crew access arm, sending him plummeting to his death on the concrete below.

8

WELCOME TO NIMBUS

Finn hammered his fist against the porthole window out of frustration, but while he regretted General Riley's sacrifice, he had to grudgingly admit that the man had done them a favor. With the crew access arm now cleared and the hatch door closed and locked, there was nothing to stop the Solaris II rocket from blasting off.

"Where's Riley?" Elara asked.

"He's gone," Finn said, resting his back against the hatch door.

"Good riddance," Ivan spat. "That man was a traitor, and he deserved to die."

Finn clenched his fists and was about to pummel some understanding into the regent successor when the capsule began to vibrate, like a ground car driving over a brick-lined street.

"I'd suggest you sit down and strap in," Ivan added, oblivious to Finn's desire to do him harm. "Unless you want to get squashed like a bug when we blast off, which I honestly wouldn't mind seeing."

Ivan and Juniper were already strapped into their seats, side-by-side. They were holding hands, like teenage lovers, but although Juniper's head was resting on Ivan's shoulders, she was looking at him, a fraudulent smile curling her lips. Elara was sitting opposite, also strapped in but with her crossbow resting on her lap. Chiefy was rammed into a seat between them.

"I see no expense has been spared on your personal craft," Finn said, stepping away from the hatch and finding a seat beside Elara.

"Of course," Ivan said, unapologetic. "What did you expect?"

Finn shook his head then found a seat next to Elara and unhooked his laser, handing it to his partner while he pulled the harness across his chest. Like everything else inside the plush spacecraft, the harness straps and buckles were adorned with gold, and there even looked to be a drinks cabinet built into the padded walls of the luxury capsule. He finished fastening the harness as the rumbles beneath his feet grew in intensity. The views through the small porthole windows that pocketed the capsule were now obscured by vapor that was rapidly dissipating into the sky around them.

"You can put the weapons down," Ivan said, nodding to Finn's cannon, which Elara had now returned to him. "All that will happen if you fire them in here is that we all die a quick, fiery death."

"You seem unreasonably calm, considering we just hijacked your spacecraft," Finn said, resting the cannon on his lap. "I would have expected you to be ranting and raging about how we're going to defile Nimbus with our unworthiness."

Ivan laughed and let his head flop against the seat's lavishly cushioned padding.

"It makes no difference either way, you'll still not be able to stop the nuclear strike," Ivan said, confidently. "Though I'm impressed you got this far. Our projections estimated only a three-point-four percent chance that you would ever set foot on Nimbus."

Finn snorted in return. "We're good at beating the odds. You should have factored that into your projections," he replied.

Ivan shrugged. "Like I said, it doesn't matter. Perhaps you believe that because you managed to infiltrate Elysium, that breaking into the president's palace will be just as achievable, but you're wrong." The acting mayor smiled. "You'll never get to see Gideon's face, but if you're lucky, you'll find a viewing gallery where you can witness the end of civilization on Earth, and wave goodbye to all of your scum worker friends."

Finn tried to get up and storm across the cabin to punch Ivan in his smug face, but the harness restrained him, and instead he was forced to endure a mocking laugh. He was still holding his cannon and he considered lasering a hole through Ivan's vile heart, but the regent successor's warning about damaging the capsule was still vivid in his thoughts.

"T-minus ten seconds to launch..." said a robotic voice.

The sudden announcement rid Finn of his ugly feelings, and instead all he could think about was that they were perched on top of seven hundred tons of violently explosive rocket fuel. He looked at Elara, and for once she didn't look glacially cool, and as his eyes swept across to Juniper and Ivan, it was clear that they were terrified too. Only Chiefy and

Scraps seemed unfazed by their imminent blast off, and as the countdown reached three, Chiefy smiled and gave Finn a thumbs up. He tried to return the gesture, but his body was suddenly pressed into the seat as the massive rocket engines ignited and pushed them skyward with over fourteen thousand kilonewtons of thrust.

Through the porthole windows, Finn saw the launch tower slip away beneath them, then the rocket began to accelerate at a dramatic rate, pressing him harder into his seat, as if he had the weight of two or three burly Metalhaven workers on top of him. The dark sky grew darker still and Finn drifted in and out of consciousness as the forces continued to build. When his eyes re-focused, he noticed that a screen had been lowered inside the cabin, above Ivan's head, showing the rocket's location relative to Zavetgrad. A similar screen was above his own seat. The primary rocket boosters had already detached, and the spacecraft passed through the troposphere and most of the stratosphere. The mesosphere was penetrated next, then a short time later the computer voice announced that they had passed the Kármán line, at an altitude of one hundred kilometers, or sixty-two miles, above the surface of the Earth.

"That means we're now in space," Ivan said, answering the question that was on Finn's mind. "Congratulations. Since the foundation of Zavetgrad, barely half-a-dozen individuals have ever left the planet's atmosphere."

"I'm sure I'm very honored," Finn replied, sarcastically.

The forces acting on Finn's body were sustained for several more minutes, but by now he'd grown accustomed to the sensation of being blasted into space. Elara shot him constant, reassuring glances, and he returned them in kind, but it was Chiefy's unflappable cheerfulness that allowed Finn to experience the journey without feeling terrified to his core.

The robot called out specific rocket maneuvers, and explained what was happening at every step of the way. Even Ivan and Juniper welcomed the foreman's input. Though they had always planned to be on the rocket when it blasted off, like Finn and Elara, neither of them had actually experienced a launch before. For everyone in the capsule, rebel, gold, and robot alike, they were in uncharted territory.

"Beginning final stage transition to Nimbus," the computer voice announced. *"Docking Port R-One is locked in. Prepare for spacecraft separation."*

"What does that mean?" Finn said, gripping the sides of his chair.

"Relax, it just means that we're done being blasted through the cosmos on the back of a rocket," Ivan said, while casually looking through the closest porthole.

A heavy thump reverberated through the capsule and Finn worried that they'd been struck by space debris or an incoming meteor. Then through one of the porthole windows, he saw the booster rockets falling away beneath them, ensnared by Earth's gravity. He was suddenly awestruck by the sight of the planet spinning below them. He looked at Elara; she was equally rapt.

Suddenly, the capsule changed course and Earth slipped away, leaving only an inky blackness in its place. For a moment, Finn saw nothing but stars, though some of them appeared to be moving. He rubbed his eyes and looked again, worried that the pressures acting on his body had somehow muddled his mind, until he worked out that he wasn't seeing stars, but other spacecraft that had departed Zavetgrad before them. With their heavier payloads, they were taking longer to reach the citadel, and some of them even appeared to be stuck in a queue. Ivan's personal shuttle wasn't affected by such inconveniences. Their craft proceeded ahead of the waiting convoy, ferrying its precious cargo to the city in space.

Then Nimbus came into view ahead of them. Finn was no stranger to the citadel, which had hung above Zavetgrad his whole life, but seeing it up close was almost as magical as witnessing his home planet from orbit. Nimbus was majestic in a way that even the golden buildings of the Authority sector, or the Regents' Cathedral in the sub-oceanic complex, couldn't hope to match. Circular, and with four giant spires shooting upward at equidistant points on its circumference, it looked like an enormous silver wheel. In its center was a large spherical module, which was attached to the main station by cylindrical conduits, like spokes on a wheel. The sphere had an iridescent silver hue and looked like a grand jewel in the center of a monarch's crown. Finn was about to ask Ivan what it was when the answer suddenly came to him, and it was so obvious he felt stupid for not realizing it sooner.

"That's Reznikov's palace, isn't it?" Finn said, though all eyes were still on Nimbus. "In the center. That's where the president lives?"

"Yes..." Ivan said, his voice breathy with excitement. "Only a handful of people have ever set foot inside it. Only the mayors of Zavetgrad, like my father..."

Ivan's voice trailed off and the bitterness, anger and resentment over his father's execution flooded back. To his credit, the younger Volkov concealed it well, but not well enough that Finn couldn't sense the hatred in his heart, and the thirst for revenge.

"Prepare for docking maneuvers," the computer voice announced.

Soon, Nimbus had grown so large outside that there was little to see, beyond metal panels and flickering lights. Finn sat back in his seat and waited, laser cannon still resting in his lap. He tapped the frame of the weapon idly, and Juniper Jones looked at the cannon, then at Finn, before smiling sweetly at him, as if the thought of blasting his head off had never entered her mind.

Several more minutes elapsed in silence until the spacecraft arrived at its destination. Thrusters hissed and the capsule made a number of small but precise adjustments to its trajectory, before there was a hard thump, and their forward motion was arrested completely.

"Welcome to Nimbus," the computer voice announced, in a bright tone. *"Humanity's Future in the Stars..."*

9

BOARDING PROTOCOLS

Finn unfastened his harness and pushed himself up, pointing his laser at Ivan Volkov the whole time. He felt strangely lighter and unsteady on his feet, which wasn't helping his aim. Elara got up next and she seemed similarly wobbly, as did Ivan and Juniper, once Elara had ordered them to stand, at the point of her crossbow.

"What the hell is happening to us?" Finn said, grabbing the wall of the capsule to help prop himself up. "I feel drunk."

"We are no longer under the influence of Earth's gravitational pull," Chiefy replied. Unlike everyone else, the robot appeared perfectly steady on his feet. "Nimbus rotates in a circular path and the force causing this acceleration is directed toward the center, simulating the effect of gravity. Your brains will adjust."

Finn looked through the nearest porthole window of the space capsule, and he could see that the stars were moving.

"I hope my brain adjusts soon," Finn said, finding that looking at a spinning starfield did nothing to abate his nausea and disorientation.

"What happens next?" Elara said. She had remained focused on Ivan and Juniper and appeared to be adapting to their strange new environment quickly.

"Next, we disembark, of course," Ivan said, in a condescending tone.

"Obviously, we disembark, but how?" Elara pressed him, more pointedly.

"There's a boarding procedure that everyone must go through, no matter who they are," Ivan said, while starting to unfasten the clasps that held his partial-pressure space suit in place. "An evaluator robot will process our entry then direct us through a gate that will disinfect our bodies, so that we don't bring any diseases to Nimbus."

Elara laughed. "You are a disease," she sneered, before looking Juniper Jones in the eyes. "You most of all."

"Then what happens?" Finn said, eager to keep them on track.

"Then nothing," Ivan shrugged. "Once we're cleared and disinfected, we can leave the arrivals area and enter Nimbus."

Elara aimed her crossbow at Ivan's throat. "In that case, we don't need you anymore."

"Wait!" Ivan said, holding up his hands. Elara had already begun to add pressure to the trigger, but she held off firing to hear what the acting mayor had to say. "Only I can unlock the door into Nimbus. It requires the DNA and retinal scan of a regent, so as acting mayor of Zavetgrad, there's no-else else alive who can get you inside that station."

Elara's free hand went to her knife, and Finn had a pretty good idea what she was thinking. Ivan did too, and quickly shot down her plan.

"The iris scanner is programmed to differentiate between

a living eye and a dead one," Ivan continued, scowling at Elara. "In case you were considering just taking my eyeball into Nimbus, and not the rest of me."

Elara released a disgruntled sigh then removed her hand from the grip of her knife. "The thought never crossed my mind," she lied.

Juniper and Ivan began to remove their partial-pressure spacesuits, which were bulky and cumbersome. Beneath the outer layer, Juniper was wearing carapace armor, complete with gold accents to denote her special rank of Commissar. Ivan was wearing a type of prefect armor, modified to include a golden chest plate with the emblem of the Authority embossed in its center. The sight of Gideon Alexander Reznikov's face brought home the reason why they had risked everything to reach Nimbus.

"Hurry up, we're wasting time," Finn said, moving over to the hatch and trying to turn the wheel. The hatch had been unsealed, but it still required a surprising amount of effort to unlock. "We may only have a few hours before Reznikov decides to launch his strike."

"Wait..." Elara said, placing her hand on Finn's shoulder to stop him from releasing the locking lever and pulling open the hatch. "What about security? How many prefects and robots are guarding the arrivals area?"

Ivan laughed and Elara set her jaw. By taunting her again, the acting mayor was playing a very dangerous game.

"What's so funny?" Elara said. The aim of her crossbow had dropped lower, and Finn could tell she was a heartbeat away from knee-capping the aristocrat.

"There is no security on Nimbus," Ivan said, still with a patronizing tone. "At least not of the kind you're thinking."

"That's bullshit, and you know it," Elara snapped. "Your old friend, Walter 'Vigor' Foster, was destined for Nimbus, to train the future prefects of the citadel."

"Yes, before he was murdered," Ivan hit back, clearly still bitter about that fact. "And the key word in what you just said is 'future' prefects. Walter wasn't scheduled to transfer here for another decade at least."

Elara narrowed her eyes at Ivan, skeptical of the man's answers, since Ivan was no stranger to lying. In that regard, he and Juniper Jones were a perfect match.

"And there's no-one guarding the entry gate?" Finn added, also doubtful.

"There are no guards because there's no need for any," Ivan replied. "No-one reaches the space citadel who is not supposed to be here." The man then waved a hand toward Finn and Elara, dismissively. "Or, at least no-one has, until you."

"I don't believe you," Elara said, still achingly close to putting a bolt into the acting mayor's gut.

"Believe whatever you like, traitor, but I give you my word that there is no-one guarding the arrivals gate," Volkov said, taking offense. "There is one evaluator robot, as I've already told you."

Finn turned to Chiefy, and specifically to the bright eyes of Scraps, who was peeking out through his peep hole.

"Are you picking up anything outside the hatch, pal?" Finn asked. He trusted Scraps' sensors over Ivan Volkov's word, any time.

"One robot," Scraps said, before narrowing his machine eyes in concentration. "Anything else... not sure."

"That'll have to be good enough, for now," Finn said. He

unlocked the door and hauled it open. There was a hiss of air, as the pressure inside the capsule equalized with the environment inside Nimbus, then Finn waved Ivan on. "You first, you majesty," he said, spitefully. "And take it slow, or Elara will turn your legs into pincushions."

Ivan removed the last elements of his spacesuit then marched through the hatch with an arrogance and imperiousness that made him suddenly look much more like his father. Juniper Jones followed, helped by a hefty shove in the back from Elara, which caused the woman to grit her teeth and glower at her in return. Elara was testing the commissar's tolerance, willing the woman to snap and give her an excuse to lash out, but Finn had learned first-hand that Juniper was supremely skilled at controlling her emotions, so that they didn't control her.

Finn exited the rocket capsule last and closed the heavy hatch behind him. Outside was a simple docking umbilical that led into a room roughly the size of the gene bank's foyer in reclamation sector four. Like that building, it was a spartan, industrial looking space, with none of the grandeur of buildings in the Authority sector. After the spectacle of Elysium, Finn found himself feeling disappointed that Nimbus wasn't somehow more impressive on the inside.

The arrivals area was cut in half by a floor-to-ceiling glass barrier that was passable only through a single, octagonal gate. Just as Ivan had said, the gate was staffed by an evaluator robot, which was cautiously watching them as they approached. Finn couldn't see any weapons, but he was reminded of how General Riley had been brutally speared through the gut by a knife-hand thrust from a robot just like the one waiting for them. The powerful machines didn't need weapons to be deadly.

"What was your plan, once you arrived?" Finn said, questioning Ivan to fill the silence as they made the long walk across the docking umbilical. "Or were you just intending to eat a nice dinner and watch while the world burned?"

Ivan snorted and shook his head. "The world is dead, anyway," the man replied, dismissively. "But if you must know, I was summoned to meet with the president. My audience is in a little over four hours from now."

"Four hours is too late," Elara cut in. "You need to move up that appointment."

"I don't get to decide when Gideon sees me," Ivan said, shooting Elara a contemptuous look. "I go when I'm told."

Elara grabbed Ivan's arm and spun the man around, pressing her crossbow into the man's gut, where his armored chest plate met his waistline.

"You'll find a way to move up that meeting," Elara snarled. "And you'll find a way to take us with you."

Ivan began to laugh, but Elara shoved the needle-like point of the crossbow bolt into his flesh, and the sharp stab of pain stole his breath away. Juniper moved toward Elara, but Chiefy raised his arm and blocked her path.

"No, let her go," Elara said, smiling at Juniper. "Let's see if the cat has claws."

Chiefy nodded then lowered his arm, but Juniper stayed where she was, her eyes flitting between the bolt that was impaled in Ivan's gut, and Elara. Then she took a pace back and held her hands in front of her stomach, in the passive repose that Finn had seen her adopt on so many occasions, when she had pretended to be his paramour.

"That's what I thought," Elara said, pushing Ivan back, but keeping the crossbow bolt, now with a thin coating of the man's blood, aimed at his gut.

"I'll do what I can to change my meeting," Ivan said, pressing his fist to the wound, as if he had a stitch from running. "But even if you do reach Gideon, and even if you could convince him to stop the nuclear strike, which you can't, it wouldn't save the planet anyway."

"Why?" Finn asked. "Earlier, you said, 'the world is dead, anyway'. What does that mean?"

Ivan regarded Finn for a moment, perhaps weighing up how much to reveal. The Regents of Zavetgrad had dealt in secrets for decades, but two hundred and fifty miles above the surface of the Earth, he wondered what use Ivan's secrets were.

"Fine, I'll tell you," Ivan said, wiping the blood from his hand onto the seat of his pants. "Maybe if you know then you'll stop trying to interfere, and just let this happen."

"Out with it, Ivan," Elara said, threatening him again with the crossbow.

"Zavetgrad is dying a slow death, and has been for more than a century," Ivan said, taking perverse pleasure in announcing this news. "The number of genetically viable babies born has been reducing year-on-year since the city was founded. In ten years, there will be no-one born with a genetic rating higher than three. In twenty-five years, the highest genetic rating will be two. In fifty years, everyone will either be sterile, if they're lucky, but more likely born with fatal genetic defects. Life expectancy will be fifteen to twenty years at best, and no medical intervention will change that. The planet is diseased, and Nimbus is our only hope." He snorted at Elara, practically spitting on the ground at her feet. "But here you are, trying to tear it down."

"How do we know you're not lying?" Finn said. He was putting on a brave face, but Ivan's revelations had shocked him. "And even if you're not lying, you could be wrong."

Ivan laughed, pushing his luck – and Elara's patience – to the limit, then gestured to the steel walls around him.

"Do you think Gideon would build all this, if there was a chance Zavetgrad could flourish?" Ivan said. The acting mayor then suddenly became more somber. "You should seriously reconsider what you are here to do. You ask if I could be wrong, but have you considered that it's you who are mistaken? By destroying this citadel, you are only dooming humanity to extinction."

Finn didn't want to listen, but Ivan's words had seeped into his ears like a poison, and he was suddenly wracked with doubt. He glanced at Elara, but she only looked angry, and if Ivan had caused her to doubt too, she did not show it.

"Enough talk," Elara said, nodding toward the gate. "Just get us inside."

Ivan sighed and shook his head contemptuously, before putting Elara to his back and walking toward the evaluator robot, which had been patiently observing their conversation.

"Welcome to Nimbus," the evaluator said, though the robot's dry delivery did not come across as welcoming. "Close your eyes then slowly walk through the gate with your arms held out to the sides," the machine added, demonstrating the pose it wanted them all to adopt.

Ivan stretched out his arms and paced forward at nothing more than a slow march. At the same time, nozzles inside the gate tunnel sprayed him with a vapor that smelled like the herbal teas the golds enjoyed, mixed with strong bleach. A wide, circular band of UV emitters also bathed his body in invisible light, until Ivan finally emerged on the other side of the gate, his armor sparkling like polished diamond.

"Thank you. Next, please," the evaluator said, and Juniper stepped forward, adopting the same pose and slow pace.

"Clear, next, please..." the evaluator repeated, and already its droning voice was starting to grate on Finn.

Elara went next and Finn watched carefully for any sign of a deception or a trap, but she passed through the disinfecting gate as easily as Ivan and Juniper had done.

"Here goes nothing," Finn said.

He stepped up to the threshold and held out his arms, then closed his eyes and marched forward, scrunching up his nose as the disinfectant mist found its way into his mouth and eyes, despite both being pressed tightly shut. Then at the other side of the gate, just before he was about to exit, an alarm sounded, and instead of UV light, he was bathed in a blood-red glow.

"Energy weapons detected," the evaluator said, with urgency. "Neutralization initiated..."

Before he could step clear of the gate, Finn was hit with a powerful electric blast that knocked him to the floor. The electronics inside his laser cannon exploded on his hip, burning his thigh, then the spear on his back exploded too, and the force of the blast slammed him, face first, into the deck plates. Elara ran to help him, and Chiefy charged thorough the gate scanner too, before the robot was also paralyzed by a similar electrical pulse.

"Emergency protocol!" Ivan called out. "Intruder alert. Do not allow them to pass!"

Elara managed to drag Finn and Chiefy through the other side of the gate, then she aimed her crossbow at Ivan and Juniper, who were both fleeing toward the exit, but the evaluator grabbed her from behind before she could release the bolt.

"We can't let them leave!" Elara said, struggling against the machine, but it was many times stronger than her. "Only Ivan can open the door. Without him, we're trapped!"

Finn struggled to his feet and unclipped his laser, but the weapon was ruined. Grabbing his spear, he stabbed the blade into the neck of the evaluator, but the machine flung out an arm and struck him hard across the chest, sending him barreling over the counter that the robot had previously stood behind.

"Chiefy!" Finn called out, his eyes bleary. "Scraps... help!"

Chiefy stormed forward and grabbed the evaluator robot's wrists, wrestling the machine away from Elara. Smoke was rising from the robot's charred circuits, but Scraps' modifications had again saved the foreman from being destroyed by an electric blast. The two robots warred for a few seconds, exchanging blows, until Chiefy overpowered the evaluator and snapped its neck. Sparks erupted from the machine's head then it toppled to the floor like a felled oak.

"Chiefy, stop Ivan!" Finn yelled, still in too much pain to run after them.

"They are already at the door," Chiefy said, poised to give chase, but even with his robotic acceleration, he couldn't hope to reach them in time. "I cannot stop them."

Elara picked herself up off the floor and scrambled to

collect her crossbow, which she'd been forced to drop while fighting the evaluator. Rolling onto her stomach, she adopted a prone position and aimed the weapon toward Ivan, but the exit door was already open, and the regent successor had ushered Juniper through.

"Take the shot!" Finn said, struggling to get to his feet. "Take it, now!"

Elara fired, but the bolt soared above Ivan's head, and the acting mayor vanished through the door, which began to close behind him. Finn scrambled forward on his hands and knees in a desperate attempt to reach the exit before it was closed to them, but it was a futile effort. The slab of metal retracted and with it, their only way of reaching Reznikov was barred too.

"You missed..." Chiefy said, sounding flabbergasted. The robot turned to Elara and frowned. "You never miss."

"And I didn't this time," Elara said, hissing and groaning as she hauled herself upright. "I wasn't aiming at Ivan. I was aiming at the door."

Finn turned back to the exit and looked more closely. The door hadn't closed fully; it had been prevented from doing so by a carefully aimed crossbow bolt that had become lodged into the inner frame.

"I'm impressed," Finn said, resting his hands on his hips.

"Still?" Elara said. "After all this time?"

"I'm not impressed that you made the shot." Finn laughed. "I'm impressed you didn't use that bolt to pierce Juniper's black heart instead."

Finn pointing this out seemed only to make Elara angry, and he wished he hadn't mentioned it.

"I still have plenty more bolts," Elara said, loading

another as she spoke. "And one of them has Juniper's name on it, mark my words."

Finn nodded then turned to Chiefy, who had stopped smoldering like an old bonfire.

"Do you think you can get that door open?"

Chiefy shrugged then interlocked his fingers and reversed his hands, as if trying to crack his joints in preparation for a heavy deadlift at the gym.

"Only one way to find out," the robot said, cheerfully.

10

OLD MODELS, NEW TRICKS

FINN CAREFULLY CHECKED his laser cannon, observing that the case was blackened where circuits and capacitors had exploded inside the weapon, after the gate scanner had overloaded its power cell. He turned to Chiefy and held out the weapon, hopeful that the robot might be able to repair it, but Chiefy merely shook his head.

"The damage is too severe," Chiefy said. "If it were not for Scraps' modifications to my own circuitry, I would also have been disabled. Permanently."

"You still have this, at least," Elara said, removing the spear from Finn's back and giving it a quick flourish. "It may not pack an electrified punch anymore, but it's better than nothing."

Finn nodded and accepted the weapon back from Elara. In truth, he'd hoped that neither the spear nor his now defunct cannon would be needed once they'd reached Nimbus, but it seemed clear that Ivan's promise that there was no security on the station had been false. The acting mayor's shout of "Emergency protocol!", which had triggered the evaluator to attack, suggested that there were likely more dangers ahead.

"We need to know where Ivan and Juniper went, and find them," Finn said. "If they raise the alarm, it could make things very difficult for us."

As he finished, red lights in the corners of the arrivals zone began to flash, and a computerized voice, similar to the one that had spoken inside the space capsule, intoned, *"Intruder Alert! Prefects to Docking Port B One."*

"I knew that bastard was lying when he said there weren't any prefects on Nimbus," Elara said. "We need to move, now."

Finn looked anxiously toward the door that Elara had wedged open with a bolt, and tightened his grip on his spear, expecting prefects to rush through at any moment.

"Scraps, can you jam the station's scanners so that the prefects can't track us?" Finn asked.

"Yes-yes!" Scraps said. The robot opened the compartment in Chiefy's chest and flew across to the destroyed evaluator. "Need bad robot's CPU!"

At Scraps' behest, Chiefy grabbed the evaluator's head and twisted it severely, snapping it away from the machine's neck.

"Work and move," Elara said, while stalking toward the exit, crossbow held ready. "This station is big, but we don't know how many prefects are on-board and how long it will take them to get here. I'd rather we're long gone before then."

Elara covered the foreman while Chiefy slid his fingers into the narrow gap between the door and the frame, and forced it open. At the same time, Scraps had flipped open the top of the evaluator's head, like popping the hood of an ale truck, and was working inside.

"Program fixed in MROM," Scraps said, while still part-buried inside the head. "But Scraps found security chip!"

Scraps emerged from the head, holding a finger-shaped circuit board containing a number of components and ICs, which the robot proceeded to feed himself. A few moments passed while Scraps digested the new processor, then he threw his hands into the air, triumphantly.

"Nimbus scanners blocked!"

"Good work, pal," Finn said, patting the robot on the head. "Now, we need to know where to go, and how to avoid these prefects."

"Ivan said that Reznikov's palace was in the center of the station, so we head inward," Elara said. She had stalked through the exit, aiming her crossbow into every nook and cranny of the space outside, not taking any chances. "Assuming he wasn't also lying about how long it would take for the rest of the Solaris rockets to leave Spacehaven, we have about four hours to stop the city from being nuked."

Suddenly, Scraps leapt onto Chiefy's shoulder, his scanner dish probing the new room, which was as industrial-looking and empty as the arrivals area.

"Someone coming!" Scraps said, urgently, before pointing toward one of the many corridors that led off from the room. "That way, quick!"

Chiefy ran ahead, guided by Scraps, and Finn was still amazed at how quietly the seven-foot robot was able to move. They entered the corridor just as bootsteps began to thump into the room, and Finn pressed his back to the wall, chancing a look at the prefect force that had been sent to capture or kill them. Six figures stormed past and entered the arrivals area, carrying firearms that were unlike anything Finn had seen before, with strange conical barrels, like siphons. Their bodies were clad in a shimmering silver carapace that resembled special prefect armor, and each wore a full-length visor that hid their faces and identities. Even so, from their physical builds and the different ways in which they moved, Finn could tell that the prefect squad was comprised of men and women, three of each.

"Come on, we can't risk being seen," Elara whispered, taking Finn's arm, and trying to coax him away. "I'm sure we'll get a proper introduction to them later, but for now we have maybe five kilometers to cover to reach the president's palace."

Finn nodded and slipped away, though he desperately wanted to stay and eavesdrop on the conversation between the officers in the arrivals hall. He had so many questions, and no answers. Were the prefects shipped up from Nimbus, or had they been born on the space station? What were the weapons they were carrying? Did the color of their armor – unique compared to anything he'd seen on Zavetgrad – represent anything important? In the end, he had to leave his questions unanswered, for another time.

Scraps scanned ahead, still perched on Chiefy's shoulder, but the robot's range was limited, and the station was massive at more than ten kilometers in diameter.

"There must be elevator cars and conveyors of some kind, to move people around the station," Finn said, as they passed from one industrial-looking corridor to another, still without seeing any signs of life. "Maybe there's even some kind of internal road system?"

"Scraps picking up monorails," the robot cut in, confirming Finn's suspicions. "But no station. No way in!"

"Keep looking, pal," Finn said, as they moved across another junction point, still without seeing a soul, other than the mysterious prefects who'd been sent to find them. "And keep your scanners peeled for people too, especially that rat Ivan and his new paramour."

"Juniper bad!" Scraps replied, before growling like a dog.

"She's also dangerous," Elara cut in. The mere mention of Juniper's name had caused her expression to sour, as if she was chewing lemon rind. "She had Ivan wrapped around her little finger. Whatever he has planned, she'll be behind it, steering the course."

Finn and the others continued through the station for several more minutes, moving through empty rooms and empty corridors, while searching for some way to access the mono-rail system that Scraps had detected, but Nimbus was a maze on a colossal scale, and without a map, the truth was that they were lost.

"Where is everyone?" Finn commented, after fifteen minutes had passed without them seeing anything but wall panels and deck plates.

"Nimbus was built to accommodate future generations, with the population increasing exponentially over time," Chiefy said, his feet gliding across the deck like ice skates.

"Sure, but there must be some people who are already here?" Finn ventured. "What about all the babies and embryos that Spacehaven blasted into orbit over the decades?"

The robot considered the question carefully before answering, and appeared to be electronically conferring with Scraps at the same time.

"Based on what Ivan Volkov told us about the rate of genetic degradation on Earth since Zavetgrad was founded, the number of viable embryos and infants that reached this citadel may have been vastly overestimated," the robot said. "Assuming the President is only interested in genetic perfection, which we have no reason to doubt, the population of this space station could be considerably smaller than anyone thought. Perhaps only in the tens of thousands, at most."

"That might mean everyone is clustered closer to the center," Finn suggested.

"Or toward the outer edges of the station," Chiefy added. "On the journey to Nimbus, I noted that many sections of the station appeared to be without power, while those closest to the edge seemed active."

"Either way, we won't know for sure, until we reach Reznikov," Elara said. Then she stopped and furrowed her brow. "Unless we can find a computer sub-station and hack into the Nimbus mainframe. Then we'd know exactly where to go, including where Reznikov is keeping his nukes."

Scraps and Chiefy conferred electronically for a few seconds then turned back to the others. Finn recognized the pleased look on his little buddy's face, and knew that Scraps had a plan.

"Scraps find network," the robot said, tracing his finger across an invisible line in the wall. "Follow hard line, find 'puter!"

"Then lead the way," Finn said, ushering the two robots ahead.

Chiefy set a furious pace and they jogged for another thirty minutes, with Scraps directing their course at each step of the way, using his finger and outstretched arm like the needle of a compass. At one point, they reached a window in the steel-gray wall that looked out onto the monorail system Scraps had talked about. A train rushed past as they stared into the dark chamber. It was sleek, like a bullet, but half the size or less compared to the bulky freight trains that circumnavigated Zavetgrad, carrying goods and materials to and from each sector.

"We really need to find a way on-board one of those trains," Finn said. His feet were already sore from stomping around on hard steel plates.

"Let's find the computer first," Elara said, also looking longingly at the train as it sped past. "Then we can find a map of all the stations and terminals, and maybe even a way to control them."

Chiefy ventured on, eventually leading the group down a long corridor that ended at a hatchway, not unlike the one in the space capsule that had ferried them to the station.

"Is this a dead end?" Finn asked. He looked back along the corridor, but they hadn't passed another junction or exit for at least ten minutes, and he hated the idea they might have to re-trace their steps.

"I believe it is a maintenance hatch, or perhaps an observation level," Chiefy said, listening closely with his auditory sensor pressed to the hatch, while Scraps tried to scan beyond it.

"Observing what?" Elara said. Her crossbow was suddenly more prominent.

"Lots of robots..." Scraps interrupted, and his mechanical eyes narrowed in concentration. "Machinery too. Maybe factory?"

"Shit, we can hardly go strolling through an industrial unit," Finn said, again looking back, anxious that the prefect might have been tracking them. "Is there a way around it without having to double back?"

"Yes-yes!" Scraps said, pointing to the wall.

Chiefy gently ushered Finn aside then thumped one of the steel wall panels with the back of his fist. A corner of the heavy metal plate popped out, then Chiefy repeated the process at the other three corners, until the panel had been released and the robot was able to shift it aside.

"We can move beneath the floor, using the interstitial zones," Chiefy said. "These are the spaces between the different areas of the station, where electrical conduits and other utilities and wiring is routed."

Chiefy invited Finn to step into the hole in the wall, but the ice-cold draught that was leaking out of it, combined with the fact it was pitch black, didn't inspire confidence.

"Did I mention I hate confined spaces, as well as heights?" Finn said.

"Just get in there," Elara said, kicking Finn's ass with the side of her boot. It was done playfully and hurt his pride more than his backside. "The sooner we find that computer room, the sooner we can swap icy conduits for a nice warm train."

Finn grouched for a moment then pulled himself inside the interstitial space. The pipes and conduits that ran through the crawlspace were either freezing cold or scalding hot, depending on what they contained, and Finn burned his hand from heat and cold three times in the first few minutes on his hands and knees. Chiefy entered last and replaced the panel to make sure that no-one could follow them, though still the only people they'd seen, besides

Juniper and Ivan, were the six prefects they'd left behind forty minutes ago.

Weaving his way through the conduit, Finn worked his way beneath the floor of the factory space that Scraps believed lay behind the locked hatchway. Through the metal grates above him, he could hear the sound of heavy machinery thumping and whirring, and the clomping footsteps of robots moving in a rhythmic fashion, like they were working on a production line. Moving his way around the edge of the factory hall, Finn maneuvered himself into a position where he could get a clearer look at the machines and the operation that was working tirelessly above them.

Part of the factory hall appeared to be dedicated to manufacturing items of clothing. Finn saw shirts, jackets and pairs of pants, all fashioned from a hardy-looking, charcoal-colored material. Another machine produced shoes, in the same dark grey hue. There didn't appear to be any variation in style or cut to account for the different body shapes of men and women, but the machine was spewing out the clothes in two distinctly different sizes. One line was producing clothes that were so small they could only have been intended for children.

Finn parked that thought then observed the second section of the factory, which was manufacturing silver canisters, like drinks flasks. The flasks were produced by one machine before being ferried to another then filled and sealed. A separate part of the operation stacked the filled canisters into boxes, which were carried onto trolleys by foremen then wheeled away.

"What they hell are they putting into those flasks?" Elara wondered.

"Unclear, but it appears to be a liquid of some kind," Chiefy said, though Finn had observed that much himself.

With the contents of the flasks still a mystery, Finn turned his attention to the foremen. The robots were rudimentary in design, and lacked the agility and dexterity of the foremen Finn was used to seeing in Zavetgrad, especially the advanced Gen-VII models, like Chiefy. Their faces were expressionless lumps with just ocular holes, mouth grilles and glowing red eyes that could neither narrow nor blink.

"They are mainly Gen Two designs," Chiefy whispered, explaining the reason for the robots' simplistic appearance and limited abilities. "Many are even Gen One models."

"I expected Nimbus to be way ahead of the tech we had in Zavetgrad," Finn said, as a Gen I unsteadily clomped its way overhead, carrying a box filled with flasks. "Why is everything up here clunky and old?"

"In Zavetgrad, it was required to improve and iterate the Foreman design, to make it more efficient and resilient," Chiefy replied. "Also, the harsh environment meant that units failed and had to be replaced on a regular basis. The same was true of much of the technology the golds employed. On this space station, there are no threats and no hardships, and so no need to replace or improve upon these older models."

Chiefy's explanation made perfect sense. Then Finn had an idea, one that could help solve all of their problems.

"Scraps, can you hack these robots, and control them?" Finn asked. "There must be at least a hundred up there, and with a force like that at our backs, I doubt even those new silver prefects could stop us."

"Two-hundred-fifty robots," Scraps said, correcting Finn

on the number of machines that were above him. "But Scraps can't hack," the robot added, forlornly.

"Like the evaluator we met, these foremen are all running programs that are stored in MROM," Chiefy said, elaborating on Scraps' answer. "We cannot affect their code."

Finn recalled how Maxim Volkov had initiated a security procedure on the housekeeper robots inside Elysium, switching their FLPs to use code stored in MROM, or Mask Read Only Memory. This was a non-volatile memory that was written-to permanently during the manufacturing process and could not be altered or reprogrammed afterward.

"Reznikov isn't stupid," Elara said. "It's a wise precaution, and one that suggests the president might even have anticipated that rebels would one day infiltrate his station."

The prospect that Reznikov might have a contingency plan already in place concerned Finn, but there was nothing they could do about it at that moment. They had to keep moving, and if the president did have a surprise waiting for them, they would have to deal with it when it happened.

"I suggest we keep moving; the computer room is not far," Chiefy said, taking the lead.

Chiefy had been forced to move through the sub-floor space on his stomach, leopard crawling like a soldier trying to sneak up on an enemy position. Scraps clung on to the foreman's back. Elara went next and this time Finn picked up the rear, still fascinated by the obsolete machines that toiled above him, and the simple clothes that they were producing. He wondered if children were already living in the citadel, or if the garments were being produced in advance of a new generation of Nimbus-born inhabitants.

Finn's thoughts then dwelled on the workhouse in the Authority sector, and how Gideon Alexander Reznikov had not hesitated to bomb the building and kill innocents, simply to make a point. From an early age, Finn remembered being told that Nimbus was a paradise and the future of humanity, and he remembered feeling jealous of the people who would get to live there. Yet after witnessing the depths that Reznikov would sink to, even killing children, he now feared just as much for the people on the space station as he did for those in the city.

Suddenly, a troop of foremen marched above him, dislodging dust and dirt from the metal gratings. The grimy cloud enveloped Finn and got into his eyes and his mouth, and up his nose. A tickle crept up on him from out of nowhere and before he could bury his face in his arm to stifle the sound, he had sneezed.

"Did you hear something?" A Gen I foreman asked. Its vocal processor was tinny and electronic.

"Be more specific Foreman 177-1," a Gen II answered. "There are hundreds of distinct sounds in this room."

The second robot also sounded processed and inhuman, but Finn could still recognize the condescending tone of a chief foreman by the way it spoke to its underling.

"It sounded like a sneeze," the Gen I clarified.

"How do you know what a sneeze sounds like?" The chief said, ramping up the level of condescension.

"I heard a perfect sneeze once," the Gen I said.

The Gen II considered this then was about to make another declaration, when Chiefy opened a pressure valve on a cooling conduit, releasing a brief but audible hiss of steam.

"There, that is what you heard," the chief foreman said,

before whacking the Gen I across the side of the head with its crude hand. "Schedule repair crawlers to inspect the floor space, then get back to work."

"I will comply," the Gen I answered, before stomping away, none the worse for being humiliated and slapped in front of its co-workers.

"Quick thinking, Chiefy," Elara said, squeezing's the robot's shoulder. "Now let's get out of here, before Finn sneezes again, or worse..."

Finn scowled at Elara, but she'd already turned her back on him and was crawling away on her hands and knees. The group made it to the far side of the factory without attracting any more attention, and Chiefy guided them out of the subfloor and back into the interstitial spaces, before repeating the process of bashing the corners of a wall panel, this time to release an exit.

Finn climbed out last, but the new room he found himself in was no warmer than the icy compartment he'd just left. Wiping the dirt from his eyes and shaking the dust from his hair, he took a look around their new location, and found it to be filled with wide rectangular boxes, connected by hundreds of wires. Each of the boxes contained an array of blinking, green lights, and altogether thousands, or even tens of thousands, of the winking LEDs twinkled at him.

"This is a computer room?" Finn asked, since he'd never been in one before.

"Correct, this is exactly what we need," Chiefy replied. He and Scraps were already busy working on a console that was stuffed between the rows of computer hardware.

"Let me know when you've found a map," Finn said, still finding dirt in places he thought he'd already cleaned. "Or, for that matter, a shower room," he added, brushing more grime from his hair.

A resonant thud echoed through the still open wall panel. Everyone froze. The thud came again, and was followed by a hollow rattle, like hailstones falling on a sheet metal roof. Then there was silence again.

"On second thoughts, stick to finding the map, and a way out of here," Finn said, inching closer to the opening in the wall, spear in hand. "I have a feeling that something is following us."

11

CREEPY CRAWLIES

Finn remained by the open panel in the computer room wall, watching and listening for the ominous sound that appeared to be getting closer. Every few seconds, there was a metallic rattle, like the scampering of tiny robotic feet, then silence again.

"How are you getting along over there?" Finn said, glancing back to Chiefy and Scraps, who were still buried inside the computer system.

"Like the foremen on this station, the computer network has not been substantially upgraded for many decades," Chiefy answered, while assisting Scraps like a nurse assisting a surgeon in an operating theater. "However, the technology and software used still constituted the state of the art at the end of the last war. We will require another two minutes to break the encryption and gain access to the outer layers of data."

The metallic rattle came again, except this time it appeared to filter into the computer room through air vents and grates in the floor. Elara had switched her crossbow for her double-headed axe and was creeping around the room, trying to follow the sound.

"Scraps, are your scanners still active? Because I'd really like to know what that noise is," Elara said, poking her axe at a vent a meter above her head.

"Scanners down while Scraps hacks!" the little robot replied. He was physically inside the cluster of computers, covered in a tangle of wires. "Won't be long!"

The robot's cheery optimism would usually set Finn's mind at rest, but on this occasion his sense of foreboding continued to grow.

"There's definitely something out there," Finn said, holding his spear in front of him, like a shield. While it was no longer able to deliver debilitating shocks, it was still a formidable weapon. "But it can't be those foremen we saw. They were way too big and clunky to move through the interstitial spaces."

Suddenly, an air-vent in the ceiling dropped to the floor, making a clanking sound like a gong. The plate-size grille spun around on its edge, like a hub cap that had dislodged from the wheel of an ale truck and gone hurtling down the road. Elara stepped on the grille to stop it rattling then peered through the opening in the ceiling that it had uncovered. For several seconds, she remained perfectly still, staring at the black hole without blinking.

"Do you see...?" Finn began, but Elara pressed a finger to her lips, and he bit his tongue, albeit unwillingly.

Several more seconds passed, then there was another percussive rattle, like a drumroll on a snare, and Elara drew back her axe, ready to swing. Finn could barely stand the tension, and he wanted to again ask what it was she'd seen, when something leapt from the hole in the ceiling. Elara swung her axe and connected with the object in mid-flight, batting the thing against one of the towering server racks. It splatted to the floor then sparks erupted from its cylindrical body, which was about half the volume of the oil can that Finn had used to build Scraps. Six legs sprang from beneath the machine then it raised its squat head and a single red light focused on Elara.

Finn angled his spear at the spider-like machine and was about to charge like a medieval jouster, when another spider jumped from the hole in the wall and clamped itself to Finn's chest armor. The shock caused him to scream in fright and he dropped his spear, before grabbing the robot and trying to tear it from his body, but the machine was dug in hard.

At the same time, the first robot scuttled across the floor toward Elara, but it was already damaged, and she was able to slice the machine in half with another well-timed swing of her axe. Two more spiders dropped from the vent, then another crawled out from beneath the server racks, and turned its red eye toward Chiefy and Scraps.

"Chiefy, look out!" Finn yelled, but he was too late.

The spider jumped like it had been propelled by a coiled spring and wrapped its legs around Chiefy's face. A drill-like probe sprang from the robot's body and burrowed into Chiefy's head, while the foreman reeled back, bouncing off server racks, and colliding with the walls, until he fell flat on his back and went as rigid as a board.

Finn tore the spider away from his chest, breaking three of its legs in the process, then slammed it to the floor and stomped on it. If it had been a real spider, the creature would have been pulped into a squelchy mass beneath his boot, but the damaged mechanical device instead limped away, its red eyes searching for somewhere to hide. Grabbing his spear, he hurled the weapon at the spider and skewered it though its center of mass, pinning it to the floor.

"Finn!"

Elara's cry spun him around, and he saw her fighting off another three of the mechanisms. One was held outstretched in her hands, its legs wrapped around her wrists, while another clung to her leg, and the third was crawling up her back, and gunning for the base of her neck.

"Hold still!" Finn said, retrieving his spear and darting toward her.

Elara froze, and for once Finn saw fear behind her emerald eyes. Fighting prefects, prosecutors and other anthropoid robots was one thing, but human beings were hard-wired to fear creepy-crawlies, and whether they were made of flesh or metal made no difference.

Finn swung his spear and slashed the spider off Elara's back before it could drill into her brain with its probe. Then he rammed the weapon between the spider on Elara's thigh and her armor plating, levering it away. The spider scuttled across the floor, and Finn chased it, trying to swat it with his spear, but the machine jinked and weaved and managed to evade him. In the corner of the room was an open floor vent, and Finn realized that if the spider managed to escape, it would alert the silver-armored prefects to their location, or send an army of Gen I and Gen II foremen after them. He threw his spear like a javelin but missed, and the spider scuttled on.

Suddenly, Scraps raced past Finn's face, rotors blaring, and dropped onto the six-legged machine before it could escape. The two small robots tussled, and for a terrifying moment, Finn thought that the spider was about to drill into Scraps' head, in the same way another of the horrific machines had incapacitated Chiefy, until he realized that his pal had outmaneuvered the other robot. Data probes were connected to the spider's head, then the machine's red eye blinked out, and it collapsed under Scraps' weight.

Finn spun around again and saw Elara hacking at the final spider with her axe. It was already in a dozen sputtering pieces on the floor, but she continued to whack it with the double-headed axe, until it was little more than a pile of metal shards.

"I think you got it," Finn said, catching Elara's wrist on the backswing. "Keep hitting that thing, and you'll hack a hole through the floor and into space."

"I hate spiders," Elara said, and she physically shivered. "I hate anything with more than two legs."

"There aren't many things with two legs you like either," Finn said, grinning, but the death stare he got in return told him that Elara was not in a joking mood.

"Chiefy!"

It was Scraps who had forlornly cried out the foreman's name, and they all rushed to the robot's side. The spider was still clamped to his head, but Scraps made short work of the machine, attaching a data probe to a port on its back and disabling it in an instant. Finn pulled the incapacitated spider away and threw it into the corner of the room, eliciting another shiver from Elara, as its spindly legs whirled through the air.

"Chiefy..." Finn said, slapping the side of the robot's face, like he was trying to wake up a drunk Metalhaven worker who'd fallen asleep at the bar. "Chiefy, are you okay?"

The spider's drill had entered through Chiefy's mouth, though there didn't appear to be any significant damage, at least in a physical sense. However, as Scraps had so aptly demonstrated, the real damage to any electronic machine was always done on the inside, to its circuits, memory chips and processors.

"Scraps checking!" the little robot said, its data probes now connected to a port on the side of Chiefy's head.

"He'll be okay, pal," Finn said, resting his hand on his buddy's head. "Chiefy has survived a lot worse than creepy robot spiders."

Chiefy's eyes lit up, and Scraps detached his interface then jumped onto Finn's shoulder.

"Chiefy?" Finn said again. The robot still hadn't moved. "Chiefy, come on, wake up!"

Chiefy's eyes blinked then the mechanical muscles in the robots face that simulated human expressions went through a series of motions, from happy to sad, angry to ashamed, and everything in between, before settling on a placid, half-smile. Finn stepped back, with Elara at his side and Scraps still on his shoulder. Then Chiefy climbed to his feet too, before fixing his glowing eyes onto him.

"Finn Brasa, you are three-per-cent below today's quota," Chiefy said, in the same asshole manager's voice that all Chief Foremen from the reclamation yards had been programmed to master. "Fifteen hours have been added to tomorrow's shift."

"Fifteen?" Finn said, pressing his hands to his hips. It was like he was right back in Yard seven, as if nothing had happened. "You can't be serious, you thick-headed metal fuck! That's outrageous..."

Finn caught himself, then narrowed his eyes, first at Chiefy, whose expression had not changed, then at Elara and Scraps, who were both choking back sniggers.

"Seriously?" Finn said, hands still on hips. "You're fucking with me, now of all times?"

"Sorry," Chiefy said, though the robot was objectively not sorry. "Was it a good joke?"

Finn wanted to be angry, but the truth was Chiefy's prank had been pretty good, and the relief of knowing he was okay felt like a pressure release valve being opened.

"Actually, yes, it was a pretty good joke," Finn said, allowing a smile. "Don't make a habit of it, though."

"Chiefy tough!" Scraps said, flexing his metal biceps. "Chiefy beat rogue program, and Scraps blocked spiders' data stream. No danger!"

"Good work, pal," Finn said, though he wasn't sure he agreed with his buddy's assessment that there was no danger. "How did you get on with finding a map in the mainframe?" he added, pointing toward the computer console that the two robots had been working on.

"There are many layers of security, but we have managed to breach the system and gain access to some of the basic systems," Chiefy replied.

The robot led them to a screen then began working at the console. A wire-frame image of Nimbus appeared on the display then began to rotate slowly.

"Nimbus is not one station, but a highly modular collection of dozens of component parts, many of which are able to function in isolation," the robot continued, while the sections in question were highlighted in different colors. Many appeared to be around the station's edge, while the central sphere, which contained Reznikov's palace, also seemed to be a distinct module. "The entire space station could be deconstructed, block by block, and reassembled in different configurations, according to need," Chiefy added. "However, as we suspected, large portions of Nimbus remain unused and uninhabited."

"Do you have enough access to put a figure on how many people are actually on this thing?" Finn asked.

"I believe so..."

The robot worked for a few more seconds, highlighting ten distinct blocks, all situated around the circumference of the station, in what the map had designated Quarter Four.

"Each of these clusters can accommodate more than one thousand human beings," Chiefy said, expanding the image and zooming in on a distinct cluster. "Carbon dioxide scrubbers in these clusters are operating at a far higher level than the rest of the station, indicating a significant level of respiration. As such, I surmise that there are perhaps ten thousand human beings alive on Nimbus at this moment in time."

The news took Finn and Elara by surprise.

"Only ten thousand, after all these years?" Elara said. "I would have guessed at ten times that figure, at least."

"It is curious," Chiefy said, cocking his head to one side. "Data that is available in the system indicates a steady population growth, but also a higher termination rate."

Finn scowled. "Don't you mean death rate?"

"Actually, the term, 'mortality rate', would be the more understood phrase to indicate deaths from illness, frailty, or misadventure," the robot corrected him. "However, the computer does not label the negative growth numbers in this manner. The heading is simply labelled, 'Terminations'."

"Well, fuck, that's ominous," Finn said. "I thought Nimbus was supposed to be a paradise."

"We thought that about Elysium too, and look how that turned out," Elara added, darkly.

"The president's palace is inside this central sphere," Chiefy said, continuing with his briefing. "Based on the data we have downloaded from the mainframe, Scraps and I can chart a course though the station that avoids the populated areas."

"How about avoiding those silver prefects too?" Finn asked.

"Fuck them, how do we avoid the spiders?" Elara cut in, with feeling.

"The spiders should no longer trouble us, since unlike the foremen, their code is alterable, at least in part," Chiefy said. "Their function is to conduct repairs all throughout Nimbus, which necessitates an ability to learn and adapt to changing circumstances."

"So, what did you do to them?" Finn asked.

"We simply programmed new variables into their memory banks," Chiefy said. "Those variables being us."

Finn nodded and noted that Scraps again looked particularly pleased with himself, which suggested that he had been the architect of the spider's modified code.

"It's a shame we can't also re-program those prefects," Elara said, at the same time as drumming her fingers against the blade of her axe.

"That would be nice, but sadly not," Chiefy replied. "Unfortunately, we are also not able to track their movements with the level of access we have achieved. It is therefore possible we may encounter them again."

Finn acknowledged Chiefy's warning with a muted grunt. From the look in Elara's eyes, and the way she was caressing her axe, Finn could tell she was eager to test the Nimbus prefects in a fight, but he would rather avoid them and their curious-looking cannons.

"Scraps can scan!" Scraps cut in, pointing to where he stowed his scanner dish.

"Then you can be our early-warning system, pal," Finn said, grateful as ever for his ingenious robot companion. His choice of words then reminded him that all of Zavetgrad was similarly under threat of attack at any moment. "Exactly how long do we have until Reznikov can launch his missiles?"

"There is no way to know exactly," Chiefy answered. The two robots then conferred wirelessly for a couple of seconds. "Based on the original timeframe for all Solaris Ignition rockets to depart Spacehaven, we have two hours and fifty minutes."

Finn sighed and his body physically deflated. That was barely any time at all, and they still had a long way to travel through a station filled with unknown dangers, and a squad of prefects that were hunting them.

"However," Chiefy added, and the rising intonation of the robot's voice gave Finn hope of a reprieve, "according to the Nimbus computer, the weather above Zavetgrad has worsened, which will delay some of the final rocket launches, unless they are willing to risk launching in dangerous conditions."

"I wouldn't put that past them," Elara said. She then appeared to reconsider her statement. "Though this is the last chance Reznikov will get to plunder resources from the city, so he might not want to take that chance."

"I agree, especially considering there is another Solaris Ignition Five rocket that has yet to blast off," Chiefy added.

"There's no way he'll risk that crashing and burning," Finn chimed in. He remembered talk of the next-generation Solaris Ignition V rockets, which had a colossal twenty-five thousand kilonewtons of lift-off thrust and could ferry almost five-hundred metric tons of cargo to Nimbus. "Reznikov will wait, which means we have another hour or two, maybe even more."

"Perhaps, but let's not bank on that," Elara said. "We head straight to his palace, put a gun to the bastard's head, and make him call off the strike."

"You make it sound so easy," Finn said.

"It doesn't have to be any harder," Elara replied, her stare hardening. "If Reznikov values his life, he'll do what we say." Elara spun her axe then patted it to the flat of her hand. "Then we'll kill him anyway and blow this space station to hell."

Finn raised an eyebrow at Elara, and so did Chiefy, but he chose not to question her murderous scheme. This was mainly because he didn't have a good alternative, though if there was a value in keeping Reznikov alive, he wanted to retain that as an option, even if Elara protested. Talk of destroying Nimbus then suddenly reminded Finn that it wasn't only Reznikov's life they were threatening, but the lives of all its colonists too. The fact they'd completely overlooked this made him feel not only foolish, but callous.

"What about the ten thousand people living on the station?" Finn asked. "We came here to stop Reznikov and save Zavetgrad, but we keep forgetting about the people who are already here."

Finn's question stopped Elara in her tracks and made her think about something besides murder. The problem of what to do with the station's population ruminated in her mind, and Finn could see her working through the options, but all the while her expression remained unforgiving.

"Here's the deal," Elara said, and Finn could already tell that the 'deal' was a bad one for those living on Nimbus. "We may be faced with a choice to sacrifice ten thousand, in order to save a million." She shrugged. "I hate to make it all about the math, but there it is. That's our choice, and we can't escape it."

Finn shook his head. "I don't accept that, not yet. Maybe we could take over the station?"

This time it was Chiefy who waded in with bad news.

"That may not be possible," Chiefy said, glumly. "The foreman robots on Nimbus are hard-wired to follow Reznikov's directives. Even if we could kill or otherwise neutralize the prefects, these robots would never follow our commands. They would remain hostile."

"How many of these old gen ones and twos are we talking about?" Finn asked.

Chiefy considered the question, while silently conferring with Scraps.

"Upwards of fifty thousand may be resident on this station," Chiefy replied.

"Well, fuck..." Finn said, his idea well and truly sunk.

"Besides, we don't even know who these people are," Elara said, sticking to her guns. "For all we know they could be worse than the golds."

Finn rubbed his eyes. He didn't have a problem fighting prefects, and he didn't have a problem killing, when it was necessary, but this felt different. This felt like crossing a line.

"Okay, but it has to be a last resort," Finn said. "If letting the people on this station die is the only way to save the city, we do it. But only if there's absolutely no other choice."

Elara smiled. "Always the hero," she said, though she wasn't mocking him. "This is why you were chosen, Finn, because you give a shit." Her eyes then hardened. "Me, on the other hand... I was chosen because I'll do whatever it takes, no matter what, to bring the Authority to its knees."

12

NIGHT AT THE MUSEUM

Thanks to the map that Chiefy and Scraps had obtained from the Nimbus mainframe computer, Finn and the others were able to progress through the station without any further incidents. Numerous times they were confronted by the spider-like repair bots, but on each occasion the machines simply went about their business, fixing wiring looms, repairing broken pipes and generally making sure that the space station didn't fall to pieces.

Soon, they had arrived at one of the many small mono-rail platforms that allowed the robotic and human population of Nimbus to traverse its vast interior. From the map, Finn had learned that there were many different rail networks inside the station, rather than one large loop. According to Chiefy, it was analogous to something called the London Underground, where many different subterranean railway lines crisscrossed England's once-great city, requiring travelers to change lines sometimes two or three times, depending on which part of London they needed to visit.

"Where does this thing terminate?" Finn asked, while

cautiously stepping aboard the narrow train. It was comprised of only two carriages, and seemed like it could ferry no more than about fifty people or robots in total.

"This train will take us roughly seventy-five percent of the distance we need to travel," Chiefy replied, while politely holding open the door for Elara. "It appears to terminate close to a cluster of large, open spaces, near to what I believe is an inhabited area of the station."

"Is that a good idea?" Finn said. He'd wedged his foot against the door, to make sure it couldn't close. "I thought we were trying to avoid the populated areas."

"We cannot avoid those spaces entirely," Chiefy replied, and the robot's calm tone gave Finn some reassurance that the machine had considered the route carefully. "However, I believe we can still navigate around the populated areas without being seem. I have calculated that this is our fastest route to the president's palace."

"Stop holding up the train," Elara said, playfully kicking Finn's foot away from the door.

"Someone is an impatient traveler," Finn said, scowling at Elara before sitting on one of the hard plastic seats that lined the train's walls.

"It used to drive me crazy when golds held open the doors for their friends, co-workers, or just other randoms who didn't have the good manners to be on time," Elara said, sitting opposite Finn, and putting her feet up on the seat next to him. "I used to enjoy tormenting them, and making them miss their trains."

"That makes you a bad person," Finn said, sweeping Elara's feet off the seat. He then reconsidered his point of view. "Though, they were golds, so I guess it's okay."

Elara smiled then swung her legs onto a seat on her side of the train instead, before shuffling back against the partition and closing her eyes, as if she were taking a nap. Finn preferred to keep his eyes open and remain alert, but the harmonious drone of the magnetic levitation system proved oddly soporific, and Finn quickly found his eyes closing of their own accord. Suddenly, he was jolted awake by the train coming to a stop, followed by the hiss of the doors opening.

"End of the line, sleepy head," Elara said. Annoyingly, despite being the one who had intentionally tried to nap, she had been wide awake and ready before the train had reached its station.

"Where are we?" Finn yawned while pushing himself vertical.

"I have no idea," Elara said, readying her crossbow. "But Scraps' scanners says that the hall just beyond the corridor outside is packed with objects, though he can't determine what exactly."

"Hopefully, not more robots," Finn said, hopping off the train and following his partner into the new part of the space station.

A short corridor ended in a T-junction and huge double-door that wouldn't have looked out of place at the entrance to the mayor's building in the Authority sector. Finn had no-idea if turning left or right would lead them deeper into the station or back toward its edge, but as it turned out, Chiefy and Scraps headed for the door instead and began working on the lock.

"Are you sure there aren't a thousand asshole gen one foremen on the other side?" Finn said, as the two robots worked the door panel.

"Sure-sure!" Scraps said. "Lots of stuff. No foremen."

The lock clicked and Chiefy inched open the door. Elara poked herself through first, since Chiefy's sizable robot body couldn't fit through the narrow gap.

"It looks clear," Elara said, moving through into the new space fully. "I don't know what this place is, but it's full of junk, like Scraps said."

Chiefy opened the door wider, and Finn followed Elara into an open space that was easily as large as the Regent's Cathedral in the sub-oceanic complex. If they'd knocked down all the interior walls on the top-floor of the gene bank office in reclamation sector four, Finn imagined it would look pretty similar, except that the ceiling in the room he was standing in was about twenty meters high.

"I believe this is a museum, of sorts," Chiefy said, approaching the nearest cluster of objects, which were set out on white pedestals, as if being displayed.

"But a museum of what?" Finn asked. He worked his way inside, still cautious of any robot spiders that might be lurking in the dark nooks and crannies, and found that the hall was filled with a wide variety of objects, from manufactured devices, to what looked like parts of old buildings built from stone and brick. Toward the center of the hall was what appeared to be part of a pylon engineered from heavy steel or iron girders, that stretched up to the full twenty-meter height of the room.

"This looks like a written language, but it doesn't make any sense to me," Finn said, stopping at a sign. "The letters all look right, but they're in the wrong order."

"Maybe it's a code?" Elara suggested, with a shrug.

"It is not code," Chiefy cut in. "It is French."

Finn scowled at the machine. "You say that like it's supposed to make everything clear?"

"France was a country on the European continent, before the last war," Chiefy explained, and Finn felt stupid for not connecting 'French' with 'France', a country he had read a little about. "This hall is filled with relics from France, recovered after the last war. The pylon is part of what was called The Eiffel Tower, which was a major landmark and attraction in Paris, the capital city. It was largely destroyed in the nuclear bombardment of the country, though it appears that some of it survived."

"And now it's here, two-hundred and fifty miles above the surface of the planet." Finn let out an exasperated sigh. "The question is, why is it here?"

"Perhaps Gideon Alexander Reznikov wanted to preserve elements from the old world?" Chiefy suggested, but Elara shook her head.

"That doesn't track. Everything we know about Reznikov suggested he wanted Nimbus to be a clean slate." Elara pointed to the remains of the Eiffel Tower, which Finn could now see was bomb damaged in places. "So why would he have all this junk blasted into space?"

"Maybe he has a sentimental side, after all?" Finn suggested, realizing that they actually knew barely anything about the president or his true motives, only what the Authority had told them. "Or maybe Reznikov is nothing but a narcissistic asshole, and this is just the greatest treasure hoard in all of human history."

"Look at this..."

While Finn and Elara had been talking, Chiefy and Scraps, who was still perched on his friend's shoulder, had moved further into the room. They were now standing in what looked like a separate exhibition space within the hall, featuring a number of relics that were all displayed with care and attention, with plenty of space and even benches placed around then.

"These object are from the Louvre, a famous museum that was also in Paris," Chiefy explained. "It was a place that stored many artifacts of significant historical value."

"You mean like a bank?" Elara asked.

"No, the Louvre was open to the public," Chiefy explained. "Anyone could visit and look upon these objects."

Elara snorted. "Sounds boring, if you ask me."

"I didn't," Chiefy replied, somewhat snootily.

Finn laughed, enjoying the robot's cool put down. Then he remembered how Chiefy had been fascinated by the Turner painting that was hung in the office belonging to Gabriel Montgomery, the now-dead Regent of Metalhaven.

"This is the Venus de Milo," Chiefy said, indicating a statue that appeared to be incomplete or damaged. "It is from ancient Greece and is almost two-thousand-five-hundred years old. It represents the goddess Aphrodite, otherwise known as Venus. The skill required to create it by hand was remarkable. It is a work of genius."

Elara looked at the statue for moment then turned up her nose at it. "If you ask me, and I know you didn't, Reznikov should have left this hunk of rock on Earth."

Chiefy frowned his metal eyebrows then moved to another object in the miniature exhibition.

"This is the Code of Hammurabi, an ancient Babylonian stele containing one of the earliest known legal codes," Chiefy continued, acting as their tour guide. "It dates to around seventeen fifty-four BC, and is a significant historical artifact."

"So, it's a book of laws?" Finn asked, and Chiefy nodded. This time Finn snorted. "Why would Reznikov save a book of laws when the bastard's idea of justice is so fucked up?"

Elara shrugged and they moved to a third exhibit, which was a painting. Elara rolled her eyes and folded her arms. Chiefy pretended to ignore her protest.

"This is the Coronation of Napoleon by Jacques-Louis David," Chiefy said, regarding the painting with reverie, despite Elara's snub. "It is a masterpiece depicting the coronation of Napoleon Bonaparte as Emperor in eighteen oh four."

"It's boring," Elara commented, and Chiefy's eyes narrowed again.

"Then perhaps you might like this better?" the foreman said, turning to another, much smaller painting of a woman. "This is the Mona Lisa by Leonardo da Vinci. It was one of the most famous paintings in the world, celebrated for the enigmatic smile of its subject."

Finn and Elara stood in front of the Mona Lisa and scrutinized it closely. Finn didn't see anything particularly special about the composition, but at the same time, he couldn't stop looking at it.

"What the hell is she smirking about?" Elara said, though like Finn, she was fixated on the image. "It makes me want to slap her across the face."

"Not possible, I'm afraid. Whomever this woman was, she is long dead," Chiefy explained.

Elara continued to play the part of unimpressed tourist, but at the same time she continued to stare into the Mona

Lisa's eyes, and Finn was also finding it difficult to look away. It was like the woman was hypnotizing them.

"Danger!"

Scraps' warning cry snapped them out of their trance, and Finn grabbed his spear.

"Where?" Finn said, scouring the room for a potential threat, but finding nothing but dusty old artifacts. "Have the prefects caught up with us?"

"No," Chiefy said, before aiming his finger between the Venus de Milo and another sculpture. "It is a foreman."

Elara turned on the machine and fired her crossbow. The bolt struck the robot on the head, but it bounced off its bulky metal shell and rebounded into the painting of Napoleon that Chiefy had shown them earlier. The robot covered his mouth in shock. Finn aimed his spear at the machine and was about to charge, but the foreman made no attempt to attack them, and appeared oblivious to their presence.

"What's it doing?" Finn said, holding his ground. "Why isn't it attacking us?"

The foreman, which was gen one design, continued to move from artifact to artifact. The robot was holding objects in each hand, but rather than weapons, it was carrying a fluffy duster in one hand and a cleaning rag in the other.

"It's a cleaner robot," Elara said, sliding another bolt into her crossbow, but not bothering to aim it at the machine.

"It would appear so," Chiefy replied, still partially distracted by the damage that Elara had inadvertently caused to the priceless painting.

The gen one cleaner robot proceeded to pluck the crossbow bolt out of the painting, before dusting the canvas surface and moving on. Finn and the others side-stepped out of the machine's way to allow it to polish the marble statues before progressing on to the Mona Lisa, where it stood contemplating the image for several seconds, before passing by, without touching it.

"It's just ignoring us," said Finn. He was stating the obvious, but the obvious still seemed unbelievable. "Are you sure it's not transmitting some kind of silent alarm to the prefects?"

Scraps shook his head. "Cleaner robot just cleaning. Not programmed for anything else!"

"Then I say we leave it to work, and get going," Elara said. "We still have several more of these museum halls to work through, before we reach the next mono-rail station."

Elara led the way, keeping a close eye on Chiefy, and refusing to allow the robot to become distracted by the many other priceless relics that Reznikov had plundered from France. The door at the far end of the hall led to another short corridor, another T-junction and another hall that was equally vast as the one they'd just left. It also contained relics from pre-war Earth, but these items were of a very different kind to those in the French museum.

"This space contains artifacts recovered from China, one of the pre-war superpowers," Chiefy said, clearly enjoying his stroll through history.

Finn stopped at three sculptures, which were quite different to the works of art that Reznikov had looted from the Louvre. The ancient warriors each had unique facial expressions and appearances, and were depicted with swords and other weapons, in addition to a kind of plate armor. However, while sculptures such as the Venus de Milo were hyper-realistic and almost too perfect, the six-foot soldiers were more stylistic in their designs.

"These are terracotta soldiers," Chiefy explained, awestruck by the discovery. "It is funerary art. These soldiers were buried with Qin Shi Huang, the first emperor of China in around two-hundred and nine BC."

"Why did the guy bury himself with clay soldiers?" Elara asked, somewhat dismissively.

"They were to protect him in the afterlife," Chiefy answered. "All were thought lost during the war, so it quite remarkable to find three on Nimbus, and in perfect condition."

"Remarkably dull…" Elara commented, unnecessarily.

Chiefy ignored Elara's philistine attitude and continued to another artifact, which was even more impressive – at least to Finn – than the incredible terracotta soldiers.

"This is the Jade Burial Suit of Han Dynasty ruler, Prince Liu Sheng of Zhongshan," Chiefy said, again acting as tour guide. "It is made from hundreds of jade plates stitched together with gold thread, and was believed to protect the wearer on his or her journey to the afterlife."

"They must have been really afraid of what came after death," Finn said. He then laughed. "I bet Liu Sheng never thought he'd end up here…"

"Neither did I," Elara said, before ushering them past the relics and toward the far end of the China hall.

Nearing the exit, they stumbled across another gen one cleaner robot, who was dusting some old vases. Their sudden arrival startled the old foreman and the robot knocked one of the vases off its plinth with his feather duster, prompting Chiefy to leap into action and catch the vase before it hit the ground and smashed. Chiefy exhaled in relief then placed the vase back onto the plinth with the care of a mother handling her newborn baby. If the machine had been capable of sweating, Finn though that Chiefy's brow would have been dripping with perspiration.

"This is a Ming Dynasty vase," Chiefy said, admonishing the gen one robot. "These were priceless, even before the last war destroyed civilization. Be more careful…"

The gen one was incapable of frowning, since it lacked Chiefy's mechanical facial muscles, but it still cocked it head to one side, quizzically, before moving on.

"How about you don't give the enemy robots a roasting?" Finn said, once the cleaner machine had departed. "We're trying to keep a low profile, remember?"

The next two halls were devoted to memorabilia and artifacts from the United States of America, which like the other superpowers, had been bombed back to the stone age during the war. Chiefy remarked how it was incredible that so much had been recovered, and surmised that some of the objects may have been stored in underground vaults that had been owned by the super-rich oligarchs and magnates that ended up founding Zavetgrad.

Conscious of time, they hustled through the hall, stopping only briefly at items that were too fascinating to be left unremarked. The first was an automobile with an aggressive stance, sloping roof, and a bulging hood with air scoops. The bold grille had a badge that featured a horse, rearing up on its back legs. Chiefy had said it was a Ford Mustang Boss 429. Finn liked it very much, and for once, Elara had agreed.

Next was a document that Chiefy had called The

Declaration of Independence. Apparently, it was the original document that was approved by the Continental Congress on July 4th, 1776. It proclaimed the separation of thirteen North American British colonies from Great Britain. Close to it was a flag called The Star-Spangled Banner. Chiefy had been awestruck by the relic, claiming it to be the original flag that had inspired the U.S. national anthem. Elara had said, "it's just a flag," and turned up her nose, before moving away.

In the second of the two halls they stopped briefly to look at a replica of a McDonalds restaurant, complete with original bistro tables and chairs, and a golden logo in the shape of an arched M. Chiefy's description of the food only served to remind Finn that he hadn't eaten in half a day, and he was disappointed to discover that the replica was not complete enough to include a functioning kitchen.

Next was an exhibit that focused on sporting memorabilia, and Finn would have sped through the space had his eye not been caught by a baseball bat that was given pride of place. He walked up to it and plucked it from its mount. It was heavy, made of wood, and looked to have been put to good use in the past, though Finn doubted that its original owner would have used it to bash the heads of prefects or foreman robots, as Finn had done with his long-defunct bat.

"That is known as the Babe's Called Shot bat," Chiefy said, unable to resist the opportunity to show his vast cultural knowledge, inherited from Scraps and, indirectly, Finn's old data device. "This is the actual bat that Babe Ruth used to hit the famous 'called shot' home run during the nineteen thirty-two World Series."

"I don't understand anything you just said," Elara said, eyebrow raised. "It's just a bat."

Chiefy shook his head. "According to history, Babe Ruth pointed to where he intended to hit the next pitch, then proceeded to hit the ball to that exact location. It is a significant piece of sporting memorabilia."

"It's just a bat," Elara repeated. "Put it down, and let's move on."

Finn went to replace the bat then hesitated, briefly considering swapping his broken spear for the sporting object, before deciding that Babe Ruth's bat had already done its fair share of hitting, and deserved some rest.

The next few halls were devoted to South America, and the largest of these contained items from Brazil. One section of the enormous exhibit was cordoned off by a floor-to-ceiling glass wall, that created a space like a giant terrarium. Inside was a dense forest that was filled with creatures, from birds and insects to hairy mammals. Finn moved cautiously closer, and it was only when he was within ten meters of the glass wall that he realized none of the creatures were moving.

"They're all dead," Finn said, staring in the glass eyes of a four-legged predator.

"Yes, they are taxidermy models, or dry-preserved actual specimens, in the case of the insects," Chiefy replied. "It is a way of preserving a species, in a sense."

"All of the creatures in here are extinct?" Elara asked.

"Yes," Chiefy said, with a touch of sadness. "Some were even extinct before the last war."

Finn shook his head and blew out a sigh. The museums were all remarkable and fascinating, but the reason for their existence still perplexed him. Then his confusion turned to anger, as he thought about all of the time, effort, and resources that Reznikov had expended, not only to send out what must have been thousands of robots to recover the artifacts from their original locations, but to then have them returned to Zavetgrad and blasted into space at the top of a rocket. And, all the while, the workers had toiled and suffered to make his personal orbital museums a reality.

"I think I've seen enough," Finn said, turning away and quickening his pace toward the exit.

Elara followed without complaint, though Chiefy could have spent weeks or even years studying the contents of the different great halls. Finn continued past works of art, gemstones, lumps of rubber, and even a perfectly lifelike waxwork replica of a man, wearing shorts and a yellow shirt with green piping, and the word 'Pelé' written beneath the number ten on his back. Oddly, considering Elara had been the one to hurry them along, she stopped and looked at the waxwork.

"Was he some sort of famous general?" Elara asked. "The uniform doesn't offer much protection if he was."

"No," Chiefy replied, grinning. "This man was far more important than any general."

Elara considered asking Chiefy to elaborate before deciding that she actually didn't give a shit, and turned away before walking headlong into a foreman robot.

"Fuck," Elara said, bouncing off the machine and rubbing her bruised forehead. "Watch where you're going."

The foreman, which was another cleaner, narrowed its machine eyebrows at her. Finn recognized it as a Gen III, still old in comparison to Chiefy, but its FLP gave it a situational awareness and intelligence that was far beyond the capabilities of the dumb Gen I and II models.

"My apologies," The foreman said, in a humble tone of voice. "Please excuse me."

The robot stepped past Elara then continued cleaning, though Finn couldn't help but notice that it had looked over its shoulder at them, before proceeding to polish a set of gemstones.

"Is it me, or that robot acting suspiciously?" Finn asked.

"Not you..." Scraps replied, warily. "Gen three linked to network. Risk we've been seen."

"Shit," Finn cursed, keeping a close watch on the robot, who was clearly doing the same to him. "Let's get to that monorail before these museums start swarming with prefects."

13

THE BENEDICTION

REACHING the next monorail station required Finn and the others to pass through another series of giant museum halls, and despite their intention to speed through the spaces, the treasures they contained were too distracting to ignore completely. One group of interlinked halls was dedicated to Southern Asia, and it was when they reached the museum devoted to India, in particular, that fascination compelled Finn to take a short break and marvel at the historical wonders contained within it.

"India was the second most populous country in the world at the time of the Last War," Chiefy said, while they stood in front of a group of startlingly lifelike mannequins wearing saree, a garment that dated back over five thousand years. "Almost one-point-seven billion people lived in India. One-point-seven billion..." the robot continued.

Finn smiled at Chiefy. Considering all the marvels they had seen in the last thirty minutes, the intelligent and introspective robot topped them all.

"One-point-seven billion... all dead," Chiefy added, and

the tone of his electronic voice took a steep downward turn. "Most of those perished within a matter of weeks. It is horrifying to consider."

"I can't imagine that many people living on a single planet, let alone a single country," Finn said. He was also now contemplating the scale of the loss, but it was too enormous to get his head around. "I got claustrophobic in Metalhaven on a trial day, and that was only with a few thousand people out on the streets."

"It must have been a warm country," Elara said, taking a step closer to one of the mannequins and letting the ornate fabric fall through her fingers. "You'd freeze to death in a matter of hours in Zavetgrad, wearing something like this."

Finn turned his mind away from dark thoughts of nuclear annihilation to inspect the saree more closely. The elegant garment was made from an ornate fabric worn as a robe, with one end attached to the waist and the other flowing over the shoulder as a shawl. Some of the mannequins had their midriffs bared, and Finn agreed with Elara that it would have been a brave choice of clothing in the sub-zero temperatures of Earth's last city.

Suddenly, music began to play, and the mannequins began to dance. Finn shot back, spear in hand, and Elara also brandished her axe, but there was no danger, and before long he was entranced by the display, in the same way that that he'd been captivated by the Mona Lisa. It reminded Finn of the dancing robots in Elysium, but unlike the grotesque erotic fantasies of the regents, this display was graceful and enchanting. With reluctance, Finn left the dancing mannequins behind, and the music stopped as soon as they had moved out of the robots' line of sight. The mannequins then resumed their previous poses, waiting for the next visitors to bewitch.

They continued through the hall, past more taxidermy models, including one of a huge cat that stood over a meter tall to the shoulder. Chiefy informed them that it was a Bengal tiger, a symbol of power and bravery in Indian culture, and that it had become extinct in two thousand and fifty-six, nine years before the end of civilization in the Last War.

The final exhibit was a bronze statue of a man with four arms, performing a dance set inside a decorative circle of cosmic fire. Chiefy had explained that it was Shiva as Lord of Dance (Nataraja), a form of the Hindu god, Shiva, and that it represented the god's roles as creator, preserver, and destroyer of the universe. It was intended to convey the idea that time was a never-ending cycle of creation, destruction, and rebirth. While many of the artifacts that Gideon Alexander Reznikov had collected across his vast museum halls seemed to lack any modern significance, the bronze statue was something Finn could understand. It highlighted how the president viewed his role as the future custodian of humanity, as if Reznikov himself was performing the dance inside the cosmic circle of fire.

Suddenly, the doors at the end of the museum room slid open and a group of foremen marched in, two abreast. Finn and the others ducked into hiding as more and more of the machines entered in a long column.

"Maybe it's a shift change?" Finn suggested, since the machines didn't appear to be forming a search party.

"Maybe, but surely there's a quicker and easier way to reach the factory rooms," Elara replied. "Scraps, are you picking up any signals?"

Scraps narrowed his little eyes. "Yes-yes, but unclear. Not shift change…"

"Buddy, if these machines are here looking for us, we need to know now," Finn whispered. Finally, the column of robots reached its end and the doors slid shut, but four robots remained in front of the exit, blocking it. "And we need another way out of this room too."

The fifty foremen that had marched into the museum quickly formed a circle, facing out toward the room. Then, in the center of the circle, Finn saw a Gen III model and recognized it as the cleaner robot that they'd bumped into in an earlier hall. The machine was no longer holding its duster and cleaning rag, and had balled its hands into fists.

"I think that cleaner robot ratted us out," Elara said, making a similar observation. "We need to get out of this room, now."

The circle of robots took two paces forward, expanding the circle. Lights then shone from their eyes and probed the room, again forcing Finn into cover.

"They're definitely looking for us," Finn said, searching for another exit, but thanks to the robot searchlights, there was nowhere they could go where they wouldn't be seen. Then he had an idea and looked at the deck plates beneath their feet. "Chiefy, is there an underfloor space here, like in the factory?"

"Yes, we could enter the sub-floor and work our way out through the interstitial spaces," the robot agreed.

The circle of foremen widened again, and their eyes probed the room, while the Gen III cleaner remained in the center, perhaps directing the actions of the other, lesser machines.

"Then do it, before we're found and become Reznikov's latest objects of curiosity," Finn said.

Chiefy pulled up a floor panel and Elara slipped inside first, followed by Scraps and then Finn. The circle of foremen had almost reached them by the time Chiefy lowered himself through the gap and carefully replaced the floor panel, which slid into place with a weighty thud, fortunately drowned out by the rhythmic stomp of metal footsteps above their heads.

Scraps lit up the dark space then gestured for the others to follow him. The crawlspace was more cramped than the area beneath the factory floor had been, and while the little robot could slip through the narrow gaps, their path was ultimately dictated by which routes were large enough for Chiefy's seven-foot frame to navigate. Eventually, after an uncomfortable ten-minute crawl, the space opened out and Finn was finally able to stand again.

"Where are we?" Finn said, placing his hand against the wall that was blocking them from moving any further in the direction Scraps had been leading them.

"Habitat zone," Scraps said.

"You mean a populated area?" Finn asked, and the robot nodded reticently, perhaps in response to Finn's exasperated tone. "Shit, isn't there another way around?"

Scraps shook his head. "Nope-nope. Must go through!"

Finn looked at Elara, but she shrugged as if to say, "what choice do we have?", and the answer, of course, was none.

"Okay, but let's try to avoid contact with the natives, if we can," Finn said, resigning himself to the task ahead of them. "If the people here are anything like the indoctrinated servants of Elysium, they won't be happy to see us."

Chiefy carefully loosened one of the wall panels then

gently peeled back the metal to allow Finn to peek through to the other side. It was another industrial looking space that, unlike Elysium with its smooth, shell-like interior, didn't try to hide its manufactured origins. With a nod of reassurance from Scraps, Finn squeezed his body through the opening and found himself on a balcony level, overlooking a hall that was many times more cavernous than even the largest museum they had passed through.

Finn worked his way closer to the edge of the balcony and discovered that the space was a self-contained village, set inside the manufactured confines of the space station. There were visible metal beams and girders left bare, rather than clad with plasterboard or something less industrialized, but there were also large areas that had been planted with grasses so vividly green that they could have been painted. The houses were all circular huts built from steel plate with thatched roofs – a curious blend of old and new. Then he saw people, flitting to and fro, going about their daily lives. He wondered if they were oblivious to the fact they were living on an engineered lump of metal orbiting high above a broken planet.

The people were all dressed in the charcoal-colored trouser suits that Finn had seen being manufactured earlier. Worn on the inhabitants, the clothes looked well-made, hardy, and practical, but unlike the saree or the chiffon dresses of Elysium's servants, the fits were shapeless, with no effort to make them look attractive. The more Finn observed the village, the more he saw, and his eyes were suddenly drawn to a group of children, playing a ball game on one of the grassy areas. The group of twenty or more boys and girls were running around freely, laughing and smiling, completely uninhibited, like the children he'd seen in Haven's residential levels. Joy was infectious, and soon Finn found himself smiling broadly too, until the damaged part of his mind forced himself to remember the horror of the workhouse, and he was suddenly tormented by guilt and doubt. These children were innocent, and much as Elara's cold logic made sense, it was wrong to weigh the survival of Zavetgrad against their right to live, regardless of what the math said was the rational choice.

"I don't know what I expected to find, but this wasn't it," Elara whispered, moving to Finn's side. "This looks..." she struggled for the right word, before settling on, "...normal."

"This balcony surrounds the habitat zone, and appears to be reserved for maintenance use only," Chiefy said, while replacing the wall panel to cover their tracks. "We can use the balcony to circumvent this room and the museum spaces, and reach the mono-rail station from the opposite side."

Following the robot's lead, Finn crept along the balcony, staying low and out of sight, though it wasn't difficult to avoid being seen, since none of the villagers in the habitat appeared in the slightest bit concerned about their surroundings. At first, Finn couldn't understand why none of the villagers were assigned to security, when he realized that they had no need to be afraid. There were no threats on Nimbus and never had been. When an animal lived without fear of predators, there was no need to be vigilant.

At times, the balcony narrowed, forcing them to progress in single file. Finn was at the rear of the line, which allowed him time to observe more of the villagers' behavior. There were areas designated for growing produce, using real soil, rather than the vertical farming units that Seedhaven relied upon to produce algae, which was the building block of almost all the food in Zavetgrad. He could also see areas devoted to cooking, painting and sculpture, and even learning. The children had long since stopped playing their ball game, and were now sitting at wooden tables, in front of a physical blackboard, while a teacher appeared to be conducting a lesson focused on math or science.

Every colonist appeared to have a role, but Finn could also see that everything was shared. There were tables close to the kitchen area where people sat and ate, but there was no payment made, either with a physical currency or chits. Most surprising of all, everyone seemed happy. Again, Finn was reminded of Haven and the community atmosphere he'd experienced in the corridors of its residential floors. Everyone was aligned and working to the betterment of their commune.

"I imagined Reznikov's vision of the future to be different," Finn mused, finally making his way through the narrow section of the balcony. "This village looks like a model of perfect society."

"Appearances can be deceptive," Elara cautioned. "Scratch at the golden exterior of the Authority sector, and you can see the decay beneath its surface. Nothing is ever as perfect as it seems."

Finn shrugged. "I don't see anything imperfect about this village."

"Sure, it looks good, but who decides who does what?" Elara said. "Who's in charge?"

"Maybe no-one is?" Finn suggested. "Maybe this is utopia. Maybe we were wrong about Reznikov, and his motives were genuine."

Elara looked so affronted that Finn worried she might slap him around the face, to knock some sense into him, but before she could do so, a holo image of a man appearing from his shoulders up materialized in mid-air above the center of the village. At first, the apparition was so bright that all Finn could see was a glowing silhouette, then the brightness faded, and the face of the man was revealed. It was Gideon Alexander Reznikov, appearing exactly like the man's depiction on the emblem of the Authority, which was stamped above the door of every building in Zavetgrad.

"Good afternoon, commune seven." Reznikov said, his voice both convivial and authoritative.

"Good afternoon, father," the commune chanted in reply.

"Please gather together for today's benediction..." Reznikov added.

A godlike hand appeared and gestured toward the grassy area where the children had been playing. The members of the commune gathered as directed, though Finn noted that one man appeared angry to have been interrupted. He was one of the artists, and prior to Reznikov's ethereal appearance, had been engrossed in creating a sculpture from a lump of smooth stone that looked similar to the material the Venus de Milo had been crafted from. Gen II foremen then marched into the village, carrying trays filled with the silver flasks they'd seen being made in the factory. The foremen walked through the commune and each villager took a flask and held it reverently in their hands. The artist took one too, though reluctantly.

"Precious children of Nimbus, today, we embrace our solemn responsibility as humanity's future in the stars,"

Reznikov began, in a sermonizing tone of voice, like a cleric or preacher.

"We are the future…" the commune replied. The artist did not chant.

"Though the world of our ancestors was turned to ash, we were not burned," Reznikov said. "We remained pure."

"We are the future…" Again, the artist did not speak.

"Today, we drink the Serenitox, the blessed elixir and symbol of our purity."

"Thank you, father, for this elixir," the commune replied, and they all raised their silver flasks, apart from the artist who held it lazily at his side.

"As we drink, we pledge ourselves to unity and to the betterment of our commune," Reznikov said.

The members of the commune drank deeply from their flasks, while the artist surreptitiously poured the contents of his onto the grass. The man had checked around him to make sure he wasn't being observed, but from their high vantage point on the balcony, Finn could see that a foreman had witnessed the deed.

"We are united…" the commune chanted.

"As we drink, we allow the Serenitox to enrich our souls, elevate our mindfulness, and strengthen our sacred bond to Nimbus," Reznikov said, in a paternal tone.

They villagers drank more of the liquid, and this time the artist pretended to join in, though his flask was already empty.

"We are as one," the commune said in unison.

"As we drink, we feel the warmth of Serenitox flowing through our veins, connecting us to one another in shared purpose," Reznikov continued.

The villagers finished their drinks then placed the flasks

onto the ground at their feet, before holding out their hands, palms facing upward. The artist joined in, though his palms faced to the ground.

"We are of one mind and one body," the commune said.

"You are children of Nimbus, and I am your father."

"Father, we love and obey you…"

"And I love you," Reznikov concluded, speaking the words with warmth and affection.

With the benediction complete, the foremen collected the flasks and assembled into a group. The villagers then gathered together in smaller groups, hugging, and kissing one another. They moved slowly and reverently, their eyes glassy and mouths turned up into turgid smiles.

"I know the effect of a drug when I see it," Finn commented. "Whatever this 'Serenitox' is, it's not holy water, that's for certain."

"I agree," Chiefy said. "The liquid appears to have had a mind-altering effect on the villagers."

"See…" Elara said, a bit too smugly for Finn's liking. "I told you this was all bullshit."

The artist then walked off the grassy area without joining in with the post-benediction celebrations, and returned to his sculpture. Without having drunk from the flask, the man was unaffected by its narcotic effects, a fact that had not escaped the attention of the foremen.

"Congratulations, commune seven, your output has exceeded your needs for this period," Reznikov said, and the villagers again turned to face their 'father', except for the artist. "Your surplus will be redistributed according to need."

Some of the foremen wheeled in carts and began loading up food and other objects that the villagers had produced, including their works of art. One of the robots went to pick up a sculpture that was being displayed beside the work-in-progress that the artist was chiseling away at. The man downed tools and began to argue with the machine, but as a Gen II, it either wasn't sophisticated enough to reply, or had not been programmed to care about the villager's objections.

"Commune member, Mateus Seven-Alpha, must I remind you that you own nothing?" Reznikov said, as the disembodied image of the president floated closer to the artist. "The commune shares everything."

The artist may have been comfortable arguing with a robot, but Reznikov's address caused the man to stiffen and look down at his feet, repentantly. Even so, Finn could tell that the villager remained angry, and became even more infuriated when the foreman proceeded to remove the work of art he'd tried to protect.

"Your new assignments have been uploaded," Reznikov continued, addressing the commune as a whole. "You will begin at the start of the next rotation."

The villagers pulled back the sleeves of their right arms and checked devices that were reminiscent of the C.O.N.F.I.R.M.E. computers that Zavetgrad prefects wore.

"But, father, I am an artist, not a cook!" the artist protested, after seeing his new assignment.

"You are what the commune needs you to be," Reznikov replied.

The artist shook his head and appeared despondent, while the rest of the commune simply got back to their lives, without protest.

"Father, please, I implore you!" the artist said, chasing

after the heavenly image of the president. "I wish to finish my work. It is more important to me than anything."

The image of Reznikov descended toward the artist, then his body, arms and legs appeared, and the president landed on the grass, towering over the man like a god.

"Your disharmony is a malaise, my child," Reznikov said, reproachfully. "You must be cured."

Suddenly, the artist was grabbed from behind by two foremen and dragged away. The man protested and struggled, but the robots were too strong.

"I love you, my child..." Reznikov said, as the man screamed and called for help, but the other villagers were too stoned to even realize what was happening.

Reznikov's image vanished, then, out of sight of the rest of the commune but clearly visible to Finn and the others from their balcony vantage, the foremen grabbed the artist's head and snapped his neck like a rotten tree branch. The artist was then unceremoniously dumped into one of the carts, and wheeled away, along with the items that had been taken from the villagers.

Finn's mouth fell open and he looked at Elara. She was similarly taken aback by the callous act or murder. A chill crept across Finn's body, seeping into his bones. It was suddenly all too familiar. Commune seven wasn't a paradise, but a prison.

"We can't let these people die," Finn said, again turning to Elara. "I don't care what we have to do, but we end this by saving Zavetgrad and these communes."

Elara nodded. She could be as cold and hard as diamond, but she wasn't nearly as ruthless as she liked to make out.

Underneath The Shadow was a decent human being, who couldn't stand to see innocent people suffer.

"Everything hinges on us finding Reznikov," Elara said. "So, let's find the bastard, and put a stop to this charade."

Elara shuffled away from the edge of the balcony then came face-to-face with a Gen II foreman. They had all been so preoccupied by the fate of the artist that they hadn't see the machine creep up on them.

"Intruder alert!" the machine intoned in its processed voice. "Prefects to my location!"

14

PREFECTS OF NIMBUS

Finn thrust with his spear and skewered the foreman through its eye socket, destroying its FLP and sending the machine reeling backward, sparks flying from its head. He ducked back into cover, as members of the commune looked in their direction and witnessed the death throes of the robot. For a moment, it seemed that they might get away without being discovered, when the disembodied head and shoulders of Gideon Alexander Reznikov reappeared in midair. This time the man was looking directly at Finn. Reznikov's serene, peaceful expression twisted in a malevolent glower, then the image vanished.

"I think it's fair to say that Reznikov knows we're here," Finn said. The president's ethereal stare had sent a shiver down his spine. "We need to hustle. No more museum outings..."

Chiefy led them out of the habitat, prising open a panel in the wall that opened into a corridor that would lead them to the mono-rail station. While the robot was working, six uniformed prefects – three men, three women – stormed into commune seven, armed with the same peculiar weapons that the squad they'd avoided earlier had carried. This time, Finn could see swords hanging from the hips of the armed men and women, and was reminded of Ivan Volkov's musketeer-inspired prosecutor regalia.

"Chiefy, hurry," Elara said.

The officers questioned the foremen, while the commune members looked on, curious but seemingly unafraid of the armored prefects. One of the robots then pointed directly at Finn, and the six officers turned to look in his direction. Opaque silver visors obscured their faces, but Finn could feel the eyes of the men and women probing him. Then they gave chase.

"Chiefy, we really need to move!" Finn said.

His laser was gone, and all they had was Elara's crossbow. She may have been a crack shot, but the weapon was too slow and too short-range to take out six prefects in full armor.

"Stop!" the lead officer called out, aiming his weapon in their direction.

Elara shot without giving a warning, but the prefect seemed to anticipate her attack, and sprang a buckler-like shield from his forearm, which deflected the bolt harmlessly onto the grass. At the same time, Chiefy finally managed to remove the wall panel, and Finn dove through the opening, followed by Chiefy, with Scraps safely contained inside his chest compartment. Elara shot two more bolts in quick succession, both of which were deflected with the same uncanny ease, then followed.

"Tough bastards," Elara said, with grudging admiration. "It takes skill to avoid a crossbow bolt."

"Skill, or luck," Finn suggested.

"You get lucky once, maybe twice, but not three times," Elara replied, as they sprang out into the corridor and started running. "Whoever they are, they're capable and well trained."

Chiefy moved out ahead, setting a pace that was almost too fast to follow. Moments later, they had burst through a door, which entered into a second commune that was almost identical to the first. The same benediction that they'd just witnessed was taking place, and the foremen robots and commune members, silver flasks in hand, were too shocked by their sudden interruption to do anything.

"Stop them you mechanical fools!"

The cry was uttered by the leader of the prefect squad, who had managed to close the gap between them, despite their head start and breathless pace. Finn saw the glowing visage of Reznikov watch him as he ran beneath it and across the lush grass, and the president's unruffled expression soured once again.

A group of foremen robots finally sprang into action, but the clunky Gen I and Gen II machines were no match for Chiefy, who brushed them aside like blades of grass blowing in the wind, before forcing open the exit door and allowing Finn and Elara to charge through.

"Which way?" Finn said, as they reached another of the seemingly unending number of crossroads in the station's corridor complex.

"Go left," Chiefy said, a heartbeat behind them.

Finn went left, then another squad of six prefects burst through the door at the far end, and Finn slid to a stop and backtracked.

"We can't go this way," Finn said, grabbing Elara's arm

and spinning her around. "We'll have to go straight on, and find another way."

With the prefects still calling for them to stop, Finn re-routed and charged down the corridor, spear in hand. The door opened just before he reached it, but this time it was a group of five foreman robots that met him. Holding his spear in two hands, he charged through the pack without slowing down, using his own armor as a battering ram. Three foremen went down, then Elara charged though, avoiding the other two, before Chiefy steamrollered the machines into the deck.

"Go left at the next junction!" Chiefy called out.

Finn managed to slow down just enough to make the turn. He expected to find another squad of robots or prefects heading his way, but the coast was clear. Reaching the door, he hammered the button to open it then charged through, straight into an energy blast that knocked him six feet back in the opposite direction. The report of the weapon sounded like a thunderclap, and Finn found that he was more disorientated than hurt.

"We must divert!" Chiefy said, closing the door on the advancing prefects before smashing the lock panel and dragging Finn to his feet. "Follow me!"

Chiefy crashed through a service door and led them through a narrow corridor that contained what appeared to be spare robot parts, tools and cleaning equipment, including the feather dusters used to keep the museum exhibits looking pristine. Smashing through the door at the far end, Chiefy took them left, circumventing the prefects that had ambushed Finn and left him flat on his back.

"What kind of weapon was that?" Elara asked, as they

continued their desperate escape. "It hit Finn square in the chest, but he's not dead, or even bleeding."

"Lucky for me..." Finn cut in. "Though it stung like hell, and made me dizzy, like being prodded in the neck with a prefect's nightstick."

"I believe it was a pulsed sonic weapon," Chiefy answered. "Based on Scraps' readings, it was operating at twenty hertz at an amplitude of one-fifty decibels, enough to induce temporary paralysis and pain."

"But it's non-lethal?" Elara asked.

"Yes..." Chiefy answered, as surprised as she was. "Perhaps it is merely a means of quelling disobedience."

"In other words, they don't want to kill their precious communists," Finn said, reading between the lines. "Up here, it's not like Reznikov can simply replenish his stock from the workhouse, like he could in Zavetgrad."

The robot continued its rampage, breaking through doors and guiding them toward the president's palace. Their detour had forced them back into the museum halls, but this time Finn wasn't paying any attention to the treasures contained within the cavernous spaces. Three halls down and they were confronted by another squad of prefects, and this time there was no avoiding them. The officers were barring the only exit, and Finn was damned if he was going to back away from a fight.

Sonic pulses swept across the hall, but Finn managed to avoid the blasts, which instead destroyed vases, sculptures and paintings that were all priceless and irreplaceable. Elara shot a prefect in the armpit, expertly finding a gap in their carapace armor, before drawing her axe and moving into close combat. Finn did the same, but began by employing some of the museum exhibits as weapons, lobbing porcelain jars, stone tablets and even funeral masks at the officers, who ducked and weaved, avoiding the projectiles with nimbleness and skill.

Closing the gap, Finn attacked with his spear, forcing the prefects onto the back foot. The officers swapped their sonic weapons for swords, proving that the elegant weapons were not merely for show. Metal clashed against metal, and Finn found the prefects to be his equal – almost. Fighting skill was one thing, but the difference between victory and defeat often came down to who had more desire to win, and Finn's desire was unmatched.

Striking down one of the men with the flat of the spearhead, Finn took a glancing blow to his back, before sweeping the leg of a female prefect and sending the woman crashing into a sarcophagus. Elara and Chiefy had ploughed through the others, though grazes, bruises and dents told a story of a battle hard won.

As they were leaving the hall, one of the prefects got off a shot that hit Chiefy in the back. The robot faltered and his steps became unsteady, before he fell face-first into the deck, the impact shaking the floor.

"Chiefy, are you okay?" Finn said, as he and Elara tried to haul the massive machine off the ground. "Chiefy?"

"I am... disoriented," Chiefy replied, trying to regain his footing, but his circuits were scrambled.

"How is a sonic weapon affecting a robot?" Finn said, glancing back into the museum. The prefects were regrouping.

"Pulses make vibrations!" Scraps said. The little robot had climbed out of the compartment and was hovering just ahead of them. "Heat bad for circuits!"

Finally, they got Chiefy to his feet, and Elara held off the officers with more crossbow bolts, which were again deflected by the prefects' buckler-shields. Chiefy recovered and set off in the lead, but as Finn followed he was hit by a sonic pulse that would have knocked him down, if it hadn't been for Elara catching him. She returned fire and this time her bolt sank in the chest of an advancing officer, and the man cried out in pain. His comrades pulled the injured officer into cover, which gave them the precious few seconds they needed to escape.

"Scraps, we've got to avoid these prefects," Finn said, still reeling from the agony and disorientation caused by the blast, which was like the aftereffect of ten pints of Metalhaven ale. "Find us a way into the interstitial zones."

"Okay-kay!' Scraps called back, before zooming off ahead like a rocket.

"Not so fast," Finn cried, fearful that his robot pal would fly straight into a sonic blast, but whether from luck or judgement, Scraps managed to avoid the prefects and lead them to another door.

"In here!" Scraps said, banging on the door. "Quick-quick!"

Chiefy arrived first and wrenched open the doors with his robotic might, as effortlessly as crushing a soda can. Elara and Finn raced inside and found themselves in what was easily the largest museum hall they had yet seen. In height and width, it was twice the size of the largest museum they had previously found, and it didn't take long to work out why. The centerpiece of the exhibition was the Shchit-Bogoroditsa, the gold dome on the Chapel of Intercession from Saint Basil's cathedral in what had been Moscow, Russia. As one of the most famous cathedrals in the world, Finn had read about it on his data device, so he knew that it was made of solid gold and probably weighed at least two metric tons. Transporting it to Nimbus would have been a titanic feat, but as one of the most prized relics of the Russian Federation, the homeland of Gideon Alexander Reznikov, no expense would have been spared in its retrieval.

"Here-here!" Scraps said, pointing to a section of the floor. "This goes to palace!"

Chiefy punched thorough the deck and tore open a hole large enough for man, woman and machine to climb into, but before he could lower Elara into the chasm, prefects burst in from all four corners of the museum.

"Stand down!" the leader of the group ordered. The man was uniquely distinguished by a black shoulder pauldron.

It was a pointless command. Finn and Elara would never stand down, not when there was the option to stand and fight.

Meeting the officers head on, Finn took the first squad by surprise, poleaxing two prefects before shoulder-charging a third and knocking the man flat. A sonic blast hit him in the chest, then swords were drawn. Behind him, Elara had incapacitated two prefects with crossbow bolts, and was fighting three more, sword against axe. Chiefy was blocking sword strikes from another squad, while using his unfeasible agility to pick them off, two at time, but still the silver-armored officers came at them, fighting with the zeal of rebels and the skill of prosecutors.

Blood was drawn on both sides, but the numbers were simply too great, and despite his efforts, Finn was disarmed and knocked down. Elara managed to fight on for a few more seconds, before five sonic rifles were aimed at her chest. Even so, she refused to give in, and it took three close-range blasts to put her on her ass, her axe spinning out of her hand.

Chiefy stood over them, then Scraps flew down to the foreman's side, and held up his fists too, bravely choosing to fight, despite his tiny size making it impossible that he could harm the skilled and heavily armed prefects. The officers surrounded them, aiming swords and rifles at their heads, but instead of going in for the kill, the lead prefect showed restraint.

"Enough of this!" the officer with the black pauldron yelled, raising a hand to order his prefects to hold their positions. "Put down your weapons, before you force us to kill you."

"I won't be your prisoner!" Elara snarled, struggling against the disorientating effects of multiple sonic blasts. "I'd rather die!"

Finn knew that Elara was serious but there had to be a better option than dying. The prefects had fought doggedly, but their show of restraint gave Finn hope that they were more principled than the corrupt prefects of Earth's last city.

"We only want to see Reznikov," Finn said, holding up his hands, which were trembling from pain. "We have to stop him from destroying the city."

The masked officer cocked his head to one side, in a manner that was unsettlingly familiar.

"What city?"

Finn frowned at the man. "Zavetgrad, of course. The only city left on Earth."

"There are no cities on Earth," the prefect answered, confused but also angry, as if he believed that Finn was trying to play a trick on him. "There is only the space yard, where foremen operate the rockets that bring us the remains of humanity's culture, for posterity."

"But you must have seen the regents who come here?" Finn asked. His brain was a muddle, partly from the sonic blasts, but also from the prefect's bizarre answer. "You must know there are people still living on the planet?"

"What are you talking about?" the prefect leader said. "The only person who travels to the planet's surface is the space yard warden, who oversees operations there. He works for the president, our father, but he was born and lives here."

"Is this warden a heavyset older man with a craggy, smug expression, who goes by the name of Maxim Volkov?" Elara asked.

There was a pause before the prefect answered, "Yes..." The other prefects looked to one another, then the leader continued "How did you know that?" The prefect paused again, then changed his question. "No, that doesn't matter right now. What matters is who you are, and where you came from?"

"I told you why we're here," Finn said.

"But that doesn't make any sense," the prefect replied, angry again. "The only surviving human beings all reside on this station."

"That's a lie, and we're the living proof," Finn said. He shook his head in disbelief. "You really don't know that some people survived the last war, and are still down there?"

"We were told that anyone who survived the downfall died centuries ago," the leader replied.

"But if everyone is dead, then who are you protecting the

communes against?" Elara said, phrasing the question as a 'gotcha'.

"Rogue robots, course," the man replied, with matching scorn. "Sometimes these machines malfunction, and need to be disabled, so they can be repaired. That's what I believed we were chasing, until I saw you."

Finn climbed slowly to his feet, hands in the air, and the barrels of multiple sonic weapons tracked him as he rose.

"I understand that you want answers, and you'll get them, but in return, I'm asking you to hear us out too," Finn said. "There are literally a million lives hanging in the balance, and what you do next, might decide whether they live or die."

Finn heard the officer exhale a breath then he gestured to his officers again, and they lowered their weapons.

"I'll hear what you have to say," the leader said, and then the man removed his helmet. Finn almost fell over from shock. It was like looking in a mirror, except the eyes staring back at him were an emerald green in color, instead of blue. "You can start by telling me your names."

15
FAMILIAR FACES

Looking at the prefect leader felt like meeting an old friend that Finn hadn't seen for years, though it was more than just the man's green eyes that seemed recognizable. Everything from the man's hair, which was thick and dark, to his angular jawline and confident stance seemed familiar. Elara had noticed too, and the appearance of the man had tamed her fiery edge to the point where they could be led away, without the threat of further violence.

At the door to the huge museum room, Finn noticed that Scraps wasn't on his usual perch on Chiefy's shoulder, and he wheeled around to look for the robot. Scraps was back where the fighting had been at its most ferocious, using a probe to collect what appeared to be a sample of blood that had splashed onto the floor.

"Scraps, come on," Finn called out, and the robot zoomed over, watched all the way by one of the prefects, who kept his sonic rifle aimed at the machine.

The prefects led them to the monorail, which ferried Finn and the others toward the center of Nimbus, though not quite far enough to reach the central sphere, where the palace of Gideon Alexander Reznikov was located. Finn hadn't envisaged making the journey under guard, but in some ways he was relieved to finally step off the train, knowing that they no longer had to traipse though endless corridors and museums, or the bizarre communes with their peculiar rituals.

Still under guard, they were then marched into the Nimbus equivalent of a prefect hub, or guard post of some kind. A squad of six prefects stood watch, though Finn again noted distinct differences between the Nimbus officers and those in Zavetgrad, most notably, how they treated their prisoners. Any of the prefects in the work sectors would have struck, electrified, groped or in some other way abused them by this point, but the Nimbus prefects were not heavy handed, and acted more like Haven's professional soldiers than Zavetgrad's thugs.

The prefect hub was home to thirty-six officers in total, including the man with the black shoulder pauldron who had removed his helmet earlier. Finn saw that the man was talking to a female prefect, who had a white pauldron on the opposite shoulder to the man's.

The two officers moved to a computer console and stood with their backs to Finn. The female leader removed her helmet, and dark hair tumbled onto her shoulders, but she was still facing away, and Finn couldn't see her face. Then the computer activated and the image of Gideon Alexander Reznikov materialized, glowing and ethereal, the same as he had appeared above the communes. It was an unreal, godlike presence, and Finn began to realize that it was intentional, so as to present the president as more than just a man.

"Have you captured the intruders?" Reznikov asked.

"Yes, father, we have them," the male prefect replied, and Finn felt his stomach tighten into a knot. "We captured four intruders, two robots, and also a man and a woman. Apparently, they stowed away from the planet, though I don't understand how this is possible. There is no-one still alive on Earth."

Finn's uneasiness eased a touch as he listened to the prefect challenge Reznikov. *Maybe he's not just going to blindly turn us in, after all...* he wondered and hoped.

"That is correct, or at least it was what we believed," Reznikov replied, playing his cards close to his chest. "My foreman and drone scouts have never encountered survivors, but the presence of your prisoners suggests their investigations may have been incomplete."

The two prefects nodded, taking Reznikov's answer on faith. It was clear that they trusted the president, which did not bode well for their chances, Finn thought.

"What have these prisoners said to you?" Reznikov continued, and Finn detected uneasiness in the president's voice.

"They spoke of a potential disaster on the planet, and implied that Nimbus may be able to help," the male prefect replied. Finn raised an eyebrow at this; it wasn't exactly a lie, but it *was* a creative way to present the truth. "They asked to speak with you directly, and seemed to know you by name."

Reznikov frowned and massaged his chin, though Finn considered the gesture to be trite and forced, as if the president was merely pretending to give the impression of confusion and shock.

"Perhaps they learned of Nimbus from the space yard, or

from interrogating a foreman that they captured," Reznikov replied. The man then looked off to one side, and his already glowing face was illuminated further, perhaps by a screen. "I directed our robot scouts to search for evidence of more survivors near to the space yard, and it seems that there may be a small faction that has remained hidden for all this time, in the caverns beneath Northern Canada." Reznikov paused, scowling at whatever information he was reading, or pretending to read. "According to our data, they are carrying dangerous pathogens that are a risk to our communes, and to our very survival." The president now looked directly at the two prefects. "We cannot risk further contamination. I must now ask of you to perform a solemn duty, but know that it is for the safety of Nimbus, and the greater good."

"What is it that you require of us, great father?" the prefects intoned in harmony.

"You must execute the prisoners at once, and cremate their remains," Reznikov said, and Finn felt his blood run cold. "The robots must be smelted down too. Then, and this is what pains me the most, anyone who came into direct contact with the invaders must be... terminated."

A silence fell across the room, and the other prefects, all of whom had remained masked, looked to one other, seeming to understand what this directive meant. Finn knew too, and he steeled himself, ready to fight.

"Humanity's survival is dependent on the purity of Nimbus," Reznikov continued, driving home his message without holding back. "A mutant virus from the planet could kill every last man, woman and child on this space station, and doom humanity to extinction. Your genetic dynasty is secure.

Your genetic line will live on. Your great sacrifice will be honored and remembered for all time."

"We understand, great father," the two lead prefects said, gravely. "It will be done."

Reznikov's image faded then then the two lead prefects turned around, but Elara was already on her feet, fists clenched.

"Come any closer, and I'll rip your fucking throats out," Elara snarled. When she had vowed never again to become a prisoner, she had meant it will all her heart. "If you're stupid enough to believe what that liar just said, then go ahead and terminate yourselves, and those drugged sheep in the communes too, but leave us out of it."

The prefects aimed their sonic weapons at Elara, and Finn stood by her side. If she was going down fighting, then he'd fight and die by her side, but instead of opening fire, the lead prefects raised their hands, and the weapons were lowered.

"Please, don't struggle," the man said.

The female leader then approached, and Finn was struck by her blue eyes and her laser-focused stare, which hit him like a sonic blast to the face.

"We don't want to hurt you," the female leader said. Like the man, she was achingly familiar, like something from a dream. "We don't want to die either, but we have to protect Nimbus. This is the last refuge of humanity. Without it, everything is lost."

"This isn't the last refuge of humanity," Finn said. He risked taking a step closer to the leaders, but they held their ground, and their nerve. "There are a million people living on Earth, in a city called Zavetgrad, and tens of thousands more living free from the Authority, in an underground silo called Haven."

The lead prefects looked to one another, but it was clear that neither had any idea what Finn was talking about.

"This place on the planet that Reznikov called the space yard is just one of many sectors in the city," Finn continued, laying it all on the line. "It's real name is the Nimbus sector, or Spacehaven as we prefer to call it."

"You came from this city?" the female leader asked.

"Yes, from another sector, called Metalhaven," Elara answered. "There are nine sectors in total, all run by the Authority."

"What is this 'Authority' you keep mentioning?" the male prefect asked. "You make it sound like Nimbus is a part of it."

"It is," Finn said, stressing this as strongly as he could. "Gideon Alexander Reznikov is the president of the Authority. The man you knew as the warden was another leader. Men like them have kept almost a million people in poverty and servitude for generations. But as soon as the last rockets from Spacehaven arrive here, they will launch a nuclear assault from this station and destroy both Zavetgrad and Haven, killing every last man, woman and child on Earth."

"Child?" the male leader said, struck by this revelation in particular. "There are children on the planet?"

"Thousands of them," Finn said, driving the message home.

The prefects all stood in silence for a time, but while Finn could feel their hesitation and doubt, he could also sense that they had not dismissed his claims out of hand.

"Why should we believe you?" the female leader said. She

approached, and her movements were fluid and graceful, like that of an assassin. "What you've told us goes against everything we have been taught."

"These robots can show you proof," Finn said, gesturing to Chiefy and Scraps. "Give them access to a computer, and they can show you images and videos from the city, and even from inside Haven. They can show you Zavetgrad, and its people. They can show our struggle against the Authority."

"All of that could be faked," the man said. "It could be a fantasy concocted to win our trust and support."

"To what end?" Elara hit back, throwing her arms out wide. "What do you think we want? We're just a couple of people and two robots. Do you think we're here to take over Nimbus?"

The woman regarded Elara severely. "No, but if what you've said is true, you could be here to destroy it."

Another painful silence fell over the room and Finn looked at Elara. They hadn't yet told the prefects everything, and if they were to win the trust of these officers, they had to be honest about it all. Even omitting the smallest truth could be enough to break the fragile bond they had established with the citadel's enforcers.

"We *are* here to destroy Nimbus," Elara admitted, and the female leader's muscles became taut. "It's either Nimbus or the planet. Over a million people, compared to a fraction of that here." She took another step closer toward the female prefect, and it was like there were suddenly two Elara Cages in the room. "Tell me, what would you do in my place? Which choice is the right one?"

The woman didn't answer, and she and Elara continued to stare into one another's eyes, neither blinking.

"My name is Finn Brasa," Finn said, and the female leader turned to him. "You asked me for our names. "I'm Finn, that's Elara Cage, and behind me are Chiefy and Scraps." The two robots smiled and waved. "What are your names?" Finn added. "You do have names, right?"

The male leader took a moment to think, perhaps weighing up the potential risk of giving his name, before presumably concluding that there was none. Or perhaps, his hesitation was simply down to the fact that no-one had ever needed to ask his name before, since everyone already knew it.

"My name is Adam One," the man said. "I am the Prefect Alpha."

Elara snort-laughed, and raised an eyebrow at the man. "Adam?" she said, cynically, before nodding to the female leader. "And I suppose you're going to tell me that she's called Eve?"

The man scowled. "Yes, but how could you know that?"

Finn laughed, the Elara and the two robots joined in. They continued laughing until it became apparent that neither Adam nor Eve, nor any of the other still-masked prefects in the room, were seeing the funny side.

"Sorry, I thought you were telling a joke?" Finn said, the skin of his face burning hot.

"What is a joke?" Eve asked.

Finn opened his mouth to answer, but he didn't know how to explain it. He considered asking Chiefy to describe the meaning of a joke on his behalf, before realizing that the robot might then spend the next hour giving everyone a detailed lesson on the origins of humor, ironically without trying to be humorous.

"So, she's really called Eve?" Finn asked, choosing instead to conveniently ignore the question.

"Eve One," the woman cut in. "I am the Prefect Omega."

"Adam and Eve, Alpha and Omega?" Elara said, still struggling to choke back laughter. "I suppose that was Reznikov's idea? What a piece of work that bastard is."

Adam and Eve were both angered by Elara speaking about Reznikov in such unkind terms.

"He is our father," Adam said, forcefully.

"Nope-nope!" Scraps said. The robot zipped forward and landed on Elara's shoulder. "Not-father!"

"It isn't meant to be literal," Adam explained, taking a kindly tone with the robot, which helped to endear the man to Finn. "We have no father or mother. We were grown here, on Nimbus. Our genetic line is new, only a decade old. We replaced the previous prefects, who were clones, like us. Genetic drift meant that their line was no longer viable, but our DNA is much stronger."

"Scraps knows!" the little robot replied, smiling at Adam as if he'd known the man all his life. "DNA good because Finn-Finn your father!"

"What?" said Finn, Elara, Adam, and Eve all at the same time.

Scraps' smile grew broader, then he patted Elara's head, affectionally.

"Finn-Finn your father," Scraps repeated, confidently. "And Elara-good is your mom!"

16

THE BEST WE CAN DO

ADAM AND EVE turned to Scraps with looks of incredulity, as if the robot had just uttered the most preposterous lie ever spoken by man or machine. Scraps, on the other hand, remained jolly and upbeat, and also suddenly devoid of fear or anxiety. Knowing that the prefects were genetically related to Finn and Elara was all the confirmation the robot needed to trust them.

"That can't be true, these people are barely a few years older than we are," Adam, the Prefect Alpha, said. "We couldn't possibly be their children. It makes no sense."

"Scraps took blood sample!" the robot said, springing a probe from one of the many compartments in his oil-can body. "Blood on floor after fight. Scraps tests it!"

Adam touched a hand to a cut on his neck, which the man had sustained during the fight with Finn and Elara. Blood was still weeping from the injury and Adam rubbed it between his thumb and forefinger, before looking back at the probe that Scraps was still gleefully waving around, like a flag.

"No offense, my little robot friend, but you will need to prove that," Adam finally replied.

"Chiefy can show!" Scraps said, pointing to the bigger robot. "Just need 'puter access!"

Adam sighed then looked at Eve, the Prefect Omega, and his counterpart. The woman simply shrugged, as if to say, "why not?". It was exactly the sort of reaction that Elara would have given in response to the same unspoken question.

"Okay, but we'll have to limit your access," Adam said.

The man gestured to the other prefects, and they all lowered their weapons and removed their helmets. Besides subtle variations in the way the men and women had cut and styled their hair, they were identical clones of one another. Adam then led them to a computer terminal and sat down at the controls, unlocking the terminal then working the system for several seconds to create a restricted account for Chiefy to use.

"You might want to get that cut tended to," Finn said, noticing that the wound on Adam's neck was still weeping. Elara smiled at him, perhaps because of the paternal concern he was suddenly demonstrating for his genetic offspring.

"We can have foremen bring in a few med kits, and some water too," Adam said, nodding toward one of the other prefects, who jumped to the task. "And some food, if you're hungry?"

"I could eat something," Elara replied. "I honestly don't know how long it's been since we ate or drank anything, or slept for that matter."

Another officer, an Adam, peeled away from the group and entered a room in the prefect hub, which was perhaps a canteen or communal space. By the time that both officers had returned, one with medical supplies and the other with flasks and food blocks wrapped in silver foil that didn't look dissimilar to the algae protein bars that Metalhaven workers survived on during a shift, the modifications to the computer were complete.

"There, you can use this terminal now," Adam said, sliding out of the seat and allowing Chiefy to take his place. The seven-foot robot barely fit in the chair.

"I hope this isn't that 'Serenitox' crap?" Elara asked. She'd taken a flask of liquid and was cautiously sniffing it and swilling it around inside the container.

"No, it's just water," Eve One replied. "As prefects, our food is different to what's grown in the communes, so we get all of our nutrients from these blocks."

"Is that what Serenitox is supposed to be?" Finn asked. "A nutrient supplement?"

Eve regarded Finn quizzically and with no small amount of suspicion. "Yes, what else would it be?" the Prefect Omega asked.

"It's just that we saw how it affected the people in the communes," Finn said, feeling a little threatened. "It seemed to alter their moods, and make them docile somehow."

Eve snorted and shook her head, and for a moment, Finn though he was looking at a spitting image of Elara.

"The benediction is a spiritual ritual, which is focused on mindfulness," Eve said. "We have our own version, though without the elixir, since it's difficult to replicate and wasted on us."

"You don't need it because all of you have already bought into Reznikov's bullshit," Elara said, pushing the prefect's buttons. "There are people like you on the planet too. Zealots."

Eve looked ready to face off against Elara, and while there was a small corner of Finn's mind that wanted to see the two women throw down, just to know who was better, it didn't serve their aims to start fighting again. Thankfully, Chiefy stepped in with a comment that distracted everyone from thoughts of violence.

"Serenitox is indeed a nutrient suspension, but it is also laden with a concoction of mind-alternating narcotics that are designed to increase susceptibility and reduce aggression," Chiefy said.

Everyone looked at the robot, and then at the screen of the computer terminal, which was displaying a detailed chemical analysis of Serenitox, including where on the station the product was manufactured, and its current stock and production levels.

"How did you get that?" Eve said, scowling at the screen.

In the few seconds that he'd had access to the computer, Chiefy had already circumvented all of Adam's security precautions. Even Finn was impressed with how quickly the robot had managed to do this. Then he spotted Scraps on the floor at Chiefy's feet, interfaced to the terminal's core hardware, and all became clear.

"How did you get this information?" Eve repeated, turning her hostility toward the robot. "And how have you broken through Adam's security lockout?"

"I'm clever," Chiefy replied with a shrug, before pointing to a sheepish-looking Scraps on the floor. "He made me so."

Scraps waved then jumped up on to Chiefy's lap and smiled innocently at Eve. The Prefect Omega had inherited her genetic mother's ability to give a probing death stare, but faced with the sweet robot face of Scraps, she couldn't stay angry.

"Just don't break anything while you're in there," Eve said, scowling a little less now. "And keep your robot fingers off data that doesn't concern you."

"Sure-sure!" Scraps said, still smiling.

Finn and Elara exchanged knowing looks. Both understood that the chances of Scraps keeping his mechanical fingers away from information that didn't concern him was precisely nil.

"What about that DNA analysis, Chiefy?" Finn said, trying to steer them back on course.

"Ah yes, it is here," Chiefy said, switching screens and showing the new data. "On the right, you can see the analysis of two DNA patterns, one Finn and one Elara, taken from the records of a gene bank in Metalhaven, one of Zavetgrad's work sectors."

"What's a gene bank?" Adam asked.

Finn sucked in a breath and let it out slowly. There was no way to explain what a gene bank was without opening a large, wriggly can of worms.

"I don't think we have time to go into that right now," Finn said, again wary of derailing the conversation. "We can give you all the information about Zavetgrad you want, but for now, let's stick to who we are, and, more importantly, who you are."

Finn could sense that Adam didn't like not knowing things, which was a trait they shared, but the truth about the man's genetic ancestry appeared to interest him more.

"I look forward to reading about this city," Adam replied,

before turning back to the screen. "Now show us this DNA comparison."

Chiefy was about to operate the console when Eve grabbed the robot's wrist and stopped the machine from punching in a command.

"Not from the blood your little robot companion scooped of the floor, if that's even where he got it," Eve said, still skeptical. She then slid a knife out of a sheath, causing both Finn and Elara to tense up with anticipation, before slicing a cut across the palm of her hand. "Use this instead."

Eve squeezed her hand into a fist and allowed a drop of her blood to fall onto to the scanner bed of the computer terminal. Adam stepped forward a moment later and cut his hand too, adding a second drop a few inches from Eve's. Both Adam and Eve then turned to Finn and Elara, with expectant glances.

"I think I've been sliced and diced enough, already, thank you," Finn said, intuiting what the prefects wanted from him.

Elara, on the other hand, simply drew her knife, sliced her palm, and squeezed a drop of blood onto the opposite side of the scanner bed, before flipping the blade and offering it to Finn, handle first. He rolled his eyes, and made a show of tutting loudly, before wiping the blade clean of Elara's blood, and adding his own to the scanner.

"As you wish," Chiefy said, activating the system, which took the blood samples, split them apart and fed them into the terminal's chemical analyzer.

The computer began to run the analysis, but since the hardware was dated in comparison to Chiefy's modern FLP, the processing time ran to several minutes. The prefects allowed this time to pass in silence. Finn's natural inclination was to fill the void with some form of conversation, whether meaningful or otherwise, but he bit his tongue and limited himself to staring contests with his brooding genetic offspring. Neither he nor Adam would budge, and Eve was even more intractable, which made for an uncomfortable few minutes.

"The analysis is complete," Chiefy said, and the relief amongst everyone was palpable. "On the right you can see the DNA from Finn and Elara, which is identical to what I already showed you."

Eve worked the console to run the comparison herself, before nodding to Adam, satisfied that Chiefy wasn't trying to trick them. The robot showed no offense at this.

"On the left is your DNA," Chiefy continued. "The top is Eve's, and the bottom is Adam's. As you can see, you are both amalgams of the DNA on the right. You are, in effect, their children."

"Let me see that," Eve said, gruffly.

The Prefect Omega shooed Chiefy out of the chair and took command of the computer terminal. Adam moved behind her, and together they worked to confirm or refute Chiefy's assertions, while the other prefects looked on, too distracted by the efforts of their leaders to even bother effectively guarding their prisoners. Finn watched the officers carefully, but it was evident after only a minute or two that Chiefy's data was irrefutable.

"So, you might be right," Eve said. The words caught in her throat, much as they would have if Elara had been compelled to make a similar admission. "I'm still struggling to believe it, but the analysis is clear."

"Now that you know we are who we say we are, there's

more you need to know," Finn said. "If I know Scraps, he's already uploaded a potted history of Zavetgrad to your databanks."

"Short-short version," Scraps said, conforming Finn's guess.

"Can I assume it doesn't make for happy viewing?" Adam asked, and the little robot shook his head, forlornly. The prefect sighed then silently consulted with Eve – the two could read each other's thoughts in the same way Finn and Elara were in tune. "Alright then, just sit tight for a while, and we'll look it over."

All of the prefects in the room gathered around the terminal, while a pair of Gen III foreman robots waited on Finn and the others, bringing food and drinks, though Finn figured that the real reason for their presence was to watch over them. Several screens were activated, each displaying a mirror image of the main computer terminal, and Finn was able to follow along, as the prefects were given a short lesson on Zavetgrad's brutal history. He could see video footage from trials, and from security cameras in the different work sectors, which had captured the brutal subjugation of reds, purples, chromes and other colors, at the hands of the prefects. Later, the condensed history covered Finn's trial then Elara's, which had sparked the rebellion that had led them both to where they were now, sat in a prefect hub on a space station more than two hundred and fifty miles above the surface of a nearly dead world.

Finn's fate, and the fates of a million or more people on Earth, now rested in the hands of another group of law enforcers. Yet, unlike the regular golds of Zavetgrad or the fanatical special prefecture, the Nimbus prefects had not been tainted by the powers granted to them. Cocooned on Nimbus, without any real threats, at least until Finn and Elara had arrived, their roles had been largely ceremonial. They had not been required, or ordered, to police the population of Nimbus, since the communes were all blissfully compliant. All they did was hunt down and disable rogue foremen. They were not oppressors, but protectors. And, despite their cynicism and mistrust, both of which were merited given the circumstances, Finn knew in his bones that they were good people at heart.

"Do you think they'll help us?" Elara whispered, breaking what had been a ten-minute silence.

Finn shrugged. "We're asking a lot. We're asking them to help us destroy the very thing they were created to protect."

"But now they know this place is rotten, they can't turn a blind eye," Elara said.

"We wouldn't, if we were in their place," Finn said, smiling at her. "And if they're anything like us, beyond their DNA that is, they won't let it stand, either."

Elara didn't seem convinced. "They each have half of our DNA." She looked at Finn out of the corner of her eye. "What if it's the bad half?"

"I don't think DNA works like that." Finn laughed, which wasn't wise in retrospect, and Elara glowered at him. He straightened his face, then his back, and cleared his throat, ready to give a more earnest answer. "What I mean is, we're not bad people, Elara. We're good people that bad shit has happened to. It's made us hard. It's forced us do things in order to survive."

"I chose to be The Shadow," Elara said, so quietly Finn struggled to hear her.

"That's not who you are anymore," Finn countered. "You're Sentinel, remember?"

Elara shook her head. "I'll always be The Shadow," she said, regretfully. "And the difference between you and me, Finn, is that you can't forgive yourself for the things you did, whereas I did unforgivable things."

Finn didn't want to let that go unchallenged, because he could see that Elara was slipping into a dark funk, but the prefects had finished their whistlestop tour of Reznikov's atrocities, and were gathering around them. Frustrated, he parked his intentions to confront Elara, and pushed himself out of the chair, as Adam One and Eve One approached.

"It would seem that we have been kept ignorant of a great many things," Adam said.

"Reznikov lied to you," Elara replied, putting it more bluntly.

"He didn't lie," Eve snapped. Her instinct had been to defend the man whom they had all referred to as their "great father". Yet the truth was inescapable, and even the hard-edged Prefect Omega couldn't deny this. "But I admit that important facts have been omitted," Eve conceded, grudgingly.

"A deliberate omission is still a lie," Elara said, not allowing Eve to diminish the significance of what they'd been shown. "Reznikov didn't want you tainted by the outrages he committed on the planet. He wanted Nimbus to be free from the past, but as noble as that sounds, it doesn't excuse what he's done. It doesn't make it right."

Eve was ready to argue but Elara had hit her with an inescapable truth. A regular prefect or captain might have dismissed her point, while a special prefect would have been too indoctrinated to believe it, but the protectors of Nimbus had not been conditioned to lie or deceive, or to believe they were in some way superior to everyone else. It was not in their nature.

"Let's say we believe you," Adam said, moving the conversation on without explicitly acknowledging Reznikov's crimes. "Let's say that there is a city with a million people and that for the reasons you outlined, our great father intends to destroy it. Even if that were true, we can't let you destroy this space station, and kill the people here."

"It's a simple numbers equation, Adam," Elara answered, sounding exasperated. "The choice is do you save a million people, or save, what? Ten thousand? Twenty?"

"The children of Nimbus do not deserve to die." Adam's answer was resolute. "What you ask is not fair."

"No, it's not," Elara admitted. "But it's the best we can do."

Chiefy then raised his hand to speak, and despite the thick atmosphere of tension that filled the room, Finn couldn't help but smile.

"What if you were to help us stop Reznikov?" Chiefy suggested. "We only need to capture the president and convince him, by force if necessary, to abort the launch. Then perhaps Nimbus and Zavetgrad could yet coexist."

Finn raised an eyebrow then looked at Adam and Eve, trying to read their expressions and gauge their willingness to turn against the man they revered as a father, if not a pseudo-deity.

"We could try to reason with him," Adam replied, and Elara immediately shook her head.

"He's already lied to you once, we were here in the room

when he did it," Elara said. "What makes you think he'll listen? More likely, he'll see that you're turning against him, and order this station's robots to hunt you down as well."

"That's not true," Eve said. The hostility between the two women was building.

"Then come with us, to the palace," Finn suggested. "Let's confront Reznikov together."

Adam and Eve glanced at one another, sheepishly, and both looked suddenly embarrassed.

"They cannot enter the palace," Chiefy cut in. Finn and Elara turned to the robot in surprise. "The prefects and colonists all have micro explosives implanted into bases of their brain stems. Should they enter the palace, these devices will detonate, killing them."

"Is this true?" Elara asked. Eve growled a sigh and nodded. "You knew this already, and you didn't think there was something fucked up about it?"

"It is for the president's safety," Adam argued, his cheeks flushing hot. "His palace is his sanctuary."

"Aren't you supposed to be his children?" Finn scoffed. "Some way to treat your kids..."

"You honestly didn't think there was something odd about being fitted with a brain bomb?" Elara said, pushing the prefects for an answer.

"Why would we?" Eve said, angrier now than ever. "We've never had a reason to question anything we've been told."

"Well now you certainly fucking do," Finn said, ramping up the pressure.

The communications console at the far side of the room began to chime, and Finn recognized the message tone from the computer in the gene bank back on Metalhaven. Adam and Eve both looked relieved for the interruption, and hurried to the terminal. Finn and Elara followed, and the other prefects let them pass. The two Gen III foremen that had served the drinks and food followed too, prompting Chiefy to stay close.

Adam waited for Finn and the others to move out of the camera's field of view then answered the incoming message. Gideon Alexander Reznikov appeared on the screen, still as a glowing head and shoulders.

"Is it done?" Reznikov asked. "Are the invaders dead?"

Adam stared at the glowing face of the president, but where the prefect had shown deference the first time he had spoken to Reznikov, now Finn could see the doubt behind the man's eyes, and the tension in his jaw and shoulders. Prefect Alpha, Adam One, was angry and not hiding it well.

"They remain alive for the time being," Adam replied. "As do the others who came into contact with them."

Reznikov set his jaw. "Why?"

"They have shown us things," Adam replied, clearly struggling to challenge Reznikov and explain his reasons. "Things about the planet that we did not know."

"They are lies," Reznikov snapped. "Dangerous fabrications. Remember why you are here. Remember what you are protecting. These people from the planet threaten humanity's very survival. You *cannot* listen to them. I require you to kill them, immediately!"

Adam allowed Reznikov to speak his piece, but his determination to question the man had not faltered.

"We tested their DNA, and compared it to our own," Adam continued, and Finn saw the president's glowing right eye twitch. "The Prefect Omega and I are an amalgam of them. We are their children."

"You are *my* children!" Reznikov roared. "I created you! I created Nimbus! I am the father of the next evolution of humanity. The vermin in Zavetgrad are nothing!"

Adam and Eve appeared to grow a little taller, and the anger that had been contained beneath the surface was starting to bleed through. Finn knew why. The president had made a mistake, and they'd all heard it.

"So, you admit that there is a city on the planet?" Eve said. Reznikov did not answer. "You admit there is a city called Zavetgrad?"

"Listen to me closely, Eve," Reznikov said. His tone was kindly but firm, and his expression was earnest. "I admit that there are things I've kept from you, to keep you pure, but understand that I did it for your own good, and for the good of humanity. These people from the planet are a relic of the past, but unlike the treasures in my museums, they are worthless and broken. They are trash, and they must be discarded, or humanity cannot evolve."

"If they are garbage then what are we?" Adam said. "We come from them, Eve and I. If these people are so worthless, then why are we any better?"

"Because I made you that way!" Reznikov roared, blowing hot and cold like a faulty air-conditioning unit. "I took the DNA from Finn Brasa and Elara Cage, and others like them, and purified it. Unlike them, you are free of the mutations that afflict those on the planet. You are perfect human beings, my children! You are the future, and they are the past. You must kill them. It is the only way!"

Adam and Eve looked at one another, before looking at

Finn and Elara and holding their anxious eyes for a few seconds longer than was comfortable, before turning back to the president.

"No," Eve said, firmly. "You have lied to us, father. You told us the planet was dead, but now we learn there are a million people living down there."

"They mean nothing," Reznikov said, dismissively.

"Is that why you intend to destroy Zavetgrad?" Adam asked.

"Come and visit me, in the palace," Reznikov said, suddenly turning amiable again, and smiling at Adam like he was inviting him to tea. "Let us discuss this in person. Let me explain."

"You didn't answer my question," Adam said.

Reznikov's eyes hardened. "Come to see me, and we'll talk. Leave Finn Brasa and Elara Cage alive for the moment, under guard. Then once we have spoken, you'll see the wisdom in my approach. You'll understand."

"Answer the question," Eve said, and for the first time, she spoke sternly to Reznikov.

"Eve, please..."

"Answer the question!" Eve snarled.

"Yes!" The boom of Reznikov's voice was like a cannon firing. "Yes, I intend to nuke the city and raze it to the ground! And Haven too, along with all the festering rejects from Zavetgrad that slithered their way inside its underground chambers. They must all be cleansed. It is for the greater good!"

Though he never doubted the president's apocalyptic ambitions, hearing the man's rageful admission shocked even Finn. He glanced at Elara, and saw that it'd had the same effect on her too. Yet if hearing Reznikov admit to plans of genocide had shocked them, it had traumatized all of the Adams and Eves in the room. Some were ghostly pale, some choked back tears, but all of them looked furious, none more so than the Prefects Alpha and Omega.

"This is wrong," Adam said, his mind made up. "We are supposed to be the protectors of humanity, not its destroyers. I will have no part in this."

"Nor will I," Eve said, with matching resolve. "You must stop, father. You must end this madness."

"No," Reznikov said. The man looked hurt and betrayed, but not repentant. "I am disappointed in you, my children." Finn and Elara stepped into shot behind the two prefects, and Reznikov's eyes fell onto them. "But, considering what you came from, perhaps I should not be surprised."

Reznikov's image vanished, then the pair of Gen III foremen leapt toward Adam and Eve, fingers pressed into blades, aimed at their throats, but the two machines didn't get within a few inches of the prefects before Chiefy had grabbed their necks, and yanked them clear. The Gen IIIs turned on Chiefy and struck the robot, but it was like a rubber mallet hitting iron. Chiefy shrugged off their attacks then crushed the inferior machines with pummeling strikes that smashed their FLPs and left them as nothing more than smoldering scrap at his feet.

"We'll get you to the palace," Adam said. "We'll help you to stop our fath..." the man paused and corrected himself. "We'll help you to stop the president."

Finn looked at all the other faces in the room, dozens of Adams and Eves, all identical, and all like Finn and Elara in so many ways. There was consensus. The prefects of Nimbus were on their side.

"But what I said before stands," Adam continued. "The people on this station cannot be allowed to die. They are no more to blame for the Authority's atrocities than you are."

"Then how do we save them?" Finn said. It was the only question that mattered.

"Nimbus was constructed over a span of many decades, built from dozens of autonomous sections that connect together like lock and key," Eve explained. Finn nodded, Chiefy had already discovered as much. "We must gather the communes together inside a cluster of these modules, and jettison them before we destroy the station."

"Will they be able to survive?" Finn asked.

"The modules are self-sustaining," Adam said. "And the communes know how to farm, and to live independently. They'll survive. It won't be easy, but they'll survive."

"More importantly, is there time to do both?" Elara cut in. Finn already knew of her objections to saving the communes. "Reznikov could launch in a matter of hours. Stopping the nuclear attack has to be our priority."

"We agree," Adam said, and Eve nodded. "But we can do both. There is a way."

Finn felt adrenaline flood his body, waking him up, and calling him to action. He was about to suggest they move out when a sobering thought gripped him like a sudden panic attack.

"Wait, what about you?" Finn asked. "What will you and the other Adams and Eves do?"

"They can return to the planet, with us?" Elara suggested. "Hell knows, we could use more people like you."

"They cannot ever set foot on the planet," Chiefy interrupted. Not for the first time, the robot had dropped a bombshell out of nowhere. "Reznikov edited their DNA. He called it purification, but in doing so, he also removed the beneficial mutations that allow Finn and Elara to withstand the high levels of radiation on the surface, with no ill effects."

The news hit Finn harder than he expected. He barely knew Adam and Eve, but it was undeniable that there was a connection between them. The prospect of leaving them behind felt like mourning someone who had died.

"We can take another section of the station, and jettison it like the communes," Adam said. "Those of us who survive will be able to live there."

"Will it be self-sustaining too?" Finn asked.

"No," Eve said, shaking her head. "But Reznikov had cryo-statis chambers shipped to the station in the early years of its construction, to preserve its original population, before Nimbus was habitable." She shrugged. "Those chambers still exist. Perhaps we can simply go to sleep, and wait until the planet has healed enough that we could return."

"That's a hell of sacrifice," Finn said. "It doesn't seem fair."

Eve laughed and shrugged again. "No, it's not," Eve said, before turning to Elara and smiling. "But it's the best we can do."

17

ONE OFFS

One of the other Adams hurried over and spoke to quietly to the Prefect Alpha. The man looked concerned, and Finn noted that the other prefects were busy gathering their weapons and forming up into the six-man squads that he'd seem roaming other parts of the station. Their helmets were back on, and they looked ready for a fight.

"We've had reports that foremen are advancing toward this hub," Adam One said, once the other officer had departed to join his squad. "It seems that disobeying our great father's wishes has consequences."

"You're just seeing the true Reznikov, that's all," Finn answered. "How long do we have?"

"A few minutes, probably less," Adam replied. "One thing that this space station is not short of is foremen."

"Luckily, most of them seem to be old generation one and two designs, which shouldn't make them too difficult to put down," Elara said, allowing her unconquerable spirit to shine through.

Eve One hurried to a weapons locker and removed two

sonic rifles. She tossed one to Chiefy who caught the weapon without his robot eyes blinking, before picking up another two and offering the rifles to Finn and Elara.

"Here, you'll need these," Eve said, while returning to the locker and recovering a rifle each for her and Adam One.

"But what use will these sonic weapons be against foremen?" Finn asked. He remembered how a rifle blast had temporarily scrambled Chiefy's circuits, but if there was an army of robots coming after them, they'd need a lot more stopping power.

"The rifles have a variable power setting," Eve said, turning her weapon on its side and showing Finn the dial. "A setting of five is enough to stun a human being, and seven should disrupt the foremen."

"What's the maximum setting?" Elara asked.

"Twelve," Eve replied. "But that might be a little extreme."

"Extreme is exactly what we need right now," Elara said. She checked her weapon and spun the power setting dial to twelve, before reaching over to Finn's weapon and doing the same to his. "Now isn't the time for half measures."

Eve considered this then shrugged and also dialed her weapon to twelve. Adam followed suit, though with some trepidation.

"To be honest, I've always wondered what a setting of twelve would be like," Eve said, while dragging out a box of spare power cells for the weapons. "We've rarely had cause to use these weapons at all, and only ever to deal with malfunctioning foremen or spider bots that have gone off-program."

One of the squad leaders approached and spoke to Eve

One. She nodded and relayed some additional orders, then the prefect hub emptied more quickly than a Metalhaven reclamation yard at the end of a shift.

"We've assigned squads to the task of moving the communes into connected habitat blocks," Eve said, explaining the reason for the sudden exodus. "Ten blocks in the east wing of the station will be enough to accommodate all of the inhabitants. Between these ten blocks are all the facilities the communes need to survive."

"What about power?" Finn asked.

"Everything is solar," Adam explained. "That's one advantage of being in space, there's an endless supply of energy."

"Water is largely recycled too," Eve added. "But we've also harvested enough ice from asteroids to support a commune a thousand times larger than the one we have here, for decades to come."

Finn nodded. The prefects had matters in hand, which meant he could now turn his thoughts to the palace and how to reach Reznikov.

"I know you can't enter the palace, but can you help us to get inside?" Finn asked.

"We can get you to it, but we don't know how to get inside," Adam said. It was the first hurdle that the Prefect Alpha had thrown at them, and it was a significant one. "When the warden, or the regent as you knew him, visited from the planet, we used to escort him to the airlock, but only Reznikov himself can open the door."

Elara nodded. "It will be a DNA-coded key. We've encountered similar locking mechanisms before."

"The problem is that this time we don't have a sample of

Volkov's DNA to fabricate a key from," Finn added. "Could we force the door, somehow, or maybe blast it open?"

Adam considered the suggestion and briefly conferred with Eve, who spent a moment running a query on the hub's computer system, but when the Prefect Omega was finished, her expression suggested she was not about to give good news.

"We'd need a dozen or more foremen to force open the door, assuming we could dig a hole in it large enough to gain leverage," Eve said. "But we don't hold any kind of explosive devices in our stores. We've never had need for such weapons, and in general it's not a good idea to set off explosions inside a pressurized space station."

"What about the nukes?" Elara wondered.

Finn raised an eyebrow at his partner. "I hope you're not suggesting we nuke the door leading into Reznikov's palace?"

"No, obviously," Elara answered, peevishly. "But from what I gather, Adam and Eve didn't even know that Reznikov had nukes on the station, so what else is here they don't know about?"

The two prefects considered this but still neither looked optimistic about finding a solution.

"It's possible that there's a weapons store we're unaware of, or perhaps there's even something contained within the museum halls that we might be able to use, but we don't know where to start," Adam said.

"I could potentially fabricate an explosive device," Chiefy suggested. "The necessary component parts will be on this station somewhere."

"How long might that take?" Finn asked.

Chiefy processed the question, whist consulting with Scraps, then shrugged. "Several hours, perhaps. Too long."

Finn cursed under his breath. They were running out of options as well as time, but he refused to give up.

"There has to be a way into that palace that doesn't involve a nuclear warhead," Finn said, trying to will a solution into existence.

"I'm sure there is, but it's not a problem that we, or any of our brothers and sisters, have ever had to consider," Adam said. "We've simply never had a reason to enter the palace, until now."

The sound of sonic rifle blasts began to filter into the prefect hub, and amongst the gunfire, Finn could also pick out voices shouting orders. Reznikov's robots were getting close.

"Let's focus on what we can do first," Finn said, trying to remain positive. "Once you have the communes clustered together, how do we jettison the modules?"

"Everything to do with the running of each station cluster is managed from the habitat control center," Eve said. "The control center manages the linkages between each section, and the flow of utilities from the primary processing and recycling facilities. From there, we can reconfigure the linkages to make the cluster of modules self-sustaining, before detaching them from the station."

"Then what happens to it?" Elara asked. "Without being attached to Nimbus, won't it just float away into deep space?"

"Or, worse, crash into the planet's atmosphere and burn up..." Finn added.

"No. Station-keeping thrusters are added to each module when they are constructed, so that they can maneuver into position under their own propulsion," Adam replied.

"They're not especially powerful, but it will be enough to move the habitats into a higher, stable orbit."

"Okay, then let's move," Elara said, readying her sonic rifle.

"Hold on..."

Finn stopped Elara before she marched out of the door and started raising hell with the foremen closing in on them. Something Adam had said was bothering him, and while it had been mentioned only in passing, his gut told him that it might be significant.

"You said that thrusters are added to the modules when they're constructed," Finn continued, addressing Adam.

"That's right," the prefect replied.

"So, what builds these modules in the first place?" Finn asked.

"You mean the Crawler?" Adam said. He was frowning at Finn, uncertain whether he'd answered the question, or even if he'd understood the question in the first place.

"Maybe; what's the Crawler?" Finn asked.

"It's perhaps best if I show you."

Adam turned to the computer and brought up a three-dimensional render of the entire space station. The image rotated then focused in on an object on the outside that looked like a super-sized version of the spider robots they'd encountered previously.

"That's the Crawler," Adam said, tapping the screen. "It's an engineering module that constantly travels around the station, repairing damage from micrometeorite strikes and space debris, while also fabricating new sections and any replacement parts that are needed."

Finn and Elara took a closer look at the Crawler. It was

difficult to judge the exact scale of the machine, but considering its size relative to the habitat blocks it was crawling across, Finn guessed that it was easily as big as a tenement building in Metalhaven.

"Can you get us onto that thing?" Finn asked. He had an idea, one that might get around the problem of Reznikov's DNA lock.

"I can see where you're going with this," Eve said, taking charge of the computer console. "The Crawler could ferry us all to the president's palace in the central sphere then use its array of plasma cutters and fabricators to build a crude airlock, bypassing Reznikov's security entirely."

"First, we'd have to get aboard it," Elara said.

"The Crawler can be accessed from the habitat control center, and we can issue a recall command from this terminal," Eve said, already inputting the command on the computer. "By the time we get there, it should already be docked and waiting for us."

Scraps suddenly jumped off Chiefy's shoulder and hovered toward the door, his sensor dish extended.

"Danger-danger!" Scraps said, pointing to the exit. All the other prefects had already left to attend to their duties, so they were the only ones left in the hub. "Bad robots coming!"

"How many, pal?" Finn said, covering the door with his rifle. Scraps gritted and bared his little metal teeth and steepled his fingers together. "Never mind, buddy, I think I get the picture," Finn said.

"Follow us, the control center isn't far from here," Adam said, and the two prefects took the lead. "The quickest route is through the waste processing chamber, but that will mean fighting through a lot of foremen."

"That suits me just fine," Elara said, adding three spare power cells for her sonic rifle to her armor. "I've had enough of being chased around this station. Wherever we go from here on in, we take the direct route."

Adam and Eve moved out into the corridor, which was already littered with the remains of robots that had gotten close to the prefect hub, before the squads had cut them down. Using their innate knowledge of the station's layout, the two officers guided Finn and the others through the labyrinthine interior of Nimbus, taking detours and short cuts that left Finn's head spinning.

To their rear, the clomp of robot feet grew louder, and the first wave of foremen charged into view, running at full speed to catch up with them. Finn opened fire, but with the weapon set to its maximum power level, the report almost burst his own eardrums, despite the blasts of sound energy being focused directly ahead.

The effects on the foremen he'd targeted were far more devastating. Finn was used to blasting robots with his laser cannon, but the sonic rifle caused destruction on a whole other level. The shots superheated the circuits in the machines' bodies and heads, causing power cells to rupture and explode like grenades, and setting fire to circuit boards and wiring looms, which fizzed and crackled like fireworks.

Between himself, Elara and Chiefy, the corridor was soon filled with the smoldering debris of dozens of Gen I and II foremen, but still the machines came at them, in wave after wave, without any end in sight.

"We're at the processing facility," Adam said, stopping at the door and using a thumb and retinal scan to access the secure area. "Get ready to fight."

"What the hell do you think we've been doing?" Elara called back.

Neither prefect heard her, because they'd already charged ahead and begun blasting the machines that were busy recycling wastewater and other organic matter for re-use. Finn and Elara backed through the door, then Eve tore the control panel off the wall and began to hotwire the circuit inside.

"What are you doing?" Finn called out, while continuing to send blast after blast into the robots that were almost on top of them.

"I'm sealing the door," Eve said, sparks casting shadows across her face. "There are more robots ahead of us, and we can't hold off them and the ones chasing after us too."

"Maybe Scraps can help?" Elara said, pulling a power cell from her rifle and tossing it, before slapping in another.

"No, I have it..."

The door slammed shut with the speed of a camera shutter blinking, crushing a foreman's arm as the robot reached out in an effort to jam it. The limb fell inside the processing facility, twitched for a moment, then lay still.

"I increased the power to the door mechanism," Eve said, wiping her eyes, which were streaming from the bright sparks that had dazzled her. "They'll get through eventually, but we'll be long gone by then."

"A little help!"

Adam and Chiefy were trying to hold off the robots that had now abandoned their tasks to deal with the intruders. Finn and the others hurried to join them and create a more effective firing squad, but there were more than a hundred foremen inside the room, and despite being lowly Gen I and II models, there were too many to fight.

"I'm down to my last cell," Adam called out, while picking off robot after robot with precise head shots.

"Here, take this," Elara said, removing a cell from her armor and tossing it to Adam.

The prefect caught the cell, reloaded, and continued to fire, not missing a shot, but even with their combined efforts, the foremen were drawing closer, like an army of the undead that couldn't be stopped.

"We might have to run for it," Finn said, ejecting a cell and reloading for a third time. "If we bunch together, we might be able to plough a line through their center."

"I have a different suggestion," Chiefy said.

The robot handed his weapon to Elara. The barrel was glowing like a red-hot coal, and it only had a dozen shots left, but Elara immediately put it to good use. She lowered Chiefy's rifle and her own weapon to her hips and began shooting like a gunslinger, knocking down robot after robot like ten pins.

"May I borrow your spear?" Chiefy added, extending his hand to Finn.

"My spear?" Finn said, face dripping with sweat from the combined heat of all the smoldering robots. "Chiefy, I don't think fighting hand-to-hand is a good idea. There are too many of them!"

"That is what I intend to rectify," Chiefy replied, calmly.

Elara raised an eyebrow, but she seemed keen to discover what the seven-foot, seventh generation foreman had in mind, and in truth, Finn was more than a little curious too.

"Okay..." Finn said, turning his back toward the robot, and allowing Chiefy to pluck the weapon from its magnetic stow. "I'll be wanting that back, though."

"Of course," Chiefy said, smiling.

Finn couldn't care less whether he got the spear back or not, he just wanted to make the point that he expected Chiefy to return in one piece, unlike his less fortunate relatives, who littered the floor of the processing hall like volcanic ash after an eruption.

Chiefy carefully placed Scraps onto Eve's shoulder, which Finn considered an interesting choice, then brandished the spear and turned to face the oncoming horde. Scraps smiled and waved at Eve before playing with her hair, and to Finn's surprise, Eve smiled back. It was the first time Finn had seen the Prefect Omega adopt an expression that was not either a scowl, frown, glower or grimace.

"I will be back shortly," Chiefy said, cheerfully.

The robot then waved to Scraps, who waved back while continuing to twirl Eve's hair, then charged into the advancing mass of robots with the force of a Solaris Ignition rocket blasting off from Spacehaven.

"Hold your fire!" Adam called out, but Finn and Elara had already stopped shooting, and the presence of Scraps on her shoulder had distracted Eve and caused her to port arms too.

Chiefy ploughed through the center of the robots, separating them like Moses parting the red sea, before spinning on the spot like a typhoon, spear outstretched. The weapons slashed though the necks and craniums of the closest robots, sending sparks flying like gushes of blood from a hundred severed arteries, but Chiefy was far from finished. Moving so fast that Finn could barely keep sight of the powerful robot, Chiefy smashed metal limbs, tore through wiring looms, crushed FLPs and pierced robot bodies like an overcharged laser cutter. The hapless Gen I and Gen II foremen had no defense, and even when one or two of the machines managed to get a grip on Chiefy, the larger, stronger and faster robot either ripped their arms from their bodies, or threw them halfway across the hall, like they'd been fired from a cannon.

Before long, only a handful of machines remained, and they were so badly damaged that they barely knew their left from their right. Feet, hands and even heads missing, the aged foremen tottered away, bashing into the recycling machinery, or simply falling face first into a pile of their fallen comrades.

"Here is your spear," Chiefy said, returning to Finn and offering him the weapon back. It was bent out of shape, mangled, and scratched to within an inch of its existence, but Finn accepted it, nonetheless. "That was... satisfying," Chiefy said, after a brief pause to reflect on the correct word to use.

"Are all the foremen in Zavetgrad like you?" Adam asked, looking at Chiefy with a mixture of admiration and fear.

"Not really," Chiefy replied, modestly.

"Not at all," Elara correct him. "Chiefy and Scraps are ones-offs."

The screech of metal alerted them to the efforts of the robots outside, who were still working to open the door that Eve had forced shut. The machines had stopped trying to break through the door itself, and were now attempting to tear a hole through the wall and interstitial spaces instead.

"That will still hold them for a few minutes yet," Adam said, unconcerned by the burrowing robots. "The habitat control room is just on the other side of this hall," he added, moving ahead, and gesturing for Finn and the others to follow. "Come on, we're close."

18
HABITAT CONTROL

Adam One reached the entrance to the habitat interlock control center first, and hurriedly pressed his thumb to the lock scanner. The device activated, scanning his thumbprint then retinal pattern, but the door didn't open.

"It's not working," Adam said, trying again without success.

"Let me try…" Eve replaced Adam at the lock controls, but her thumbprint and retinal scan also failed.

"It's Reznikov, he's already started to lock you out," Elara said.

"Then we're finished," Adam replied, hammering his fist against the door. "Without the Crawler, we have no hope of reaching the president's palace."

"We're not beaten yet," Finn said, determinedly.

He stepped back and waved Chiefy forward. Scraps was sitting on the larger robot's shoulder and had already sprung an array of tools from his compartments, ready to start hacking.

"This station uses old computer tech that hasn't been

updated for years," Finn said, as the little robot hopped onto Eve's shoulder, so he could gain access to the lock panel. "Scraps and Chiefy have been able to hack into the very best security systems the Authority has thrown at us. This won't be a problem."

"Piece of cake!" Scraps said, setting to work in earnest.

"What does cake have to do with this?" Adam said, frowning at the little machine.

"Nothing at all," Finn cut in, smiling at his genetic offspring, though this did nothing to alleviate the man's confusion. "Don't worry about it, it's just Scraps' way of saying that it will be easy."

The door mechanism cycled on cue and Scraps snapped his little fingers then pointed to the now disabled lock.

"Piece of cake!" Scraps repeated, and this time Adam understood.

"Let's hope it's also a 'piece of cake' for you to break into the habitat control systems," Adam said, stalking inside the room.

The control center was dark and the cold air inside the room was stale and musty. Finn guessed that it hadn't been used for months, maybe even years. Lights flickered on as Adam and Eve entered, cautiously checking the space for robots that may have been left dormant since the last habitat operation had been executed. Finn followed, and discovered that the center was larger than he'd expected. The floor area was similar to the suite inside the gene bank in Metalhaven where the rebels had set up their HQ, and was set out on two levels. There was a semi-circular bank of control consoles on the lower level, and a smaller mezzanine floor, which appeared to be where the center managers, either human or robot, overlooked and directed operations.

"This reminds me of the rocket launch control room I saw in Spacehaven," Finn commented, as the unhappy memory of his trial resurfaced in his mind. He scanned his eyes across the dozens of stations and felt suddenly overwhelmed. "We'd need three full squads of your prefects to run this place. Are you sure we can do everything we need to do on our own?"

"It's all in hand," Eve said, as she and Adam ran up the narrow metal stairs to the mezzanine level. "The other squads will have done much of the preparation for us. From here, we just need to execute the command."

Finn and the others followed the two prefects to the mezzanine floor and found them already sitting at control stations, but the computers were as stubborn as the door lock had been, and refused to respond to their commands.

"Hey, Scraps, we could use your help getting into the system," Eve said, waving the robot over. "I hope this is a 'piece of cake' for you too."

Scraps flexed his arms like a body builder at a championship contest, before hopping onto the computer terminal beside Eve and plugging himself into it. Within a matter of seconds, every computer terminal in the control center sparked into life with a thrum and a beep, then a giant TV screen, not unlike the displays that used to show footage of the trials, powered on.

"Piece of cake," Scraps said, folding his arms across his oil can chest in a triumphant manner.

Eve smiled at the robot then got to work. The TV screen was

split into dozens of picture-in-picture segments, each displaying a different part of the station, but as Eve worked, the smaller images were replaced by a larger one, showing the cluster of habitat blocks on the circumference of Nimbus. Finn could see Earth slowly rotating in the background, and it put into perspective just how far, figuratively and literally, they had come from the reclamation yards of Metalhaven. While he was gawping at the blue planet, he became aware of a rhythmic thump vibrating the floor panels beneath his feet. It occurred at set intervals of a few seconds, and seemed to be getting louder and stronger.

"Do you feel that too?" Finn asked, and Elara nodded. They both turned to Chiefy, but the robot shrugged.

Suddenly, the image switched again, and the face of an Adam appeared in the center, blown up many times larger than life.

"This is Adam Nineteen," the prefect said, reporting in. "We've moved all of the commune inhabitants together into sections seven through sixteen. We're ready here."

"Do they know what's about to happen to them?" Finn said, addressing the prefect on the screen.

"No," the officer replied, somewhat sheepishly. "We told them it was a safety drill. If we told them the truth, there would be panic."

Finn blew out a sigh. He thought that the colonists deserved to know that they were about to be jettisoned into space, without the full support network of Nimbus to back them up, but he understood the prefect's reasons for secrecy.

"Will they be able to survive?" Elara asked, which was perhaps the more important question.

"We chose these habitats because, between them, they have everything the colonists need," Adam Nineteen replied.

"They have power, water, reclamation, and the ability to grow food. It won't be easy, but they'll adapt."

"Nimbus was based on the idea of the commune," Adam One cut in. "Reznikov, for his failings, knew that life in space would be difficult. He designed this station, and its society, around the idea of self-sufficiency. They have everything they need to survive. Whether they live or die is down to them."

"What about the Serenitox?, the drug that Reznikov feeds the colonists to keep them docile and compliant?" Finn asked. "Down on the planet, the Authority laced our food and drink with narcotics too. We became quite dependent on them, some more than others."

Adam and Eve exchanged anxious looks, and it seemed obvious that the Serenitox question was more complex than answering whether the communes had sufficient material resources to survive.

"Serenitox was designed to encourage compliance and harmony," Eve began. "Nimbus aspires to the idea of utopia, but it is not one, not yet. The plan was to attain that level of societal cohesion over decades, even centuries. The president aspired to the idea of the perfect communist civilization, with collective responsibility."

Elara snorted. "That's just more crap that Reznikov fed you. He and his descendants have maintained absolute power for over two centuries. Do you really think he'd give it up?"

Eve shrugged. "Two hours ago, I would not have questioned it, but now..."

"Now, you know that this space station is built on a lie," Elara said, as ever, putting her point forward bluntly. "Reznikov doesn't care about the perfect communist society, what he really wants is to become a god. That's why he appears to you as a glowing aura. It's why he won't let you defile his palace by setting foot inside it. He believes he's better than you, and if that's what he thinks of his perfect humans up here on Nimbus, imagine the disgust he has for the people on the planet."

Elara's speech landed with the weight of a right hook from Chiefy, and while it hadn't strictly been necessary to ram home the point that Nimbus was corrupt, it didn't hurt to reinforce the stakes.

"Sir, we must launch the habitats now, before we are locked out of the system," Adam Nineteen interrupted. Finn had almost forgotten that the man was still waiting. "The longer we delay, the more anxious the people here will become."

Adam One nodded then pressed a button on his console, before turning to Eve. She let out a heavy breath then pressed a corresponding button on her console, before turning a dial ninety degrees to the right. There was a heavy thump that momentarily distracted Finn from the regular beat that had continued to drum through the floor, then the display switched, and they watched as the communes detached from Nimbus with sudden bursts of thrust, and began to float away from the station, like chunks of ice breaking off a glacier and drifting into the ocean.

Adam and Eve stood up from their consoles and the group gathered together to watch the habitats push away from Nimbus using their individual thruster packages, then perform an intricate ballet of maneuvers to align with one another. All the while this was happening, Finn could hear the *thump, thump, thump* of something reverberating through the deck, but neither prefect seemed concerned, so he put it to the back of his mind. Finally, the ten communes connected and locked together as a single unit – a miniature version of Nimbus. The thrusters fired again, this time in unison, pushing the new commune into a higher orbit, where it caught the light from the sun, and glowed like a giant halo above the earth.

"It's done," Adam said, shutting down his station.

The thumps continued, and without the spectacle of the connected communes to distract him, Finn was now growing anxious.

"What the hell is that sound?" Finn said, as the next thump shook his bones and rattled the dials and switches on the consoles.

"That's the Crawler, heading this way," Eve replied, as if it should have been obvious to Finn. Four more thumps shook the floor in quick succession and Finn worried that the mezzanine was going to collapse. Then there was silence. "And now it's here," Eve added. "We should move quickly, before the president realizes what we're doing."

Adam opened a door at the rear of the mezzanine and the warmer air in the control room was suddenly pulled through it, like a ghostly breeze. Adam stepped inside and lights blinked on to reveal a narrow corridor that ended in a ladder.

"Follow me," Adam said, slinging his rifle and beginning the climb. "I hope you're not afraid of heights."

"What was that?" Finn said. A chill ran down his spine.

Adam scowled at Finn, but Elara moved past and slapped him on the back, heartily.

"Just don't look down, and you'll be okay," Elara said. Instead of appearing concerned, she was smirking.

"Thanks for tip," Finn replied, grumpily.

Dreading the climb that lay ahead of him, Finn waited for the others to go first then grabbed the lower rungs of the ladder and began to pull himself up. The metal was freezing cold, and if it hadn't been for his gloves, his skin would have stuck to the rungs like glue. Leaning out to get a clearer look ahead, he saw that the top of the ladder was shrouded in darkness, making it seem that the tunnel went on without end. He shuddered again, and began to pull himself up, all the while keeping Elara's advice in mind.

Lights flickered on as Adam continued his climb, but several minutes elapsed and still there was no end in sight. The air inside the narrow tunnel that the ladder traversed became colder and colder, and Finn's labored breaths fogged the air, turning to ice crystals the moment the plumes of moisture-rich vapor touched the bare metal of the ladder.

"Not long now," Adam called out. More lights flickered on ahead of the prefect and finally Finn could see a hatchway. "Just remember not to look down."

Finn looked down.

Dizziness and nausea overcame him, and he pulled his body tight to the ladder, clinging on like a barnacle to a Seahaven ship's hull.

"He said don't look..." Elara had climbed down and was hanging off one side of the ladder, oblivious to the two-hundred-meter sheer drop below them. "And so did I..." she added, unhelpfully, before extending a hand. "Come on, I'll help you."

Elara took hold of Finn's arm, and guided him the rest of the way, just as she had guided him every step of the way since he'd first set foot inside the crucible as an offender on trial. She had been his rock, and she was still looking out for him, even if sometimes her help came with a dollop of snark or sarcasm.

The hatchway hissed and Adam threw it open. Above it was an airlock and a short distance beyond that was another hatch, though the metal was weathered and beaten-looking. Adam spun the lock wheel, bleeding more stale-tasting air into the passageway, before climbing inside the Crawler. Adam and Eve worked fast to power up the Crawler's environmental controls, which had been set to minimal power mode while the vehicle was unmanned.

By the time Finn arrived and the hatch was closed and locked behind him, his hands and fingers were numb, and his body was trembling from cold as well as fear. The cabin of the Crawler was frostier than an evening shift in Yard seven, and Finn realized how quickly his tolerance for icy temperatures had waned after all the time he had spent inside the luxurious, heated accommodations in the gen bank and Authority sector. The only time he could remember feeling colder was after Chiefy had hauled them out of the Davis Strait and onto the ingress platform, shortly before he and Elara had infiltrated the regent's sub-oceanic complex. He'd lived with cold all his life, and it hadn't bothered him before. Now he detested it.

"We'll pilot the Crawler using full manual controls," Eve said, occupying the co-pilot's seat in the cabin. "That way, there's no chance that the computer systems can be overridden."

Finn nodded then examined the small cabin that they all now occupied. The compartment, which was located at the front of the Crawler, like a spider's head, was little larger than the cockpit of a skycar. There were two main control stations, and nowhere behind it that seemed designed to accommodate passengers, forcing Finn, Elara and the two robots to squeeze inside as best they could. The advantage of this was that their combined body heat quickly warmed up the freezer-like space.

Adam grabbed two stick-like control yokes while Eve controlled the Crawler's power levels and forward velocity. The machine lurched ahead, and Finn was unbalanced by the rocking motion of the Crawler as it took giant strides across the surface of Nimbus, like a boat navigating rough seas. Through the cockpit glass, Finn could see the communes, still glowing under the light of the sun. The he saw the moon, brilliant and white, and so large he felt like he could reach out and touch it. Then there was the Earth itself. From their unique vantage, strolling across Nimbus on the back of a titanic mechanical spider, Finn could finally see Earth in its entirely. He'd read about the different continents on his data device, during cold, lonely evenings in his squalid room in Metalhaven, but to see them from space was awe-inspiring and terrifying in equal measure.

Elara moved to Finn's side and hooked her arm though his, and together they looked down on the planet that had once been home to billions. He could see the desolate part of Northern Canada where the very first regents had established Zavetgrad, across the Davis Strait from Greenland, which was home to Haven, deep beneath its frozen plains. Elara pulled him closer, and he could feel the warmth of her breath on his neck, and her closeness helped him to feel more at ease. He felt like he should say something, as if the profoundness of the moment necessitated something profound in response, but instead they simply watched in silence, until the central sphere containing Gideon Alexander Reznikov's palace consumed the view ahead of them, and Earth was gone.

"I'll try to latch on as close to the palace as possible," Adam said, still working the levers to maneuver the Crawler. "Reznikov's throne room is in the topmost part of the central sphere, so that he has an uninhibited view of the planet."

"Then what's the rest of it used for?" Elara asked.

Adam and Eve thought for a moment, each looking to the other for inspiration, then both shrugged.

"To be honest, we don't know," Eve admitted. "I've always assumed he used it to house more of the historical artifacts that he recovered from the planet. Perhaps his favorite exhibits."

"I don't think that's what he has stored there," Finn said, as the crawler stretched its giant legs across the gap between outer Nimbus and the central core. "I reckon it's where he's storing the nuclear missiles."

Elara frowned then leaned over the top of Eve to get a clearer view at the surface of the central sphere. It was dotted with circular marks, like craters in the moon, but instead of being chaotic and irregular, the circles that littered the sphere were all the same size, and arranged in an organized pattern.

"Missile launch silos?" Elara said, and Finn nodded. Elara laughed, wearily. "That's why Reznikov didn't want you entering his palace. It has nothing to do with preserving the sanctity of his domain, or any bullshit like that. He just didn't want you to know he had a nuclear arsenal capable of leveling an entire continent stored there."

Adam worked the controls for a few moments longer then released the yokes and pulled a series of smaller levers.

The Crawler stopped moving then sank lower, its legs gripping the surface like pincers.

"I'm locked on," Adam said, turning to Eve. "Now let's see if we can build you a door."

The Prefect Omega set to work, closely observed by Scraps, who jumped onto the officer's shoulder, and was quietly twirling her hair, though Eve didn't appear to mind. A series of thumps and thuds shook the cockpit then sparks began shooting into space, flashing past the glass like streaks of fire. On the monitors, Finn could watch the Crawler's array of plasma cutters slicing into the space station's hull, but at the same time as destroying, the machine was also creating. Other tools were busy fabricating a box, and as the object took form, Finn recognized it as an airlock.

The Crawler continued to work for several minutes, while it weaved the airlock into place, like a spider spinning a silk web. Then the tools fell silent, and the sparks stopped flying. Adam returned to the control yokes, and with a deftness of touch that an artist such as Michelangelo or Da Vinci would have been proud of, the prefect maneuvered the Crawler's hatch above the new airlock and docked the machine with a weighty thump.

"There, it's done." Adam said, again releasing the controls.

The two prefects stood up and turned to them, and Finn realized that the time to say goodbye had arrived without him even realizing it. A sudden and overwhelming sadness gripped him, the like of which he'd experienced only a few times before, such as when Owen had died, or after he'd been forced to abandon Elara, injured and bleeding in the test crucible. It seemed ludicrous to feel such sorrow, when he barely knew the man and woman stood before him, but there could be no denying the intimate connection they shared. They were both a part of him and a part of Elara, as if they were their own flesh-and-blood children. And now, Finn realized, he was about to walk away, and never see them again.

"I wish we had more time," Finn said.

"If you succeed, then time is what you'll buy us," Adam replied. "Time for the planet to heal, and maybe time for us to work out a way to return."

"I hope so," Finn said. He took Adam's hand then clasped his other on top of it. "It's just a shame we won't be around to see it."

Adam shrugged and smiled. "Who knows what will happen. A few hours ago, I didn't even know you existed." He bowed his head a little. "I'm glad I got to meet you, and to see what I came from."

"We shouldn't linger here too long," Eve said. She was a pragmatist, like her genetic mother. "Reznikov will have seen the Crawler and no doubt have sent foremen to this location."

Eve turned to Elara, and it was like there was a force holding them apart, like two strong opposing magnetic poles.

"I wish I could come with you," Eve said, her hand going to the grip of her sonic rifle. "I wish we could fight Reznikov together."

"So do I," Elara said. She took a step closer, overpowering the force between them with her unconquerable strength of will. "You're a good soldier." She paused and Finn could see that the words were a struggle. "You're a good person, Eve. Better than I am. I'm glad I got to meet you, if only for a short time."

Eve sprang forward, and suddenly she had pulled Elara into a tight embrace. The two women remained interlocked for a several seconds, before the necessity of their mission compelled them to separate.

"Good luck," Eve said, now looking at Finn, since holding Elara's gaze was proving too difficult. "And don't forget about us."

"Never," Finn said, taking Eve by the shoulders and smiling at her.

Scraps suddenly leapt from the control station and wrapped his arms around Eve's neck. The little robot was sobbing electronically, but he didn't want Eve to see the sadness in his eyes. Jumping from Eve to Adam, he hugged the man, burying his head into his neck, before sprouting his rotors and leaping into the airlock without saying a word.

Following Scraps' lead, Finn stepped onto the ladder and climbed down, keen to not drag out the inevitable and made it harder than it already was. Elara went next and Chiefy followed last, waving and saluting to the two prefects, before closing and sealing the hatch behind him.

The long, cold climb helped to clear Finn's head, and soon he was at the base of the ladder, and in front of the hatchway that the Crawler had fabricated. He spun the locking wheel and pulled open the door, flooding the icy passageway with hot air that was heady with the scent of incense. Readying his sonic rifle, he moved through and found himself in a space that felt instantly familiar. If he hadn't known better, he would have sworn he'd climbed all the way back down to Earth, and beneath the ocean into Elysium.

Elara was quickly at his side, weapon in hand, and they

stood guard while Chiefy closed and sealed the airlock hatch. As before, the seven-foot robot was acting as escort and guardian to Scraps.

"It's nice to know that's how they'd turn out," Finn said, as the tell-tale thump of the Crawler's feet reverberated through the floor and walls. The two prefects were already heading away.

"Who?" Elara asked.

Finn scowled at her. "Our children, of course," he said, knowing full-well that Elara had understood his meaning.

"Who says I even want children?" Elara said, though she was fighting to contain a smile. "Besides, we already have dozens of them."

"That's true, we do." Finn nodded and sighed. "And I hope that one day we get see them again."

19

THE CORONATION

WALKING through the president's palace felt like the first time Finn had set foot inside the Regent's Cathedral in the sub-oceanic complex. The place was simply too quiet. There were no foremen robots or evaluators, or machines of any kind, only sweeping, curved corridors that undulated elegantly like the inside of a conch shell. Yet despite their advance going unchallenged, Finn took each step forward with caution, steeling himself for an ambush that he expected to arrive at any moment.

"This place gives me the creeps," Elara said, also stalking forward, alert and on edge. "I can barely tell up from down. Why the hell did Reznikov build this place to look like the inside of an egg?"

"I think it's supposed to be heavenly or ethereal, or some shit like that," Finn said, trying to find the joins where the lustrous silver floor met the lustrous silver walls and sky, but everything appeared to be seamless. "I think the president is taking this 'great father' idea to extremes, like he believes he's a deity, not a man."

"I'll be happy to prove just how mortal Reznikov is," Elara said, with feeling. "So long as we can find him, that is."

"I can show you the way," Chiefy said, picking up speed and moving ahead of Elara. "There is a major structure a hundred meters ahead, behind that partitioning wall."

Finn focused his eyes forward and squinted them, but he couldn't see a wall, only more silvery nothingness.

"Are you sure?" Finn said, following closely behind Chiefy, which seemed like the safest place to be. "It feels like I'm inside a cloud. I can't even tell which way we came from anymore."

"That is the idea," Chiefy answered. Scraps was sitting on the machine's shoulder, scanner dish deployed. "The space surrounding the president's palace has been designed to confound the human mind. Only robots can successfully traverse it."

"Like a moat around a keep," Finn said, remembering pictures of ancient castles from his data device.

"Your analogy is crude but not incorrect," Chiefy said. The robot hadn't intended to be unkind, but Finn still felt a little offended. "Except this is a moat for the senses, and if you are not careful, you will drown."

Chiefy held out his hands and Finn and Elara each took hold of one, allowing the robot to guide them through the amorphous space that seemed to become more incomprehensible the longer they spent inside it. Soon, Finn could barely stand to keep his eyes open, such was the crushing sense of nothingness that enveloped him, but the darkness didn't help to abate his dizziness.

"I feel drunk, or ill, or both," Elara said, staggering forward. "I think I want to go back."

"There is a powerful infrasonic field permeating this room," Chiefy said. "In humans, it is known to produce the sort of effects you are experiencing."

"Can't you shut it off?" Finn said. He was no longer just dizzy, but afraid, and it wasn't just a casual unease, but a primal fear, like Elara's fear of spiders, or his fear of heights.

"The field dissipates once we are beyond the partition," Chiefy said. "We must keep going. If you remain too long in this space, the consequences will be serious."

"They already feel pretty fucking serious," Finn said, barely able to put one foot in front of the other. He wanted to turn and run back to the airlock, and he tried to release the robot's hand, but Chiefy kept a firm grip on them both.

"Do not struggle," Chiefy said, picking up speed and practically dragging Finn and Elara forward. "We are almost there."

"Let me go!" Elara growled, fighting the machine, but still Chiefy pushed on. "Damn it, Chiefy, I have to get out of here!"

"Not long now..." Chiefy said, maintaining a smooth, reassuring tone.

Finn hammered at the robot with his fist, yelling at the machine to let go, and Elara struggled to free her axe, perhaps with the intention of hacking herself free, but her hands were shaking, and her eyes were bloodshot and wild. Finally, she managed to free the double-headed axe and she swung it, but there was no power in the strike, and the weapon merely glanced off Chiefy's arm with a dull clunk.

"I would prefer it if you didn't try to remove my arm," Chiefy said, as Elara swung again, and missed, almost hitting herself in the process.

"Let me go!" Elara roared.

Then, suddenly, Chiefy released them, and Finn and Elara collapsed to the floor. Finn kept his eyes shut and he curled his body into a fetal position, still tormented by a dread sense of anxiety. Then he felt a needle prick to his neck and he shot upright to see Scraps on the floor beside him.

"That hurt!" Finn complained, rubbing his neck. Then he looked around the room and the enveloping emptiness was gone, replaced by regular walls and floor tiles. The only strange thing about the space was the ceiling, which mimicked the sky, complete with clouds and even birds. "Are we through? Did we make it?"

"Yes," Chiefy replied, calmly. "You should start to feel better soon. The drugs that Scraps administered will help."

"Thanks, Scraps," Elara said. She picked herself off the floor and grabbed her axe, which she'd dropped when Chiefy had thrown her to ground. "And sorry for trying to hack your hand off," she added, looking at the foreman robot with apologetic eyes. "I don't know what came over me."

"Powerful infrasonic fields have an interesting effect on the human mind, so you were not fully in command of your senses," Chiefy replied, still smiling. "Even so, apology accepted."

"Is that real?" Finn said. He was looking at a grand cathedral, which stretched maybe forty or fifty meters into the fake sky. "I still don't trust my eyes."

"That is real," Chiefy confirmed. "It is what remains of the Cathedral of Vasily the Blessed, also known as Saint Basil's Cathedral, a unique Byzantine Christian church that originally resided in Red Square, Moscow. There was another piece of it in the Russian museum hall."

"The gold dome?" Elara asked, and Chiefy nodded. "Why leave that piece in the museum hall, if the rest of it is here?"

"The part of the church where the dome originally resided is missing," Chiefy explained, pointing to the spot where the missing piece should have fitted. "Like all the major powers, The Russian Federation was destroyed during the last war."

"Why bring this here?" Elara asked. "It must have taken dozens of rockets to haul it up to the station, brick by brick."

"The Reznikov who founded Zavetgrad was a Russian citizen," Chiefy said. "Perhaps, this was his way of maintaining a link to his ancestral past."

"I think we should ask him, personally," Finn said. His mind was clear again, and he was keener than ever to find the president of Zavetgrad. "Scraps, can your scanners locate the throne room?"

Scraps nodded. "Yes-yes! Just ahead. Not far now!"

Finn checked his sonic rifle and reduced the power level to a setting that would stun a human being, rather than kill. They needed Reznikov alive, at least until the nuclear strike had been aborted. After that, he honestly didn't know what came next, though he expected Elara had a pretty good idea what to do. She had chosen not to reduce the power setting of her rifle.

Chiefy led them inside the rebuilt remains of St Basil's Cathedral, but it quickly became apparent that only the exterior of the church had been reconstructed. Instead of brick and stone, the interior of the building was assembled from the same lustrous, silvery metal that the prefect's armor had been made from. And, unlike the original cathedral's claustrophobic, labyrinthine corridors, its replacement was spacious and airy, as if it were bigger on the inside than the outside.

Chiefy guided them to a long flight of shallow steps that climbed to a grand, arched double door, which also looked to have been reclaimed from Earth. Standing at the foot of the steps, Finn was still surprised, and concerned, that there had been no resistance to their approach. He hadn't even spotted a single spidery repair bot scuttling around, fixing up the opulent hall, or just polishing the floor tiles. The place seemed dead, like the city that the cathedral had been salvaged from.

"The throne room is behind that door," Chiefy said.

Finn detected hesitancy from the robot, who remained rooted in place at the foot of the steps, rather than guiding them to the top.

"What's wrong?" Finn asked. "Is there someone waiting behind those doors? Or something?"

Chiefy nodded, and Finn could see that Scraps was also anxious. The little robot had climbed onto Chiefy's back and was peeking from behind the machine's anvil-sized head. Suddenly, the doors creaked open, and a blinding silvery light flooded through the gap, as if the room beyond was home to a captive star. Finn shielded his eyes, then after a few seconds the glow faded, and he could see two figures standing at the top of the steps.

It took Finn a moment to adjust, but even then, he couldn't believe what he was seeing. Ivan Volkov and Juniper Jones stood in front of the doors, which were now fully opened, revealing the grand throne room behind them. The acting mayor and commissar had changed clothes, and Ivan was now wearing full Regent's robes, complete with an exquisite, patterned cloak that reflected all the colors of

Zavetgrad from red to gold, with the addition of an ethereal silver trim, which appeared to be the color that represented the tenth sector, Nimbus.

Juniper had shed her carapace armor and was wearing a dress that was even more elaborate than Ivan's robes. The outer layer was worn like a cloak. It had long sleeves and a train that flowed out two meters behind her. Gold embroidery ran along the tail and sides of the dress, while beneath it was a velvet bodice and floor-length, pearlescent silver-satin skirt.

"What the fuck is this?" Finn said, though not loud enough for Ivan or Juniper to overhear. "A coronation?"

"I think it's more than that," Elara answered. "I think it's a wedding..."

"This is as far as you go, Heroes of Metalhaven," Ivan called out, and his voice was amplified through the room, as if the walls were speaker cones. "Once again, you have violated a sacred space and left only death and destruction in your wake."

"Death and destruction are why we're here, Ivan," Finn called back, his unamplified voice sounding puny in comparison. "Once we've stopped the nuclear strike, we'll be more than happy to see the back of this place."

Ivan laughed and the booming sound of his voice reverberated Finn's chest.

"Don't pretend like you're not here to destroy Nimbus," Ivan said. "I know you too well, Finn. I know that you'd never risk leaving this citadel intact, even if you got what you wanted, and the missiles were aborted."

"Then what happens now, Ivan?" Finn said. "We're not here for your wedding, or whatever the hell this is."

"This is the first step toward a new begging..." Ivan was now sounding much more like his deceased father. Confident. Arrogant. Selfish. "Gideon has blessed us all by making me his adopted son, while Juniper will become the mother to a new generation of rulers."

Ivan pressed a hand to Juniper's belly, and the commissar swelled with pride. In contrast, Finn's hairs stood on end and his skin shivered with cold.

"She's pregnant?" Finn said. "With Reznikov's child?"

"Not yet, but soon," Ivan said, proudly. "Juniper will carry the first of a new generation of regents, and I will be the prince's guardian and tutor."

Elara took a step forward, but Ivan didn't flinch, even when the barrel of her sonic rifle was aimed toward him.

"Do you think Reznikov is a fool?" Ivan said, scornfully. "That will not work in here."

Elara pulled the trigger, but the sonic rifle didn't fire. She checked the power cell and tried again but still nothing, and even a fresh cell made no difference. Ivan smiled and laughed while Elara struggled and became more and more frustrated. Eventually, she threw the weapon down, and drew her knife.

"I don't need a rifle to kill you," Elara said. "I'll just cut out your black heart instead."

She stormed forward but as soon as her boot hit the bottom step, she was blown back, as if she'd walked into an invisible electrified fence. At the same time, Finn felt a wave of dizziness and nausea hit him, like he was back in the space beyond the partition wall, at the mercy of the infrasonic field.

"There are sonic emitters above the door," Chiefy whispered, as Elara picked herself off the floor, to the sound of Ivan's continued laughter. "Scraps will attempt to disable them."

Finn looked for the robot, but Scraps had already vanished from the foreman's shoulder. He peered around the room, searching for his pal, but he couldn't see any sign of him. Ivan and Juniper had remained focused on Elara, who was still struggling to regain her balance after being hit by the powerful sonic blast. While the new royal couple had been focused on mocking Elara's discomfort and embarrassment, they had also not seen Scraps slip away. What they needed was time, and Finn knew the best way to delay Volkov was to simply give the man opportunity to bluster.

Elara finally regained her footing and was about to charge again, teeth gritted, but Finn held her back, gently shaking his head.

"Your new prince will have no subjects," Finn said, while looking into Elara's eyes, imploring her to wait. "Your bright new future has already ended."

Ivan laughed again, and Elara almost snapped, but she had understood Finn's silent request for her to stand down, and grudgingly held her ground.

"I suppose you're referring to the ten communes you jettisoned earlier," Ivan said, in a bored, offhand manner. "It is no matter; we will recover them soon enough." The man shrugged. "Besides, we have enough seed and embryos stored on this station to grow new communes, and with our growth acceleration technology, mastered from decades of genetic experimentation conducted inside Zavetgrad's many gene banks, we will be repopulated within a generation. All you've done is set us back. Everything we need to survive and thrive is already here."

"Then we'll just destroy the station, and everything in it," Elara snarled, shaking herself free from Finn's hold. "We'll burn it all, and end your perverted dynasty before it begins."

"There she is!" Ivan said, laughing and pointing to Elara. "There is the Iron Bitch of Metalhaven! The true Elara Cage."

"You've never seen the real me," Elara hissed. "But you will. Soon."

Ivan dismissed Elara with a waft of his hand.

"I'm still baffled as to why you're fighting to save Zavetgrad," the new regent said. "Like I told you already, in fifty years, everyone on the planet will be sterile, and the planet will die."

"The workers of Zavetgrad are stronger than you think," Finn said, taking his chance to engage Ivan and keep the man talking in the hope that Scraps, wherever the robot had gone, was busy circumventing the sonic security device. "You and your aristocratic relatives always underestimated us. And there's still Haven. If that place taught me anything, it's that there's hope for Earth to recover. I won't abandon it, even if you have."

"I admire you for how far you've come, Finn, I really do" Ivan said, in a thickly condescending tone. "A lowly worker, revered by his kind, and risen to Nimbus. It is quite a story, and also why your DNA was chosen for the new generation of prefects, though we should have anticipated your rebellious nature, and edited out those unfortunate traits." Ivan shrugged again. "We will know better for next time."

"There won't be a next time," Finn said. "This ends, today."

"You can't stop us, Finn," Ivan said, almost pleading with

him to see sense. "I wish you would stop this foolishness and just accept your fate."

Ivan and Juniper stepped apart and another figure emerged from inside the throne room. At first, Finn thought it was Reznikov himself, but then he recognized the man's stern face.

"Voss?" Finn said, as the Chief Prosecutor and Judge General of Zavetgrad reached the top of the steps and began to slowly descend them. He hadn't seen the leader of the prosecutors since the test trial, and had started to believe he was dead.

"What are you doing here?" Elara said, drawing her axe from its stow, and wielding it alongside her knife.

"Did you think I'd abandoned my duties?" Voss said. The man was wearing his old prosecutor armor, and looked like a medieval knight, complete with a modified broadsword housing an electrified blade. "I am Apex, the lead prosecutor," Voss continued, proudly. "You two are my mistakes, and I'm here to correct them."

Elara let out a cry then charged at Apex, managing to make it part way toward him before a sonic blast knocked her flat and sent her tumbling to the foot of the steps. Chiefy ran to Elara's aid, but in doing so he strayed too close to the throne room, and was also hit by a powerful blast that overloaded the robot's FLP and sent the machine crashing to the ground, smoke and sparks rising from his head. Finn threw down his nonfunctional sonic rifle and drew his spear, but unlike Elara, he was patient. He waited for Voss to come to him.

"I always said it was a mistake to promote the victors of trials to the ranks of the prosecutors," Voss said, flourishing his sword. "You might be strong, but in your hearts, you will always be worker scum."

Voss charged at Finn and swung his sword, which crackled as it split the air and connected with Finn's spear, dumping thousands of volts in his body, and crippling him with pain. Finn fell to his back and Voss moved in for the kill, but Elara was on her feet, and she charged at him, axe held high. To Finn's astonishment, Voss didn't move or try to parry, and just as Elara was about to strike, a sonic blast hit her again, and knocked her clear.

"This is not your crucible, Shadow," Voss said, as Elara writhed in pain a few meters away. "Here, I am the hunter, and you are the prey."

Finn recovered and lunged with the spear, but Voss parried, and another crippling jolt of electricity ran through his body, dropping him to his knees. Elara dragged herself to her feet and threw her knife, but Voss deflected the blade with his vambrace, displaying the skill and reflexes that had earned him the position of Chiefy Prosecutor.

Undeterred, Elara pressed her attack, swinging her axe like she was trying to fell a great oak, but Voss dodged and weaved and parried with his armored forearms, to the soundtrack of Ivan Volkov and Juniper Jones laughing and cheering. Finally, she struck a blow to Voss' chest, but the blade didn't penetrate the man's silvery armor, and Apex swatted Elara away like an irritating fly.

Finn roared with rage and threw his spear like a javelin, but incredibly Voss deflected it in mid-flight, and the weapon crashed harmlessly into the stone steps. He pushed away from the ground and charged, intending to tackle Voss and rip out the man's throat with his teeth if he had to, but a sonic blast smacked him in the chest, and he was down again. Finn's vision blurred and pain pulsed through every inch of his body. He tried to stand, but he only reached his knees before Voss was standing over him again, sword raised like an executioner's blade.

"I'll grant you the mercy of a quick death," the Chief Prosecutor said. "It is more than you deserve, but I remain an honorable man."

"You're not an honorable man," Finn said, spitting blood at Voss' feet. "The Prosecutors of Zavetgrad were nothing but murderers, and you're the worst of them all."

"Say your prayers, Redeemer," Voss said, his muscles tensed. "And prepare to meet your maker."

Voss swung the sword, but before the blade could sever Finn's head from his body, Elara launched herself at the man like a missile and tackled him. Unbalanced, the flat of the blade hit Finn instead of the edge, which saved his neck, but didn't spare him from the crippling jolt of electricity. Voss hit the ground hard, rolled through the impact, and was back on his feet in seconds, but Elara had recovered even more quickly, and she faced the man without fear, axe in hand.

"You fool!" Voss roared. "You can't stop me!"

Elara was wild like one of the mutated beasts Finn had fought beyond Zavetgrad's wall, and she had abandoned all reason. Whether she could hurt Voss no longer mattered. She was only rage and violence, contained within the shell of a woman who would stop at nothing to kill her enemy.

Voss lowered his sword and beckoned Elara to attack, a smile on the man's face. Ivan and Juniper continued to laugh and cheer. Finn wanted to call out to Elara to stop, but he couldn't move, and couldn't speak. Instead, all he could do was watch as Elara ran at Dante Voss and swung her axe, but instead of being struck back by a crippling blast of sonic energy, her blade landed true. A look of confusion swept across Voss' face, then was fixed in place, as the axe sliced cleanly through his neck, and the Chief Prosecutor's head thudded into the ground at Elara's feet.

Finn forced himself to stand then finally saw Scraps, covered in a mass of wires and circuits that he'd yanked out of a panel in the wall, while no-one was paying the robot any attention. Then Finn's eyes moved to the top of the stairs, but Ivan and Juniper were already gone.

20

GIDEON ALEXANDER REZNIKOV

Finn wrapped his fingers around the handle of Dante Voss' electrified broadsword and deactivated the current coursing through its blade. He gave it a few test swings and found that the weapon was nicely balanced and felt good in his hand.

"No point in letting this go to waste," Finn said, placing the weapon into his magnetic back scabbard. He then looked at Voss' headless body and winced. "I think this technically makes you 'Apex' now, don't you think?"

"That title died with him," Elara said. His partner was looking toward the open palace doors, Voss' blood still dripping from the blade of her axe. Finn saw that she'd also recovered her knife, which was safely back in its scabbard. "We're the last two Prosecutors of Zavetgrad. After us, there won't be any more."

Finn nodded, then stepped over the headless corpse so that he no longer had to look at it.

"Should we go after Ivan and Juniper?" Finn asked. Partly, he wanted to settle his personal score with his former classmate, but he was also keenly aware that Elara and Juniper had unfinished business.

"No, they don't matter now," Elara said, still focused on the entrance, as if she was expecting an army of foremen to charge through the doors at any moment. "All that matters is Reznikov, and stopping the launch."

Suddenly, Chiefy sat bolt upright, and his eyes flickered chaotically, as his FLP sparked into life and the robot's core operating system rebooted. Scraps was anchored to the robot's shoulder, data probes plugged into Chiefy's electronic brain through ports in the side of his head.

"Did we win?" Chiefy said. Smoke was still wisping from the robot's singed circuits.

"Not yet," Finn replied.

Voss had been an unexpected challenge, but Finn suspected that greater ones still lay ahead of them. He offered the robot his hand and helped Chiefy to stand, though the Gen VII foreman remained a little unsteady on his feet.

"How are you feeling?" Elara asked. "You took a hell of wallop from that sonic cannon."

Chiefy considered the question at the same time as running a self-diagnostic, during which time his eyes flashed vividly, like the blinking LEDs in the computer room they'd hijacked.

"Several of my sub-processors have been destroyed, and my fine motor functions are impaired, but I am not severely damaged," Chiefy replied.

"Chiefy okay!" the smaller robot added, while patting Chiefy's head. "Scraps fix at home."

Finn laughed and nodded. Not matter what was thrown

at him, Scraps could still somehow manage to remain hopeful, but home was still a very long way away.

"You're right, pal," Finn said, choosing not to sully the robot's mood with his more pessimistic opinions. "And thanks again. I've lost count of how many times now you've saved our asses."

Scraps began to count on his fingers, but then ran out of fingers and shrugged, causing both Finn and Elara to laugh. It was a much-needed moment of levity, but it didn't last long. A looming threat of nuclear annihilation had a tendency to suck the joy out of any situation.

"Let's hope the president has time in his busy schedule to receive us," Finn said, turning back to the entrance into the throne room.

The group climbed the long, shallow flight of steps, and Finn was relived to find that the sonic cannons remained quiet. Before long, they had entered the president's personal chambers. The change in setting was stark. Instead of ambiguous, curved silver walls, the throne room was breathtakingly ornate.

Finn drew the sword he'd taken from Voss and cautiously stepped into the chamber, with Elara by his side, bloodied axe held ready. The floor looked like marble with gold inlay that sprawled across its polished surface like glowing vines. Huge stone columns reached up to a vaulted ceiling that was so tall, Finn could barely make out the detailed frescoes that had been painted there, all of which appeared to depict Reznikov in a variety of regal poses.

They moved deeper into the chamber and walked past deep aisles on both sides that were accessed through a series of stone arches. Each of the side-rooms had been set out as a different living space. There was a library, an elaborate bedroom, sitting room, study, dining room and more. There was also a single android-like servant in each room, similar to the humanoid mannequins in Elysium that had frolicked for the amusement and titillation of the regents.

The mannequins, all women, wore elaborate gowns with wide skirts, fitted bodices and ornate embroidery. The necklines were low, and the dresses were figure-hugging, rather than voluminous. Curiously, all of the dresses were made from a silken yellow fabric, a bright primary color quite distinct from Authority gold that Finn had never seen used anywhere in Zavetgrad, or even inside the sub-oceanic complex. None of the android women attempted to stop them as they passed.

At the far end of the room was a flight of steep steps that led up to the throne itself, set five meters above floor level. The throne was silhouetted against a towering altar that reached up to the center of a circular window, ten meters in diameter, through which a silvery light flooded the chamber. As Finn approached, he realized that there was a man sitting on the throne, also shrouded in darkness, but given away by the glint of a crown and bejeweled armor.

Tightening his grip on his new sword, Finn reached the foot of the steps and was able to see the man more clearly, and recognize the face of Gideon Alexander Reznikov. It was obvious that the president had seen them too, but Reznikov didn't stir, and instead simply watched them right back, his eyes impassive and his mouth adopting a half-smile, like in the Mona Lisa painting in the France museum hall.

The president's clothes were just as ornate as the throne in which the man sat, lazily slumped to one side, as if he'd been anticipating Finn's arrival for some time, and had grown bored waiting for him. Pearlescent silver-white robes flowed over the arms of the throne and the man's golden-colored silk pants, while a diamond-studded gold cuirass covered his chest. Reznikov's skullcap crown was decorated with jewels and delicate filigree, with a fur border. Yet despite the splendor of the man's appearance, it was Reznikov's baby-smooth face that captured Finn's attention the most. The president looked younger than even his youthful prefects did.

"Congratulations," Reznikov said, and his voice thundered throughout the room as if a thousand mouths had spoken the word. "I never imagined that anyone would breach my palace walls, and in almost three centuries, no-one has."

Reznikov stood up, and brushed his robes behind him with a theatrical flourish, before taking a step toward them. Finn and Elara both brandished their weapons, and Reznikov stopped, one step down from the top.

"You have nothing to fear from me," Reznikov said, his smooth voice still bombarding them from all directions. "I merely wish to pay tribute to you both. You are a testament to the enduring will of humanity. You are the reason I built Nimbus, to preserve that essence for all time."

"You can have Nimbus without destroying Zavetgrad," Finn said. "There's no reason for you to murder a million people in cold blood."

Reznikov frowned and took another step toward them. Finn flicked the switch on the hilt of his sword and a crackle of power raced across the blade, compelling the president to halt his advance.

"You misunderstand," Reznikov said, holding up his

hands to them in a conciliatory manner. "Zavetgrad cannot be saved. In time, it will succumb to the creeping death that infected the planet at the culmination of the last war. What I offer is mercy, not murder."

"That's not your choice to make," Elara cut in. "You don't have that right."

"I alone have that right, since humanity would not exist if it was not for me," Reznikov replied, with a firmness that was amplified a hundredfold by his throne room. "But survival is not enough. Humanity is weak and corrupt. The corruption that led the leaders of Earth to all but annihilate one another is ingrained into your faulty DNA. It must be wiped out, and that is why Nimbus is so important." Reznikov took another step toward them then halted of his own accord before he was threatened again. "Only the best of humanity exists here. Here, I will wean human beings off their desires to cheat and lie, swindle and murder. Here, I will breed a new kind of humanity, one that is pure and good."

"That sounds to me like playing god," Finn said.

"Call it what you will," Reznikov replied, his words shaking Finn's chest. "The truth is that Zavetgrad cannot be saved." The president then shrugged, causing his flowing robes to ripple like waves in water. "But you've been told this already, many times, and still you have come to me, so there is no point in discussing it further."

"You're right," Elara said. She spun her axe then drew it back, ready to hack the president's head from his shoulders, as she had done to Voss moments earlier. "The time for talking is over."

"I have called off the missile strike." Reznikov's words

stunned Elara and she froze, axe still held high. "See for yourself."

The president snapped his fingers and a computer console rose from the floor beside his throne. The display flickered on and showed a row of twenty-four missiles, tucked snugly into their launch silos, not far from the chamber in which they all stood. There was also a single analog clock on the display, and its needle was stuck at the ninety seconds mark.

"If you prefer for Zavetgrad to suffer a slow, painful death, its inhabitants crippled by mutations and radiation sickness, then so be it," Reznikov said. "My missiles – my mercy – will not be delivered. You have your victory."

"You're lying," Finn said.

"Have your robot check for himself," Reznikov answered, turning his keen brown eyes toward Scraps. "A fine machine. One I would very much like to study."

Scraps blew a loud raspberry at Reznikov then gave the president the middle finger, before sprouting his rotors and flying toward the computer console. Chiefy remained close to his robot companion, but also kept his distance from Reznikov as he climbed the steep steps. Like Finn, the foreman could sense that there was something dangerous about the president, like a deadly trap that was on a hair trigger.

"Bad man right," Scraps said, after he'd spent a few moments interrogating the computer. "Missile launch aborted."

Reznikov smiled then clapped his hands together, and the sound was like a grenade exploding next to Finn's hand.

"Good!" the president bellowed, and the floor shook like

an earthquake. "Now that's over with, please allow me to show you my vision for humankind."

Reznikov climbed the rest of the way down the stairs, keeping well clear of Finn and Elara, who watched his every step, weapons ready. A previously hidden door slid open to the side of the throne and the president extended a hand toward it.

"Please, it is the least I can do to reward your tenacity and bravery," Reznikov said. "Not even the mayors of Zavetgrad – all vile creatures in their own way, as I'm sure you agree – have seen what I am about to show you." Reznikov adopted a beseeching look, like a needy puppy. "Please come with me. Then, perhaps, you will realize that I do have the best interests of humanity at heart."

Reznikov strolled into the room, leaving Finn and Elara too shocked to even move. Eventually, curiosity got the better of them both, and they stalked toward the secret door. Finn expected to be ambushed at any moment, but all he found was the president waiting for them, alone and still smiling.

"What the fuck just happened?" Finn said, as Elara crept to his side.

"I don't know, but I still don't believe him," Elara answered.

"Launch stopped," Scraps said, landing on Chiefy's shoulder with a gentle thump. The two robots had filed in at their rear. "No understand. But true!"

Finn stepped forward, intending to enter the secret room, but Elara caught his arm and stopped him.

"What are you doing?"

"Well, we can't just stay here," Finn said, still keeping half an eye on Reznikov. "I want to see what's in that room, and hear what he has to say."

"Whatever he says will be a lie," Elara replied. "We should just kill him now, and be done with it."

"Maybe it will come to that," Finn admitted. "But we need to get close, and be smart. Something tells me that Reznikov is not nearly as defenseless as he appears."

"Please, come," Reznikov called out, his words still echoing throughout Nimbus. "You will want to see this, I promise." The president now stood beside a rectangular block that looked like a sarcophagus, except that it was built from a dull, steel-colored metal, rather than stone. Finn entered the room, and Elara stuck by his side, despite her doubts. The room was cramped, and she'd swapped her axe for the black-bladed combat knife that General Riley had given her. Of all the many weapons that The Shadow could wield with consummate skill, Finn knew that she was quickest and deadliest with a blade.

Reznikov backed away to allow Finn and Elara to climb onto the metal block without them coming too close to one another. Unlike its sides, the top of the sarcophagus was a single sheet of pure crystal glass, or some other perfectly transparent material. Inside the sarcophagus was a body and Finn recoiled from it.

"Who is this?" Finn asked.

Reznikov's smile broadened. "That is me. The original Gideon Alexander Reznikov, and founder of Zavetgrad."

"What?"

The word leaked from Finn's mouth like an obscenity, and all he could do was stare at the dead body, perfectly preserved on a feather bed, hands resting serenely on his stomach. The man was perhaps in his mid-sixties, and despite the efforts of the preservers, radiation burns to his face and neck were evident.

"I don't understand," Finn said. He looked from the corpse to Reznikov, and the likeness was undeniable.

"He's a clone," Elara said, unimpressed by the spectacle that Reznikov was showing them. "There has only ever been one Reznikov, all this time."

"Very good, my dear," the president replied, in a patronizing tone that was typical of the regents and senior golds that Finn knew so well. "But I am not a clone, at least not anymore."

Finn risked getting closer to Reznikov, close enough that he could almost reach out and touch the president, yet still the man showed no fear of him, and continued to smile. Up close, Reznikov was beautiful. He was six-feet-two-inches tall, toned, athletic, and presented an aura of imperiousness that only the ultra-privileged could carry off. Yet, there was something not quite right about him too. Finn looked closer then finally saw the cracks in the man's skin, where the different synthetic flesh-like panels butted up against one another. It was almost seamless, but not quite.

"You're not real," Finn said, drawing back from the man. "You're a robot. A facsimile."

"I am Reznikov in every way that matters," the president said, stepping down from the sarcophagus and continuing deeper inside the room. "Please, come with me, and you will understand."

Finn and Elara jumped down from the sarcophagus, and followed Reznikov, who had his back to them, seemingly without a care in the world. Finn wondered if that was the reason why Elara had showed restraint. She may have been a killer, but there had to be an impetus for her to strike, and Reznikov was not giving her one.

"These are me also," Reznikov said, pointing to a line of eight burial urns, each of them identical to the last. "These were the first eight Reznikov clones, each of whom succeeded the last. Of course, I was already old and decayed by the time my cloning technology was ready, so each version did not last long. Then genetic drift finally forced me to sustain my form in another manner."

"You mean as an android?" Finn asked.

"Not quite..." Reznikov said smoothly, before taking two steps closer to Finn. He recoiled and Elara thrust her knife at the president, but Reznikov simply leaned forward, as if offering his neck for slaughter. "See for yourself," the man added, calmly ignoring the weapon that was poised to kill.

Finn reached out and touched Reznikov's face. Elara tensed up, ready to cut should the president try anything, but the man did nothing other than continue to smile.

"It's warm," Finn said, surprised to discover that the synthetic flesh was not cold to the touch. "And I can feel a pulse..."

"Of course," Reznikov said, drawing back. "I'm as real as you are, Finn Brasa, in every way that matters. And better in ways you cannot understand."

Reznikov turned his back on them again, and Finn could see that Elara was considering ending the president's life at that very moment, but something made her hesitate. It was the same something that was compelling Finn to follow the man. Curiosity. The truth. He wanted answers.

They moved on, past pairs of cylindrical vats that were

set into the walls, opposite one another. Inside each vat was mannequin-like figure, apparently in stasis. The first were crude looking, inhuman gargoyles, but as they walked further into the room, the designs became more human and lifelike, until the android-like forms inside the vat were almost identical to the man standing in front of them. At the end of the row, the final four vats were mysteriously missing.

"Sixty-three years ago, my consciousness was cultivated inside an engineered organic brain," Reznikov said, while admiring one of his other selves. "It took over two-hundred years of experiments in genetics, cloning, and memory transference to achieve that momentous feat, and with each iteration I grew closer and closer to becoming the perfect human being."

Elara laughed. "So, that's what Zavetgrad was really all about." She shook her head at the man. "The gene banks. Stealing our DNA. It was all to preserve you."

"No, not just that," Reznikov hit back, and for the first time, the president's silky-smooth composure showed signs of cracking. "I am a visionary, Miss Cage, perhaps this planet's greatest, and certainly its last. Only I can bring about the creation of a genetically pure communist society, free from the sins and immoralities of our past. It is why I *must* succeed. Surely, you see that now?"

"What I see is a lunatic, playing god," Elara said, unmoved by Reznikov's impassioned speech. "And I've seen enough to know that this mad-science experiment has to end."

Elara swept forward, and in the blink of an eye, her knife was at Reznikov's throat. A trickle of blood ran down the man's neck and stained his exquisite robes.

"If you can bleed then you can die," Elara hissed. "Then, finally, there will be no more Reznikovs."

The president laughed and the sound reverberated throughout the room, shaking dust from the sarcophagus and from the tops of the urns that had been resting in the tomb for generations.

"But my dear, there are already more of me," Reznikov said, pointing to the missing four vats.

Suddenly, the door leading into the tomb chamber slammed shut, and the liquid inside the vats gushed out onto the floor, like the blood from Voss' severed neck, turning it into an ankle-deep pool of slimy fluid.

"No!" The cry came from Scraps. "Countdown started!' Missiles active!"

There was another heavy thud, but this was more than simply a door slamming shut, and Finn suddenly felt like the entire palace was moving.

"What have you done?" Finn cried.

"I have detached the central sphere from Nimbus and set it on a course for Earth, where it will burn up in the planet's atmosphere," Reznikov said, still absurdly happy, despite the knife at his throat. "But before that happens, my missiles will destroy Zavetgrad, and Haven too."

"But you're stuck here with us," Finn said. "You'll die too!"

"This body is obsolete, and my replacement is already active, safe inside Nimbus," Reznikov said. "I will endure. Nimbus will endure. My communes will be returned to the space station, and they will live on with me as their father. Then, finally, the darkest chapter of humanity's history will be closed."

21

THE EFFIGIES

Elara drew the nine-inch blade across Reznikov's throat, cutting deeply. Blood gushed from the open wound and spilling onto the floor, where it mixed with the fluid from the vats to create a murky brown soup. Elara threw the dead body to the ground, but no sooner had it landed with a splat than more of the android-like forms of Gideon Alexander Reznikov came to life. The beings were a horrifying mix of barely-human gargoyles, disfigured effigies, and true-to-life replicas, and all of them turned their vengeful eyes toward Finn and Elara.

"Scraps, get us out of here!" Finn yelled, as one of the Reznikovs came at him, fingers outstretched toward his throat.

Finn struck the monster with his sword, slicing a deep gouge into the creature's side and flooding its terrifying, misshapen body with electricity. The failed Reznikov experiment fell to the ground, writhing in agony and splashing the goop from the vats into Finn's face. It tasted salty and bitter, and it made him retch.

"We have to get that door open!" Elara yelled. She'd sheathed her knife and was hacking at another of the Reznikov beings with her axe. "Chiefy, see if you can force it open!"

Chiefy charged down the long line of vats, all of which were in the process of releasing their synthetically-engineered replicas of Gideon Alexander Reznikov, all failed experiments of one form or another. Finn struck down a second monster and its misshapen eyes barely registered the impact. None of the beings appeared to contain the consciousness of the president, and while they were evidently alive in some sense, they possessed only a beast-like intelligence, driven by survival instincts and rage.

"The door is too heavy," Chiefy called back, as Finn and Elara continued to hack and slash at the monstrosities. "It will need to be unlocked."

"Scraps?" Finn called out. He thrust his sword through the chest of a misshapen Reznikov then looked for the robot. "Scraps, where are you?!"

"Here-here!"

It took Finn a moment to spot his buddy, who was on top of the sarcophagus that contained the preserved body of the original Gideon Alexander Reznikov. There was a computer terminal built into the rectangular structure that Finn hadn't spotted previously.

"Trying hack!" the robot called back. "Need key!"

"We don't have a key, pal," Finn said, fighting his way toward the little robot. Other monsters had seen and heard Scraps too, and were heading his way. "You'll have to find another way, or we're dead!"

Chiefy began to fight his way toward Scraps, but a dozen

of the twisted Reznikovs had surrounded him, and were trying to pull the robot down into the swamp at their feet. Chiefy fought them using his immense robotic strength, but even a Gen VII robot had its limits, and soon the foreman had been wrestled to his knees.

"What about another exit?" Elara shouted, while hacking at some of the monsters that had piled on top of Chiefy. "There must be another way out?"

"Nope-nope!" Scraps called back. "Need key!"

A Reznikov reached for Scraps and the robot leapt into the air, and angled it rotors at the naked man-like effigy, slicing off its fingers with the blades of the spinning propeller. Finn charged through three more beasts then jumped onto the Sarcophagus and began slashing his powered sword into the advancing mass of bodies, but even maimed, dismembered, and electrocuted, they still came at him, like mindless zombies.

"What kind of key, pal?" Finn said. "Maybe it's in here, somewhere?"

"DNA key!" Scraps called back. "Reznikov DNA!"

Finn felt a wellspring of hope rise up inside him.

"Reznikov DNA is something we're not short of," Finn said. He grabbed one of the effigy's hands and severed it at the wrist, before throwing the mass of synthetic flesh at Scraps. "There. Use that!"

Meanwhile, with Elara's help, Chiefy had pulled himself free, and the pair were retreating toward the sarcophagus, fighting back-to-back. Scraps caught the severed hand and analyzed it with a probe. The little robot's mechanical features were twisted with revulsion.

"No good!" Scraps said. "Synthetic. No blood!"

Finn cursed then searched for one of the Reznikov mannequins that looked closer in appearance to the man they had spoken to in the throne room, and fought his way toward it. Despite looking much more like the Reznikov Finn knew, the effigy had a blank expression and vacant eyes, suggesting that there was nothing inside its lab-grown brain but a base compulsion to kill.

With hands grabbing at his neck and arms, Finn fought off the monsters trying to restrain him, dumping electrical shocks into their bodies, and sending them reeling. Then, with his target in sight, he plunged his sword into Reznikov's heart and drew it out. He expected to see blood gushing from the wound, but the fluid that coated his blade was not blood, but rather some manufactured approximation of it.

"It's no use," Finn said, backing himself against the wall. "None of these Reznikov's have any real blood in them."

"Can you reach the one I killed?" Elara called out. She and Chiefy were protecting Scraps, while the little robot tried desperately to crack the computer and open the door.

Finn looked for the version of Reznikov that Elara had killed with a swift cut of her knife, but the body was gone.

"It's gone!" Finn cried out. "They must have taken it!"

"Get back here, I have an idea!" Elara yelled.

Three more Reznikov effigies grabbed him, and he wrestled the creatures off him, throwing them into the sludge before stabbing them through their synthetic hearts. The monsters were relentless, but he managed to fight his way back to the sarcophagus, where Chiefy and Elara gave him some cover.

"What's this idea?" Finn said, kicking a lifelike Reznikov

in the face and causing the man to glower at him like an angry dog.

"We have the real Reznikov right here," Elara said, motioning toward the glass cover, through which the original president could still be seen, resting peacefully. "Just smash the glass and take what we need."

"I am afraid that won't work," Chiefy said, while crushing the skull of a malformed creature. "This body has been embalmed, and very little of the original organic material remains. What is left is either too complex to extract without lab equipment, or tainted by the chemicals used in the embalming process."

"Then what can we use?" Finn said. "There must be something!"

"Only Reznikov's blood will work," Chiefy said. "But without the version of the president that Elara killed, we cannot obtain a sample."

"Shit, wait..."

Elara stepped away from the fighting and Finn covered her, swinging his sword with all his might, but the heavy weapon was causing his muscles to tire, and each subsequent strike hit with less force.

"Here!" Elara said. She had pulled Riley's knife from its scabbard, and was holding it aloft like King Arthur wielding Excalibur. "Reznikov's blood is on the blade."

Elara tuned toward Scraps and held out the weapon, but at the same time, a grotesque effigy of the president scuttled across the top of the sarcophagus and bumped into Elara, sending the weapon spinning though the air. Without thinking, Finn dove for the knife and caught it in mid-flight, dropping his sword in the process. The bodies of the remaining Reznikovs cushioned his fall, but soon he was face down in the quagmire of vat liquid. Somehow, he kept the knife held high so that Reznikov's blood wouldn't be washed off the blade. Unable to breathe, he tried to pull his face out of the liquid, but hands were pressing down on the back of his head, trying to drown him.

Finn cried out, but his shouts were lost in bubbles of stinking goop. He struggled and fought, but there was no way to get up. The mass of bodies pushing down on him was simply too great. Desperate to breathe, panic gripped him, and his body's survival mechanism kicked in, forcing him to suck in a lungful of liquid instead of air. Then he was yanked off the floor and thrown on top of the sarcophagus like a bluefin tuna being pulled out of the ocean and onto the floor of a fishing boat. A huge robotic hand slapped his back, striking the salty fluid from his lungs, and he coughed and retched, until finally he could breathe air again.

"Tell me you got the knife..." Finn wheezed, flopping onto his back, and realizing that the black blade was no longer in his hand.

"I got it," Chiefy said, while stabbing Finn's electrified broadsword into another effigy. "Scraps is formulating a key."

"Tell him to formulate faster!" Finn said, spitting more of the disgusting liquid from his mouth.

The tomb door slid open, and the vat liquid gushed into the throne room, sweeping out the bodies of the dead Reznikovs with it. Chiefy grabbed Finn and slung his limp, soaking wet body over his shoulder, before leaping from the sarcophagus and sprinting toward the exit. From his inelegant perch atop the seven-foot machine, Finn could see Elara running behind them, Scraps tucked in beneath her arm.

Reznikov monsters reached for her, but she ducked and weaved, evading them with the dancer-like skill and agility that had saved her life on countless prior occasions. Then they were outside, and Elara slammed her hand onto the door mechanism, compelling it to shut, and trapping the remaining effigies inside the tomb, with the body of their ancestor.

"We have to reach the missile control room," Finn said, as Chiefy set him down. "We have to stop the launch manually. It's the only way."

"It's already too late…"

Elara had climbed the steps to Reznikov's throne and was peering through the enormous window behind it. The bright blue orb of Earth was clearly visible, growing larger by the second as the sphere, now detached from Nimbus, hurtled toward its eventual fiery demise inside the planet's atmosphere. However, it wasn't Earth that Elara was watching, but twenty-four streaks of light that were on a parallel course to it, accelerating away from the palace with the ferocious power of rocket engines.

"The nuclear missiles have all been launched," Elara said, turning from the window to look at Finn, her face drawn. "Zavetgrad and Haven will be destroyed."

22

FOUR-MINUTE WARNING

Finn refused to be beaten, not after they'd come so far. He searched around the president's throne room then spotted the computer terminal that Reznikov had used to convince them that the launch had been aborted. It was still raised up on a plinth beside the throne and the screen was active.

"Scraps, can you use that computer to abort the missiles?" Finn asked, pushing his weary legs up the steps to where the terminal was waiting.

Scraps arrived before him, courtesy of his spinning rotors, and wasted no time linking his data probes to the device. While the little robot worked, Finn stood next to Elara and anxiously looked out of the window, watching the nuclear missiles streak away from the station, on course to destroy the last vestiges of humanity on Earth.

"Can't abort!" Scraps said, bashing his fists onto the console. "Manual abort only!"

"Where's the control room, pal?" Finn said, holding the

little robot's body and turning Scraps to face him. "We don't have much time."

"Not far!" Scraps said, the robot pointed to Chiefy. "Chiefy shows the way!"

"How long do we have until those missiles reach their target?" Elara said. The possibility they could still stop Reznikov's plan had jolted her from her funk.

"Based on the current orbital position of Nimbus, and the rocket platforms that the missiles are using, we have just over seventeen minutes," Chiefy said.

Finn winced. That was no time at all. "How quickly can we reach launch control?"

Chiefy's broad metal shoulders sagged. "Fourteen minutes, if we run all the way," the robot answered. There was an ominous pause, before he added, "and assuming we do not meet much resistance."

"What kind of resistance?" Finn asked.

"Reznikov activated every robot inside this sphere," Chiefy said. "They are all coming for us."

"Then we fight our way through," Elara said. She ran down the steps, axe in one hand and blood-stained knife in the other. At the bottom, she stopped and turned to the others. "Well, what are you waiting for? We have sixteen minutes to save everyone on Earth. Let's move!"

Finn felt like he was back in the prosecutor barracks in the Authority sector, being beasted from pillar to post by his old mentor, and it focused his mind like a shot of adrenaline to the heart. Flicking the switch on the handle of Voss' broadsword, Finn swept ahead and took the lead, with Scraps flying overhead as their guide.

"Stay behind me and pick off what I don't manage to take

down," Finn said, the crackling electricity from the blade lighting the way forward. "I don't care if a hundred foremen stand in our way, we don't stop until we reach the missile control room."

It didn't take long for Finn to meet resistance. Reznikov's servant androids charged out from the aisles and side rooms, but their waiflike bodies, clad only in silk court dresses, were no match for Finn's electrified broadsword, and he cut them down, one swing at a time. The expressions on the faces of the women, so human in their imitations of rage and pain, stuck in Finn's mind, but had to remind himself that they were automatons, not people. They were programmed, not alive. That was what he had to tell himself, because the alternative was too unsettling to consider.

By the time Finn had exited the throne room, dozens of Gen I and II foremen had already entered the piazza, where Dante Voss' decapitated body still lay on the stone steps. Finn didn't stop running, and headed straight for the center of the pack, keeping half an eye on Scraps, ahead and above him, like a guiding light.

The robots tried to form a blockade, but Finn charged at their center, like a cavalry brigade trying to punch through an enemy line. Finn used the sword like his old baseball bat, jabbing and swatting at the robots as they moved toward him, and relying on its electrified punch, rather than Finn's muscles, to deal damage and clear a path.

Chiefy had detoured to reclaim Finn's old spear from where it had come to rest on the steps, after his failed attempt to throw it at Voss. The seven-foot robot was devastating enough without a weapon, but with the bent and mangled spear in his hand, Chiefy was able to crush the foreman like a wrecking ball smashing through a weather-beaten tenement block wall.

And then there was Elara. Finn had seen her fight enough times to understand her aptitude and capacity for violence, but she was operating on a whole other level, like she was in a trance. Robot bodies were not easily damaged by a simple axe or a knife, but Elara knew exactly where to hit the machines, and she was ruthless in her pursuit of robot murder. Servos were severed, gears crushed, and control lines were cut with a speed and precision that even Chiefy would have struggled to match. Before long, there was a pile of disabled robots in her wake, and she had broken the line and pushed through into the shapeless space beyond the throne room's courtyard, where the Crawler had first deposited them inside the central sphere.

"The infrasonic field is gone," Finn called out.

He'd expected the nausea to hit him the moment he'd entered the space, which had acted like a moat, protecting Reznikov's inner sanctum.

"Scraps turned off!" the little robot called back, before altering course to head past the airlock that the two prefects, Adam and Eve, had hastily constructed to get them inside. "Hurry, this way!"

Finn wanted to call back, "which way?", since inside the nebulous silver room, left looked no different to right, and he could barely tell up from down. Then he saw the faint outline of a door, and he had to pull up sharply to avoid running headfirst into a solid barrier.

"Chiefy, it's locked!" Finn said, hammering his fists on what he assumed was their exit, but the door wouldn't budge.

"Stand aside!"

The sudden cry caused Finn to jump back in shock, which was fortunate, since a moment later, Chiefy ploughed through the door like a battering ram, missing him by mere inches. The robot fell and tumbled into a passageway on the other side, warping the metal wall panels and sending sparks flying, like a ground car colliding with crash barriers at the side of an autoway. The robot was back on his feet in an instant and running again, spear in hand, before Finn's frazzled mind caught up with what had happened.

"Don't just stand there!" Elara said, racing past Finn a second later and charging into the corridor. "Move!"

Finn spun around and saw at least a hundred foremen bearing down on them. The robots were piling inside the space from other hidden entrances and concealed passageways, so that it appeared to Finn that they were coming out of the walls as if by magic. Then, amongst the mechanical mass of machines, he spotted the organic motion of bodies. The tomb door had been unsealed, and the surviving Reznikov effigies were charging after them like predators with the scent of blood on their tongues.

"Finn, run!" Elara yelled, and this time he didn't need telling twice.

Turning on his heels, he sprinted after Chiefy and Elara, who were already twenty meters ahead of him, and showing no signs of slowing down. Chiefy smashed through another door then the passageway veered sharply to the right. The light level dropped, and the temperature plunged below zero as they moved from the inhabited part of the central sphere and into the interstitial spaces. He listened to the hard clatter of robotic feet then saw Chiefy racing down a steep set of stairs, one of many that crisscrossed the metal framework that comprised the heart of the sphere.

Finn's breath fogged the air as he reached the top of the stairs and descended as fast as he could, without risking going head over heels. Then the pursuing foremen burst through the end of the corridor, practically fighting with each other to be first to run him down. Their momentum was so great that some of the machines toppled over the railings and tumbled into the hollow center of the sphere, disappearing into the cold, dark abyss.

Anxiously, Finn glanced back, then saw the Reznikov effigies clawing their way to the front of the pack. Most were examples of the president's ghoulish earlier efforts to recreate his body, but there was also a lifelike Reznikov imitation amongst them. Nimbler and stronger than the others, the naked synthetic man, driven by some base programming built into its lab-grown brain, squeezed through the clunky mass of robot bodies, and burst ahead.

Finn turned around and began to climb down the stairs backward, sword held ready as the Reznikov replica sprinted across the gangway and launched itself at him. Finn thrust his sword and sliced open the effigy's gut, but the momentum of the tackle bowled him over, and soon they were plummeting down the stairs as one intertwined mass. The sword bounced down ahead of them then spun away into the dark center, its blade crackling like bottled lightning. Finn felt the effigy's hands around his neck, but he was still falling, and could do nothing to stop the man from squeezing his throat shut.

He hit the landing at the bottom of the stairs hard then rebounded into a solid bulkhead wall. Finn's armor saved him, but the impact still pressed what little air was inside his lungs out of his constricted throat. It sounded like a man taking his dying breath. Instinct took over, and Finn wrestled himself free of the imitation Reznikov and kicked the man away. The effigy's stomach was cut open from his sternum to his belly button, and his intestines were hanging out, but still the monster came at him, relentless.

Fighting to keep it from clawing out his eyes, Finn spun an elbow strike into the creature's face, then grabbed its arm and threw it to the deck. At the same time, fifty or more robots were clattering down the stairs, while the remaining Reznikov monsters, all grotesque mistakes of science, climbed over the top of them, using the mass of machine bodies as a slide. The effigy at his feet attacked again, but this time Finn evaded it and hammered a knee strike into the man's lower back, cracking vertebrae and incapacitating it. Grabbing the thing by its throat, Finn hurled the Reznikov replica over the railings and into the heart of the sphere.

Then he ran, and he didn't look back.

Eyes streaming, lungs burning and body screaming at him to stop, he almost collided with Elara, who was coming the other way, her face a tortured mix of concern and fatigue.

"What happened to your sword?" Elara said, noticing Finn's empty hands.

"I lost it," Finn said. "And I'm fine, thanks for asking," he added, pissed that Elara's first thought was about his missing weapon, rather than his safety.

Elara's expected sarcastic response went unspoken, because she had already pushed past Finn and launched herself at a group of foremen that had managed to make it down the stairs ahead of the effigies. The sharp edges of her double-headed axe flashed faster than Finn could see, and two of the robots were left broken, and blocking the narrow passageway. Elara spun around and grabbed Finn's arm, dragging him with her.

"Chiefy's found the missile control room," Elara said. "We're almost there."

Elara led them through the maze of passageways, chased every step of the way by the sound of their pursuers, until finally Finn spotted the welcome sight of Scraps and Chiefy. The two robots stood to the side of a heavy pressure hatch door, both neck deep inside a control panel that had been torn open.

"How much time do we have left?" Finn asked, resting his hands on his knees. He felt physically sick from exhaustion and his whole body was shaking.

"Just under four minutes," Chiefy replied, his voice remarkably calm and assured.

A group of foremen burst around the corner in an entangled mass, then began swarming toward them. It was like the sphere had been flooded by liquid metal, and the deluge was gushing toward them like a tidal wave.

"Chiefy, we need that door open..." Finn said, trying to channel some of the robot's calm, but his voice was trembling worse than his body.

"Ten seconds..." Chiefy replied.

"In ten seconds, we'll be dead!"

The pressure hatch swung open, and Finn practically fell through it. Elara jumped inside next, followed by Scraps, then Chiefy ducked through and slammed the heavy door directly into the faces of four Gen I robots, smashing them like egg crates. Chiefy spun the lock wheel then tore a steam pipe away from the low ceiling, and fed it through the spokes, like threading a needle, to make it impossible to open the door again.

"Three min-mins!" Scraps yelled, waving his arms, and urging them to follow him.

Finn climbed to his feet and compelled his body to move through sheer force of will. The corridor quickly widened into a control room, with a long glass window that looked out into a missile launch bay, except every one of the twenty-four silos was empty.

"Quickly, abort the missiles," Elara said, reaching the control console and steadying herself against it.

"Wait!" Finn said. Everyone looked at him like he was insane.

"Wait? We have less than three minutes until a million people are turned to ash!" Elara hit back.

"What if we can change the course of the missiles?" Finn said. An idea had come to him. He had no idea if it could work, but they still had perhaps sixty seconds to find out. "What if you can alter their course so that the missiles return and hit Nimbus instead? That way, no more Reznikov. No more Authority."

Elara's eyes widened. His idea had caught her interest. "Is that possible?" she said, looking to Scraps and Chiefy.

"Maybe-maybe!" the little robot replied, then plugged himself into the launch control computer, and set to work.

"Can he do it?" Finn said, looking at Chiefy with imploring eyes. The robot had been curiously silent on the subject.

"Normally, altering the course of a ballistic missile would require an extended period of careful planning and detailed computations," Chiefy began.

"Yes or no?" Finn said. He didn't want a physics lecture, just an answer.

"A gravitational slingshot maneuver could achieve what you are asking, but it is highly complex and would have to be executed with precision."

"Damn it, Chiefy, yes or no!" Finn yelled.

"I... do not know," Chiefy finally admitted.

Finn cursed and Elara's chin fell to her chest. Chiefy then shrugged and looked to Scraps for the answer, but the smug smile on the little machine's face told Finn everything he needed to know.

"You've done it?" Finn asked.

Scraps pointed to one of the monitors, which was displaying a simple diagram of the earth-moon system, along with the trajectories of the twenty-four nuclear missiles. Now, instead of impacting on the surface, the deadly weapons were projected on a course around the planet, and back again.

"Piece of cake," Scraps said, beaming a smile at them.

Finn felt like the weight of a hundred foremen had just been lifted from his shoulders, and he sank to the floor, with his back pressed up against the launch control console. Elara flopped down at his side, and grabbed his arm, pulling him close. He felt her head rest on his bruised shoulder, and it hurt like hell, but he didn't care.

"Ingenious," Chiefy said. The larger robot was examining Scraps' handiwork on the computer. "These computations are incredibly sophisticated. In one hour, thirty-two minutes and forty-nine seconds, the twenty-four nuclear missiles will have orbited the Earth and intercepted Nimbus. At the velocity they will be traveling at, the warheads would not even be necessary, but suffice to say that the combined energy of the kinetic impact and the atomic detonations will reduce the space station, and everything on it to atoms." The foreman turned to Scraps and shook his little hand. "You are a very clever little robot!" he said, proudly.

"Yes-yes!" Scraps said, completely without ego. "Finn made me so!"

23

RAPID ORBITAL DECAY

An alert flashed up on the missile launch computer, robbing Finn of the euphoria he was feeling and replacing it with a dread sense of unease. He rushed to the terminal and stared at the screen, but the alert wasn't related to the missiles – they were still on a perfect course back to Nimbus – the warning concerned the sphere, and its own imminent demise.

Alert! Rapid Orbital Decay detected... a heavily processed computer voice announced at ear-splitting volume though a PA system in the room. *All personnel must evacuate. Time to atmospheric impact, one hour, seventeen minutes...*

Finn dragged himself to his feet then planted the palms of his hands onto the launch control computer to stop himself from falling flat on his face. The warning alert continued to flash at him in bright red letters, and he cursed and shook his head.

"Is there any way to alter the course of the sphere, like you did with the missiles?" Elara suggested. She was always looking for a way out, always refusing to be beaten. "Maybe we can put the sphere into a stable orbit again?"

Chiefy looked to Scraps, since he was the expert at conducting intricate orbital maneuvers, but the little robot shook his head, forlornly.

"Nope-nope," Scraps said. "Thrusters too weak!"

Despair threatened to overwhelm Finn, but he shook it off and tried to channel some of Elara's doggedness.

"I don't suppose Reznikov thought to add any escape pods to this sphere?" Finn asked, glancing at Chiefy over his shoulder.

"Actually, he did," the robot replied, ever cheerful. "There are a number of evacuation pods dotted around this space module. It would have been foolish not to include them."

Suddenly energized, Finn pushed himself away from the missile control console and spun around. "Please tell me that we can reach one of these pods in less than one hour and seventeen minutes?"

"One hour and fifteen minutes now, but yes," Chiefy said.

Finn excused the robot's unnecessary pedantism because at that moment he could have grabbed the seven-foot machine and planted a kiss on his mechanical mouth.

"Then why the hell are we still standing around here?" Finn said. "Let's go!"

From the sterile seed-extraction bays of a gene bank to the reclamation yards of Metalhaven, and especially the crucible where he had barely scraped through with his life, Finn had found himself in a great number of places that he'd wanted to escape from, but none more so than Reznikov's presidential sphere. In a little over an hour, the kilometer-wide structure that had once occupied the central part of Nimbus, would burn up in the Earth's atmosphere, spreading its scorched and twisted remains across hundreds of miles of the dead planet. Finn intended to be long gone before that happened.

Scraps led the way, guiding Finn and the others through the interstitial spaces of the sphere. With the pressure hatch into the control room firmly jammed shut, the foremen were unable to pursue, and before long the horde of robots, together with horrifying last few Reznikov effigies were far behind them.

The route was tortuous and at times perilous, as they were forced to climb across sheer drops, navigate bare framework floors, and squeeze between gaps that elicited feelings of extreme claustrophobia. It was like traveling with General Riley through the caverns beneath Zavetgrad, except the dangers were far greater. This time, instead of the threat of being mauled by a mutant fish, or eaten by mutagenic lupus, failure meant being cooked inside the sphere as it plummeted to Earth and turned into a giant, superheated fireball.

Forty minutes into their scramble to safety, they were forced to move back into the sphere's main internal spaces. Finn checked for foremen or evaluator robots, but all he found were repair spiders, scurrying around and looking for anything that might need fixing. Startled, three of the arachnoid machines wheeled around and raised their two front legs as threat gestures, but Elara was in no mood to take shit from anyone, let alone repair bots. Sliding to a stop, she drew her axe and clashed it across the armor on her thigh, causing sparks to fly and skid across the polished floor. The three spider bots lowered their legs, looked at one another, then scampered away in the dark corners of the room.

"At least they're smart enough to know when they're

beaten," Finn said. He didn't blame the spider robots for running. He might have done the same.

Pushing on, Finn's mind began to wander and for some reason his thoughts dwelled on the Mona Lisa, whose mysterious smile had captured his attention. He thought of it and the many other treasures that Nimbus contained, all of which would soon be reduced to elemental matter. Centuries of human history, including some of its greatest achievements, were contained within the space station, ironically transported there for safe keeping. Then he realized that Da Vinci's masterpiece had been considered lost for close to three hundred years already. Ninety-nine percent of the population never knew the painting had even existed. Perhaps that was for the best, Finn thought. *A clean slate...* In the centuries to come, he hoped that humanity would create new wonders and a history it could be proud of. Once that had been little more than a pipedream. Now, it was a real possibility.

Finn's body was on the brink of total exhaustion when Scraps finally slowed to a hover in front of an innocuous looking door that was no different to hundreds of similarly innocuous doors that the robot had led them past for the last hour.

Alert. Rapid Orbital Decay. All personnel must evacuate. Time to atmospheric impact, twenty-three minutes...

"Please tell me this is an evacuation pod, and not just another door on the way to the pod?" Finn said, resting his back against the wall, breath heavy.

"This it!" Scraps said, while unscrewing the lock panel with one of his many tools. "Almost there!"

Scraps' hands worked faster than Finn had ever seen them

move before, and within seconds the lock had been circumvented, and the door slid open. Elara moved in first, axe in hand, and checked the corners, before waving the others inside. The knowledge that they were almost free gave Finn a burst of adrenaline and energy, and he hustled into the room. It was about the same size as his apartment in the prosecutor barracks, where Zoe, the floor coordinator from the workhouse who'd helped to rescue many children from the burning blaze, had since taken up residence. He idly wondered what state his bed was now in, after several days of partying and bouncing.

"This is it," Elara said, peering through a port-hole window and into a heavy airlock hatch, similar to the one they had moved through to enter Nimbus in the first place. "It's plenty big enough for all of us."

"But how does it work?" Finn said.

Scraps was already on the case. The little robot had landed on a computer console that was set atop a metal plinth, like a lectern. The computer sparked into life, then bright lights inside the evacuation pod flickered on, and the pressure inside the airlock began to equalize with the sphere.

Alert. Rapid Orbital Decay. All personnel must evacuate. Time to atmospheric impact, nineteen minutes...

"No worries!" Scraps called out. "This only take a min-min!"

A red light above the airlock hatch suddenly turned green, and Elara grabbed the locking wheel and spun it with all her strength, before pulling back on the handle and hauling the heavy door open.

"Get inside," Elara said, stepping back.

Feeling suddenly euphoric again, Finn considered making

a joke that it should be, 'ladies first', but the severe look on Elara's face said she was in no mood for any kind of antics, and the thought came and went within a microsecond.

"Chiefy, you first," Finn said, turning to the hulking machine. "I'm guessing you know how to work this thing and get it ready."

"I don't," Chiefy replied, though the robot did not appear distressed by this. "However, I believe I can figure it out."

"Figure it out quickly," Elara cut in.

The slightest hint of a smile brightened Elara's expression then suddenly her eyes widened with surprise, and a sonic blast smacked her in the chest and knocked her to the floor. Finn looked for the shooter, and at the same time a second blast hit Chiefy in the head. The robot was disabled, and he toppled through the control console, smashing it to pieces and sending Scraps fleeing, rotors spinning wildly.

Finn's training kicked in and he ducked and rolled, avoiding two more blasts that thumped into the floor and smashed a wall panel to his rear. Finding cover, he chanced a look at his attackers then punched the floor so hard he drew blood. It was Ivan Volkov and Juniper Jones. Both were still in the ceremonial outfits that Finn had last seen them wearing in front of Reznikov's throne room, except that Juniper's flowing train had been cut loose. Both were also carrying sonic rifles.

"Come out, Finn!" Ivan yelled. "Come out and I'll kill you quickly. It's more than you deserve!"

Scraps flew out of the shadows and collided with Juniper's head, stunning her, and knocking the commissar into Ivan. The regent successor fired frantically at the machine as Scraps buzzed around his head, before finally lashing out with the weapon like a club, and knocking the robot to the floor. Finn got up and charged, tackling Ivan though the midriff just as he was about to blast Scraps at close range and reduce the robot to a mess of broken parts. The sonic rifle skidded away, and Finn tried to wrestle Ivan into submission, but Ivan had lost none of his fighting prowess, and before long, the man had shaken Finn off him, and climbed to his feet. Ivan raised his guard and was about to attack, when the man saw the smashed console, still partly covered by Chiefy's inert body, and cursed bitterly.

"You fool, you've killed us all!" Finn roared, realizing that their only chance of escape was now gone.

"Me?" Ivan spat. The accusation repulsed him. "I was to be the guardian of the new human race, and now look what you've done. The communes set adrift, Nimbus and the president's palace doomed, and for what? So that a few hundred thousand diseased, worthless rats can live for another two generations at most?" Ivan spat at Finn's feet. "The truth is that you doomed humanity the moment you chose not to die inside that crucible."

"None of that matters now," Finn said, shaking the stiffness out of his arms then closing his hands into fists. If they were all going to die anyway, he would be the one to kill Ivan. "I'm still a Prosecutor of Zavetgrad, and I think there's time for one last trial."

Finn attacked, throwing punches and kicks at Ivan, but the man blocked and evaded, displaying the superior skills that had defeated Finn once before. This time, however, there was a difference. This time Finn had nothing to lose, and he would stop at nothing to make sure Ivan died by his hands.

Countering, Ivan landed hard blows into Finn's face, but he barely felt the impacts. He was too full of bile and rage. Blow after blow landed, and soon Ivan had all but punched himself out. The man's guard dropped, and Finn unloaded everything he had in a single flurry of raw hatred. The bitterness he felt for every humiliation and degradation that he'd suffered at the hands of prefects, foremen and gene bank doctors was concentrated into his fists. Every injustice that he'd suffered and every atrocity that he'd witnessed were focused into each swing of his arms. If at that moment he could have punched the frozen ground beneath Metalhaven, he would have split the earth in two.

Ivan Volkov reeled back, teeth and blood spilling from the man's mouth, but Finn didn't relent in his assault. He forced Ivan against the wall and kept punching, until bones were broken, both in Ivan's face and in his own knuckles, but the pain just spurred him on. Eventually, gravity won and Ivan crumpled to the floor, barely alive.

"Stay where you are!"

Heart thumping and chest heaving, Finn saw Juniper Jones, aiming a sonic rifle at his chest. She was trembling, but whether it was because of the violence she'd just witnessed, or because she feared her own death, Finn didn't know.

He ignored Juniper – she could not hurt him now – and looked for Elara. She was still dazed, but had managed to climb to one knee, her hand pressed to Chiefy's chest for support. Scraps was with her, and Elara was shielding the little robot behind her back.

"Get away from the escape pod!" Juniper yelled, motioning at Finn with the rifle.

"Where are you running to, Juniper?" Finn said. The

fight had gone out of him, and all that remained was regret. "Even if the escape pod still worked, there's nothing left for you in Zavetgrad. The Authority is gone."

"Zavetgrad needs me, now more than ever!" the commissar hit back. Her finger was on the trigger of the sonic rifle, but like the rest of her, it was shaking with fear.

"You're the last thing Zavetgrad needs, or ever needed," Finn said, inspecting his broken fist. At that moment, he didn't care whether Juniper shot him or not. They were all dead anyway.

Alert. Rapid Orbital Decay. All personnel must evacuate. Time to atmospheric impact, twelve minutes...

"Besides, in twelve minutes, we'll all be burned to a crisp," Finn said. He sighed and lowered his hands to his sides.

"Pod still active!" Scraps said, peering up at Finn from behind Elara. "Could still launch!"

Finn frowned at the robot then looked at the smashed control console. "How?" he asked.

"It doesn't matter how, only that we can still escape," Juniper said, suddenly enlivened. "We can all go home!"

"She's not coming back with us," Elara hissed, her voice unsteady. "I'd rather die than let that bitch live."

"There's another choice, Finn," Juniper said, inching closer to him. "We can escape, together. Just you and I..."

Finn laughed. "Me and you? Ha! Just like old times!"

"Don't be like that," Juniper said, angry at Finn's sarcastic dismissal of her suggestion. "I know you loved me, despite what I did to you. You can't deny the connection we had."

Finn laughed again and shook his head. Out of the corner of his eye, he could see that Elara was watching, but there was more to her now than rage. There was concern. There was doubt.

"Our love was real, Finn, not like what you feel for Elara," Juniper continued, lowering her rifle by a few degrees. The commissar was gone, and instead his old paramour was standing before him. "You don't love her, not really. It's guilt that keeps you together."

"What the fuck are you talking about?" Finn spat. "We're about to die, and you pull this shit on me now?"

"Elara saved your life, and you think you owe her something because of that, but you don't," Juniper said, still inching closer. "What you feel for her is gratitude, that's all..."

"You don't know what you're talking about," Finn said.

They were hurtling toward Earth three times faster than a speeding bullet, and Juniper was talking about love. It was insane, but he too stunned to do anything but listen.

"Our love was pure, Finn," Juniper continued. She was vulnerable again, like the woman who'd called at his door in the prosecutor barracks, all coy and embarrassed. "You know, deep down, that I'm right. You know that I'm the only one who can free you from the torment of Owen's death." Juniper nodded toward Elara, who was back on her feet, but still shaky. "She can't help you. She would have killed Owen in that trial if it had come to it."

Finn felt his gut twist. He glanced at Elara, and she was looking at him too, but her eyes didn't try to contradict the truth that Juniper had spoken.

"See, she won't deny it!" Juniper yelled, triumphant. "She's a cancer, Finn, and so long as you're together, you can never heal. You can never be happy..."

Juniper was careful to keep the barrel of the rifle aimed at

Finn, while she took his broken hand into hers. Her touch was warm and soft, and in the air was the scent of her perfume, exactly as he remembered it.

"Together, we can change the city, for the better," Juniper said, speaking in hushed, reassuring tones. "Zavetgrad needs leadership. You can't believe that these workers can govern on their own. It'll be chaos, and within a year or two, all will be lost. Humanity needs you, Finn, but for you to save Zavetgrad, you need me by your side. Together, we can be the mother and father of a new Earth."

"They're just words, Juniper," Finn replied, softly. "A honeyed potion poured into my ear, just like you always did."

"I'll prove it to you..."

Juniper looked over to where Ivan Volkov was still slumped against the wall. The man's face was puffy, and his mouth bloodied and raw, but Ivan clung to life with the persistence of a cockroach. Then Juniper stepped back, wheeled the barrel of the sonic rifle around, and blasted Ivan in the head, killing the man instantly. Finn jerked away. He was no stranger to killing, but witnessing the act of murder still had the capacity to shock him.

"There, it's done," Juniper said, lowering the rifle to her side. "Now, there are no more aristocrats, no more entitled golds." She turned back to Finn and pressed her left hand above her heart. "You and I, Finn, we can change the world." She looked again to Elara, and hatred oozed out of her every pore. Hatred and jealousy. "All you have to do is kill her."

"You're right, Juniper..." Elara's mouth dropped open and tears welled in her eyes. "I hate you for being right, but that doesn't change the truth."

Juniper glowed like on the first day he'd met her, then she

nodded and turned to Elara, raising the sonic rifle to her shoulder. Elara didn't even try to resist. Her eyes simply fell to the floor and her shoulders sank. For the first time ever in her hard, cruel life, she was beaten.

"No. I have to be the one to kill her," Finn said.

Juniper stopped with her finger still on the trigger of the sonic rifle, and looked at Finn out of the corner of her eyes. The paramour was gone and the commissar had returned.

"You almost had me convinced," Juniper said. She laughed then shook her head, lowering the rifle to her hip. "It seems that you picked up a few tricks from me about the art of deception."

"I suppose I learned from the best," Finn said, shrugging. His gambit had failed and Juniper had seen through his attempt to trick her.

"I meant what I said, Finn, at least about Zavetgrad needing you," Juniper added, bitterness and disappointment now coloring her words. "It would have been fairer to say that *I* need you, so that *I* could become ruler of the city by your side." She shrugged. "I'll find another way, though. Few men are as resistant to my charms as you are."

"Still so suspicious," Finn said, throwing his arms out wide and trying to shrug off Juniper's remarks. "If you really loved me and trusted me then you'd give me that rifle."

"Do you really believe I'd give you this weapon?" Juniper said, mocking Finn now. "Do you think I'd let you kill me, so you can run away with your precious Elara and live happily ever after?" She laughed. "Maybe you're not as smart as I thought."

"You want proof?" Finn said. Juniper may have seen

through his attempts to deceive her, but at some level, deep down, she wanted to be wrong. She wanted Finn to love her.

"There's nothing you could say to convince me," Juniper said. "And we're out of time." She pulled the weapon to her shoulder again.

"I swear to you on the ashes of Owen Thomas, my Metalhaven brother, that I won't kill you."

Juniper hesitated again, then twisted her hips toward Finn so that she should interrogate his eyes and his body language more closely.

"You actually mean that?" Juniper said, surprised to discover that Finn wasn't lying.

"Yes…" Finn said. Then he nodded toward Elara. "I won't kill you, because she will."

Elara threw her combat knife like a missile and the blade pierced Juniper's chest and sliced into her heart. For a second or two, the commissar simply stared down at the blade embedded into her flesh, a look of confusion on her face. Then she looked at Finn, but if Juniper had hoped for compassion, she was looking at the wrong man. With nowhere else to turn, she stumbled toward Ivan's corpse, reaching out for him, desperately, before collapsing on top of the regent successor's mutilated body, and exhaling her last breath.

Alert. Rapid Orbital Decay. All personnel must evacuate. Time to atmospheric impact, eight minutes…

Finn ran to Elara and she wrapped her arms around him, squeezing so tightly that every bone in his body creaked like old metal.

"I thought I'd lost you…" Elara whispered into his ear.

"Never," Finn said. He drew back and kissed her. "At

least, not so long as we get off this station in the next few minutes."

Chiefy powered up and sat bolt upright. Scraps was entangled inside a mass of wires that were sprouting from the foreman's head and chest.

"I am... impaired..." Chiefy said.

"Don't worry, we'll get you out of here and fix you up back in Metalhaven," Finn said, as he and Elara helped the robot to stand.

"But the control console is smashed," Elara said, looking at the electronic rubble at Chiefy's feet. "We can't launch!"

"Scraps, you said that the evacuation pod is still active," Finn asked his little robot pal, and Scraps nodded. "So how do we launch it?"

"It must be jettisoned manually," Chiefy interrupted.

Finn cursed and looked to Scraps for confirmation. The little robot nodded and steepled his fingers. Like Finn, Scraps understood the terrible implications of what Chiefy had just told them.

"Someone has to stay behind to trigger the launch," Chiefy said, spelling it out for everyone in plain terms. "It is the only way."

Finn closed his eyes and let his head loll back onto his shoulders. It seemed that fate had dealt them one last, cruel blow. Elara then rushed away from Finn and picked up the sonic rifle that Juniper had dropped. Finn watched her, hoping that she had a plan to use the rifle's components to fix the computer, but she had a different idea in mind.

"Get inside the pod, and take them with you..." Elara said, aiming the weapon at Finn.

Alert. Rapid Orbital Decay. All personnel must evacuate. Time to atmospheric impact, six minutes...

"Elara, what are you doing?"

Finn moved toward her, and Elara shot him in the chest. The weapon had been dialed down to a lower power setting, but it was still enough to stop him dead and put him on his ass.

"I'll knock you out with this if I have to," Elara said, ratcheting up the power level by one notch. "Don't make this harder than it needs to be. It has to end this way."

"What way?" Finn snapped, climbing to his feet. "What are you talking about?"

"Juniper was right about me, I am a disease," Elara said, her eyes welling with tears. "But you're a good man Finn, a good man who is punishing himself for a stupid mistake that you'd take back in a heartbeat if you could."

"Elara, please, we don't have time for this..."

"You deserve a second chance," Elara continued, ignoring Finn's pleas. "I made a choice to become The Shadow. I made a choice to kill innocent people. The ends don't justify the means, no matter what anyone says. And The Shadow is who I'll always be, not Sentinel, or any other name you want to call me."

Alert. Rapid Orbital Decay. All personnel must evacuate. Time to atmospheric impact, four minutes...

"I'm sorry, Finn," Elara said, tears now streaming down her face.

Finn moved for her again, but she fired the sonic rifle and blasted him over the threshold of the escape pod.

"Elara, no!" Finn cried, trying to stand, but he was too weak. "You can't leave me!"

"I'm sorry," Elara said again, the words barely audible. "I love you..."

Suddenly, Chiefy swept toward Elara, and at the same time she turned and shot the robot point blank. Sparks flew, but Chiefy didn't go down, and managed to club Elara across the side of her head, knocking her out cold. She fell, but Chiefy caught her, then dragged her dazed body inside the evacuation pod. Scraps flew inside too, and landed on Elara's chest, looking fretful and concerned.

"Good work, Chiefy," Finn said, cushioning Elara's head against the cold steel floor with his hands. "Now find a way to trigger the launch, so we can all get out of here!"

There was no answer, and Finn looked up to see that Chiefy had already exited the pod. Scraps flew toward the door, but the powerful Gen VII foreman slammed it shut before the smaller robot could escape.

"Chiefy!" Scraps yelled hammering at the porthole window. "Chiefy no!"

Alert. Rapid Orbital Decay. All personnel must evacuate. Time to atmospheric impact, two minutes...

Finn struggled to his feet and staggered to the hatch, alongside his robot pal.

"What are you doing?" Finn called out, banging on the door. "You can fix this, Chiefy. You can fix anything!"

Chiefy shook his head. "Not this time..." The robot began to work on the manual controls then an alert blared inside the evacuation pod.

Evacuation pod armed. Launch in t-minus twenty seconds, and counting...

"Thank you for my life," Chiefy said, returning to the

window. Then he looked Scraps in the eyes and smiled. "And thank you for being my friend."

Thrusters fired and pushed the evacuation pod clear of the dock. Finn barely managed to cling on to the escape capsule then rapidly accelerated away from the president's sphere. The last thing Finn saw, before grief overcame him and tears blurred his vision, was Chiefy's smiling face, waving them goodbye from the window.

24

BACK TO EARTH

Finn staggered away from the hatch then was hurled against the spherical wall of the evacuation pod as its reaction control thrusters fired, in a desperate effort to slow their approach velocity. His leg slammed against one of the metal seats, hard enough to bruise his muscles through the thick armor plating. Hissing with pain, he saw Elara sliding across the floor and he dove for her, landing just in time to cushion her impact with his own body.

Warning, approach velocity too high. Reduce speed. Reduce speed...

"Scraps!" Finn called out, while hoisting Elara into one of the seats and strapping her in. She was barely conscious. "Scraps, where are you!"

There was no answer from the robot, and Finn grabbed a handrail, fighting the forces that were acting on him and managing to pull himself to his feet. Through one of the array of small porthole windows that surrounded the spherical pod, he could see Earth approaching fast. Then through a window to his right, he saw Reznikov's palace begin to burn up in the planet's atmosphere.

"Scraps!" Finn called out again, but still there was no answer.

Finn searched the pod then found the little robot, still clamped to the hatch, through which they had both seen Chiefy for the last time. He dragged himself over to the robot and pressed a hand to his oil can back.

Warning, approach velocity too high. Reduce speed. Reduce speed...

"Pal, we need your help," Finn whispered. He knew the robot was hurting, but Scraps was their one chance to survive. "The evacuation pod is flying out of control. You're the only one who can stop it."

"Chiefy..." Scraps said, peering through the porthole into empty space.

"I know, pal, I'm sad too, but we can't think about it right now." Finn pulled himself closer so that Scraps could see his face out of the corner of his sad, mechanical eyes. "Chiefy sacrificed his own life to save ours, but right now we're still in trouble."

Scraps turned his head a little. "Still danger?"

"Yes, pal," Finn said. "The pod is out of control, and I don't know how to fix it."

Scraps nodded then finally managed to tear his eyes away from the porthole, before climbing onto Finn's shoulder. The robot looked around the pod then saw Elara, strapped to a chair, her head lolling from one side to the other as bumps and shimmies hammered the pod.

"Elara!" Scraps yelped, and the robot leapt from Finn's shoulder and flew to her side.

"She'll be okay," Finn said, though in truth, he had no idea how badly hurt she was. "Fix the pod first, then we can help Elara."

DANGER, approach velocity too high. Reduce speed. Reduce speed...

Scraps stroked Elara's hair then scampered over her legs and hustled to a control panel at the front of the capsule. Springing tools from his body, the robot got to work, while Finn dragged himself into a seat beside Elara and waited. Through the portholes, he could still see Reznikov's sphere, now consumed by fire, but he could also see Nimbus in the background, illuminated brightly by the light of the sun. Somewhere near to it were twenty-four nuclear missiles, though he didn't know how close the weapons were to striking their target.

Without warning, he was thrown forward, as if he were in a ground car that had braked suddenly. He gripped the arms of his chair and tried to support Elara's head, then as abruptly as the force had appeared, it vanished, and all was suddenly calm. It was like they were on a Seahaven boat in the middle of a hurricane, and the vessel had passed into the eye of the storm.

"Pod safe," Scraps said, scampering back across the seats toward them. "Entry course set."

"Entry course?" Finn said, not understanding the robot. "Do you mean that we'll make it back to the planet?"

Scraps nodded. "Yes-yes..." he said, though without his usual vivacity. "Land near Zavetgrad. Outside fence."

"Well done, pal," Finn said, speaking the words as one long, relieved sigh.

Finn rested a hand on Scraps shoulder, and the robot

grabbed his index finger and squeezed it tightly. The robot's grip was surprisingly firm, and his mechanical fingers were sharp, but Finn didn't flinch or try to pull his hand clear, despite the pain. Scraps needed him at that moment, and after everything the little robot had done for them, enduring a little discomfort was the very least he could do.

Finn then looked at Elara and gently moved her head so that it rested more comfortably against the back of the chair. There was lump and a bruise where Chiefy had hit her, but all told, she didn't look in bad shape. Still with one hand in Scraps' grip, he searched around his seat for an emergency medical kit, and found one clamped to a pillar, behind his head. He unhooked the cigar box sized case and dropped it onto his lap, struggling with the latch, since he only had one free hand.

Scraps let go of Finn and hopped closer, sitting down on Elara's lap so that Finn could open the med kit. Inside was the expected first aid equipment, including an aerosolized stimulant designed to rouse someone who had lost consciousness. In a situation where you were falling to earth in a metal box no bigger than a sky car, Finn imagined that it was an important consideration to make sure everyone remained conscious and able to attend to their tasks.

"How about this?" Finn said, showing the compact aerosol to Scraps. "Will this wake her up?"

"Yes-yes," Scraps said. He was scanning Elara, his mechanical brow furrowed in concentration. "Elara-okay. Can wake."

Finn flipped the cap of the aerosol then sprayed it over Elara's nose and mouth. Immediately, her eyes shot open, and she coughed and spluttered, while rubbing her eyes, at the same time working more of the stimulant compound into her system. Some of the spray blew back into Finn's face, like getting a whiff of second-hand smoke from a narcotic laced cigarette, it woke him up too.

"What happened?" Elara said, now gripping the arms of the chair to steady herself. Her disorientation was to be expected, considering that the last time she had been conscious was when they'd all still been inside Reznikov's presidential sphere. "Where are we?"

"We're safe," Finn said, squeezing Elara's wrist. "We're in the evacuation pod, heading back to the planet. To Zavetgrad."

"But... how?" Elara said. She looked at Scraps, who smiled sadly back at her, then scanned her eyes across every other seat in the capsule, her frown becoming more pronounced with each empty place she looked at. "Where's Chiefy?"

Scraps wailed and wrapped his arm around Elara's waist, hugging her tightly. She gently put her arm around the robot then looked to Finn for an explanation.

"He sucker-punched you, then did the same to me," Finn said, putting it as plainly as he could. "Chiefy sacrificed himself, so that we could escape."

Elara let out a gasp then pressed her throbbing head against the seat and closed her eyes. "That wasn't how this was supposed to happen..." she said. "It was supposed to be me on that space station. Chiefy never put a damned foot wrong. He was good. I'm the one who deserved to die."

"Chiefy disagreed," Finn said. He wanted to add that he disagreed too, and that he was glad Elara was alive, despite what it had cost, but he was conscious that Scraps was listening. It didn't make him feel proud to admit it, but it was the truth, just as it was true that Chiefy was more deserving than either of them.

"It's not right," Elara said, opening her eyes and hugging Scraps more tightly to her side.

"No, it's not right," Finn agreed. "But we'll have to live with it. It will be our penance."

"Forgive..." Scraps said, peeking up at Finn and Elara. "Chiefy would want."

"There's nothing to forgive, Pal," Finn said. "Chiefy did what he thought was right. That's all any of us can do."

"No. Not forgive Chiefy," Scraps said. "Forgive yourselves."

Finn blew out a heavy sigh. That was a much harder request to honor.

"I suppose we can try," he said, looking at Elara. Forgiveness came harder to her than anyone he'd ever known. "We'll do it for Chiefy."

Elara nodded weakly, then looked through one of the portholes. Reznikov's sphere was already glowing like metal in a forge. Before long, the palace began to break apart and the smaller fragments quickly burned up, streaking fiery paths across the sky like a cataclysmic meteor shower.

"Will the burning pieces of the sphere hit anything?" Finn asked, transfixed by the lightshow. "Anything important, I mean."

Scraps shook his head. "Impact over North America," the robot explained.

"Everything there is dead already," Finn said, relieved to hear that they hadn't saved Zavetgrad from nuclear obliteration, only to see it bombarded from orbit by thousands of tons of burning metal. "It's nothing but scorched wastelands and blackened bones."

"Maybe it won't always be that way," Elara said, taking up Chiefy's role by adding a touch of optimism to the gloomy discussion. "Time is all we need. Time to heal."

"It's good to have hope," Finn agreed. "Without hope, what's the point of going on at all?"

Elara shrugged. "Right now, the only reason I want to live is so I can have a hot shower, and a pint of ale. Maybe five pints."

Finn laughed. "I think given the state both of us are in, five pints of Metalhaven ale would probably be enough to kill us." He thought about it some more, drumming his fingers on the metal arm of his chair as he did so. "But what the hell, I'm game if you are."

"Look-look!"

Scraps leapt out of Elara's lap and jumped onto the sill that ran around the circumference of the evacuation pod. He stopped at a porthole behind Finn, that was aiming out toward space, instead of inward toward the blue planet, which was looming closer by the second.

"Look at what pal?" Finn said.

"Nimbus!" Scraps answered, chirpily.

It took Finn a moment to locate the orbital citadel, but even without its central sphere and the ten commune habitats that they'd already jettisoned, it was still the biggest object in space, besides the Earth and its moon.

"What are we looking for?" Finn asked.

From their current angle, Nimbus looked barely any different, besides the doughnut-like hole in its center, where the palace had once been. Then space was suddenly lit up by a succession of massive explosions, primordial in their power, like the birth of the universe itself. Finn had to squint his eyes as the fireball built and expanded, so that for a moment, it appeared like there were two suns.

"That's not something you see every day," Elara said, forcing her eyes wide despite the painful glow. "And it's not something anyone will ever see again."

"Let's hope so," Finn sighed. "And let's hope that the last Reznikovs were on that thing when it blew.

Scraps straightened up, standing as tall as his little legs would allow, then the robot saluted sharply.

"Bye-bye, Chiefy," Scraps said. "Thank you."

Finn shuffled in his seat and wrestled with his harness so that he could turn to face the glowing remains of Nimbus. He shot up a salute, or the best imitation of one he could remember. Elara did the same.

"Goodbye, Chiefy," Finn said, bidding farewell to the robot who had displayed more humanity in his short life than any actual human being that Finn had ever met. "And thank you," he added, solemnly. "Thank you for Earth."

25

HURRY UP

An alarm blared inside the evacuation pod, snapping Finn back to the sobering reality that they were still hurtling through space in a metal box, on a crash course for Earth. After winning his trial, Finn's incredible journey from Prosecutor of Zavetgrad to rebel leader and revolutionary had exposed him to countless alarms, each one instilling a sense of dread. The alarm blaring at him now beat them all.

Warning, objects on collision course. The computer announced in a robotic voice. *Recommend evasive action.*

"What objects?" Finn said, turning to Scraps for the answer. The little robot then pointed to the glowing remains of Nimbus.

"Space junk!" Scraps said. "Traveling fast!"

The explosive power of twenty-four nuclear missiles had reduced Nimbus mostly to dust, but parts of the station had escaped being atomized in the nuclear fire, and been propelled into space, in every direction, including theirs.

"Can we maneuver to avoid this junk?" Finn said. If ever there was a time he wanted Scraps to nod and smile, it was now, but the robot shook his head, and Finn's rollercoaster ride of emotions continued. "Then what can we do?" he asked, somewhat desperately.

"Nothing!" Scraps said with a shrug. "Twenty seconds to atmosphere. Move now, we dead!"

"But if we don't get out of the way of this flying junk then we're dead too!" Finn said, not understanding why Scraps wasn't already back at the controls, ducking and weaving the evacuation pod through space.

"Move... dead for sure," Scraps explained, wagging a finger at Finn. "Not move... might live!"

"And those are our only two options?" Finn said, deeply unimpressed by the little robot's answer. "Die, or might die?"

Elara then did something that Finn could never have anticipated. She laughed.

"Sit back and relax," Elara said, resting her throbbing head ahead the cushioned padding of the seat. "All we can do is ride it out and hope our luck holds."

Finn felt like continuing his protest, if only to release the frustration that was pent up inside him like magma in a volcano, but he realized there was no point. Elara was right, and so was Scraps. Their survival was now in the hands of cosmic forces. Perhaps, Finn wondered, it always had been.

He suddenly realized that his body was being pressed more firmly against his seat harness, as if some invisible hand was trying to shove him out of the chair. Through the porthole window closest to the front of the spacecraft, he noticed that their view of the blue planet was now tinted red.

"Deceleration," Scraps explained. "We hit atmosphere."

The evacuation pod began to shake as friction buffeted the craft. Finn tried to force his breathing into a more regular rhythm, but the truth was he was terrified. Elara reached across and took his hand, shooting him a quick smile. If she was also scared then she was hiding it well, as she always did.

"Heat shield holding!" Scraps said. The robot was finally back at the control station, examining the readings from the evacuation pod's sensors. "We okay!"

Finn nodded then tried to concentrate his attention on the stars outside, rather than the flames that were steadily encroaching around the ship. Streaks of light began to flash past, like rockets in a firework display, and he focused on them, finding the chaotic pattern to be oddly soothing, until he realized what the streaks of light were, and panic flooded his gut again.

"Missed!" Scraps said, pointing to the streaks, which were actually fragments of Nimbus.

"Thank fuck for that," Finn said. It was like standing in front of a firing squad and hoping that every single one of the soldiers missed.

Scraps then pointed toward what remained of Nimbus. "More coming though," he said, less brightly.

"You could have kept that part to yourself," Finn replied. He didn't know how much more of the torment he could take.

The buffeting grew more intense and the forces acting on Finn's body increased sharply. It was like he was in a skycar piloted by Lieutenant Thorne, while she was throwing the craft around to avoid incoming fire.

"Entry interface!" Scraps called out, now having to shout to be heard. "Altitude, seventy five miles!"

Finn had no idea whether being seventy-five miles above the surface of the Earth was a good thing or not. All he knew was that they were getting closer to the ground. A sharp clank rang out inside the cabin and Finn glanced over his shoulder to see more space debris rocketing in their direction. Something had hit them and taken a gouge out of the craft's armor, but it was still flying, and still in one piece.

"We okay!" Scraps yelled. "Close one!"

"Too close," Finn called back. "What happens next?"

Scraps pointed to the forward section of the spacecraft, but Finn could only see red. Earth, if they were still heading toward it, was entirely obscured by flames.

"Peak heating!" Scraps shouted.

"What does that mean?" Finn yelled back.

"It means we either make it through the atmosphere in one piece, or we cook," Elara shouted. She was squeezing his hand a lot more tightly now, and Finn could practically take her pulse by the throb of the veins in her neck.

Warning, ablative heat shields at forty percent.

Finn gritted his teeth and waited. There was nothing else he could do.

Warning, ablative heat shields at thirty percent.

More debris raced past and the capsule was hit again, but the same forces that were turning the escape pod into a superheated lump of metal were also eroding the debris, and what little had got through lacked the mass to do any significant damage.

Warning, ablative heat shields at twenty percent. Critical failure imminent.

"Scraps!" Finn called out, but the little robot simply smiled at him and held up an "okay" sign with mechanical thumb and forefinger.

Warning, ablative heat shields at seventeen percent. Critical failure imminent.

Finn pressed his teeth together so tightly he thought they might crack under the pressure. The ship continued to shake like a belly dancer and the fire outside turned the cabin a blood red. Then the view through the windows suddenly cleared and Finn saw dark clouds instead of swirling flames. The spacecraft jolted from side to side, and Finn watched as Scraps wrestled with the controls. Thrusters fired and the pod reorientated. Then light burst in through the windows, and at last, Finn could see ground beneath them. It was little more than a frozen, mostly dead wasteland, and on any other occasion, Finn would not have welcomed the prospect of landing beyond Zavetgrad's tall fence, but all he wanted now was to feel solid Earth beneath his feet.

Approaching parachute deployment altitude, the computer voice announced. *Brace, brace, brace...*

Finn grabbed his harness then sheets of white material bloomed above them, and the pod decelerated rapidly, jolting him against the straps, which cut into his already battered and bruised flesh. Multiple parachutes deployed and filled with air, each one forcing the pod to swing violently in a different direction, making Finn feel nauseous and disoriented. Finally, the capsule leveled out and the strain on his body ebbed away like heat escaping beneath his old apartment door in the Metalhaven tenement block where he'd lived most of his life.

"We okay!" Scraps said, abandoning the controls and climbing up onto Elara's lap. She put her hand on the robot. Her other was still gripping Finn's tightly.

"Shouldn't you be flying this thing?" Finn asked.

"Course set," Scraps said, nuzzling into Elara like a cat. "Now, we wait!"

Finn waited, but he didn't have to wait long. In only a few minutes, the evacuation pod had dropped low enough to make out details on the ground. Finn could see the little village that he and General Riley's squad had passed through before entering the caves beneath Zavetgrad, and from his high aerial vantage, he could also see that it hadn't been the only one. Dozens of similar villages pockmarked the landscape, all evidence of humanity's struggle for survival. A struggle that all of them had lost.

Then a gust of wind spun the pod around and Finn saw Zavetgrad for the first time since he and Elara had blasted off from the city at the top of the Nimbus Solaris II rocket. For all its many faults, Zavetgrad alone had refused to succumb to the freezing temperatures and radiation-polluted skies. If anything could be said in favor of Gideon Alexander Reznikov it was that he'd built the city to last, but it wasn't the president who was responsible for humanity's survival inside its walls. That was down to the enduring will of its people, no matter whether they were blues from Seahaven or chromes from Metalhaven. The people had endured, and Finn knew in his bones that they would endure for centuries more to come, in spite of Reznikov's dire predictions otherwise.

"It doesn't look any different from up here," Elara commented. "Metalhaven, Seedhaven, Volthaven... they all look the same."

"If the Metals haven't taken over those sectors yet, they soon will," Finn said. "The Authority is gone. If the golds that are still alive have any sense, they'll realize it's over."

"Or, maybe not," Elara said.

She tapped Finn on the shoulder and pointed through a window on the opposite side to where Zavetgrad was fast approaching. Finn released his harness, which seemed unnecessary now, and climbed up onto the seat. It took him a moment, then he spotted a long convoy of Authority gold ground cars exiting Zavetgrad through the south gate from Makehaven. The electrified fence appeared to have been deactivated.

"Are they fleeing, or did Trip and Briggs let them go?" Finn wondered out loud.

"I doubt that very much," Elara said, and Finn knew she was right. The two rebel leaders were not the benevolent types. "But I think I know who did."

Elara pointed through one of the boxy windows that was aimed toward Zavetgrad, and Finn shuffled his position again to get a clearer view. Landed in the Authority sector, and on rooftops surrounding the capital, were dozens of skycars, but none of them belonged to the now defunct ruling class of Zavetgrad.

"Pen…" Finn said, suddenly realizing who would have sanctioned such a merciful act. "Well, she always was the forgiving kind."

"If it was down to me, I'd string up every last gold by their necks, and hang them between tenements buildings in each sector, like wet socks."

Finn raised an eyebrow and examined Elara's cold, hard expression, but there was no suggestion she was joking.

"Maybe it's a good job it's not up to you then," he said.

Elara shot him a dirty look and he held up his hands in submission. "I don't mean anything by it, only that we're too close to this to be objective. Perhaps what this world needs less of is rough justice. We've seen enough of that. Maybe a little compassion will go a long way."

Elara snorted then returned to watching the convoy. If the escape capsule had been armed with missiles or guns, Finn felt sure that she would have altered course and strafed the convoy until it was burning just as brightly as Nimbus had done.

"Landing soon!" Scraps said, cheerfully.

The parachutes suddenly detached and fluttered away in the wind, but the evacuation pod didn't drop like a stone. Instead, the whoosh of retrorockets firing filled the cabin, robbing it of the calming silence that had persisted during their slow descent. Then the windows were obscured by huge cushions that inflated in the blink of an eye. Finn returned to his seat and grabbed the arms of the chair. Seconds later, there was a hard thump, then the cushions deflated like punctured tires and the stillness resumed, punctuated only by the rasping sound of Finn's breath, and the *plink, plink* of metal panels rapidly cooling in the sub-zero temperatures outside.

"We home!" Scraps called out, waving his hands in the air.

The hatch through which they had last seen Chiefy exploded outward and went cartwheeling across the rocky, snow-covered terrain. Freezing air blew inside, and Finn shivered. The shock of the arctic weather felt like being doused in ice-cold water. He got up and moved to the open hatch, with Elara at his side. They could see Zavetgrad in the near distance, no more than four or five hundred meters away. Ground cars were already headed in their direction.

"Looks like we have a welcoming committee enroute," Finn said, as he climbed outside. Snow crunched beneath his boots.

Elara followed and Finn noted that Scraps was now clamped to her shoulder. She sucked in a deep breath of air then coughed bitterly as the cold tightened her throat and made her choke.

"I've missed this," she said, still wheezing.

"I haven't," Finn replied, still shivering. Elara narrowed her eyes at him, and he shrugged. "Okay, maybe I have, a little."

Finn caught the sound of a low growl in the wind, and he checked the rocks around their landing site, feeling a familiar sense of foreboding. Then he saw the beasts, slowly stalking toward them. Mutagenic lupus, or mutated wolves. He'd come across them before, and on that occasion, the monsters had not gone away hungry.

"We might be in trouble," Finn said, pointing out the pack of six mutant animals to Elara, but unlike him, she wasn't concerned.

Elara pulled her axe from its stow on her armor then faced down the pack leader, which had moved out into the open, curious to learn what its prospective meal was doing. The wolf howled then Elara then let out a howl of her own, while clashing her axe against her chest plate, sending sparks flying into the air all around her. It was so sudden and unexpectedly terrifying that Finn forgot all about the wolves, and worried whether his partner had gone mad. The wolves appeared to share Finn's concern. The lead beast sniffed the air for a few seconds, then released a long, low growl and bared its teeth.

"Come on!" Elara shouted, cursing into the wind. "Try it, I fucking dare you!"

The mutagenic lupus growled again, then to Finn's astonishment, it slowly wheeled around and led its pack away toward the setting sun, and into the encroaching darkness. In that moment, the mutant wolf had proved itself smarter than one hundred percent of the fools who had chosen not to run when The Shadow had faced them down.

A growl of another kind filled the air, but it was the mechanical growl of a ground car motor, rather than the guttural snarl of a wolf. Three of them pulled up in front of the evacuation pod, and it was only then that Finn realized they were special prefect vehicles. He reached for a weapon, but found that he had nothing. Then the side door on the lead ground car was thrown open, and a familiar face appeared inside it.

Principal Penelope Everhart stepped out into the snow and shivered. She was smothered by an enormous greatcoat that, judging by the orange patch on its shoulder, had once belonged to the Head Prefect of Stonehaven. Beneath the coat, Pen was still dressed in her usual suit and the same court shoes that she'd worn in Haven. Both were wildly inappropriate given their arctic setting. Finn and Elara approached the woman and stopped a few meters away. Neither knew what to do next. Pen scowled at them both then threw her arms out wide.

"Well, hurry up and get into the damned car, already!" Pen called out. "It's freezing out here!"

26
REGENT HOPE

The principal's motorcade drove into the Authority sector and cheers erupted all around them, as if there were bombs falling. Finn and Elara were in the lead car with Pen. Scraps was scrambling around the tops of the seats, moving from window to window and waving at the seemingly endless lines of people who had gathered on the streets, or who were hanging out of apartment block windows, to celebrate their return. The fact that there were workers inside the Authority sector was remarkable enough, but it was the total lack of prefects that shook Finn the most. Not long ago, the oppressive police officers would have viciously beaten any worker who'd dared to sully the golden streets of the capital. Now, there wasn't a single prefect to be seen, anywhere.

"I can't get used to the fact the prefects have all gone," Finn said. It was too momentous for him to let pass without comment. "Is it like this in every sector?"

Pen nodded and smiled. She'd removed the enormous greatcoat, since the inside of the skycar was as warm as Haven.

"The days of prefects patrolling the streets with electrified batons is over," Pen confirmed. "Most left with the convoy you saw departing Zavetgrad, but some chose to stay, and face the repercussions of their actions."

"What will happen to them?" Finn wondered.

"There will be hearings, trials if you will, where we'll assess their crimes, and judge them accordingly," Pen said. "Before the Last War destroyed civilization, many countries had functioning legal systems. Some of those texts survived, and formed the basis of the legal system we adopted in Haven. In fact, our laws are based on the legal system of a country called Sweden, though I confess to knowing absolutely nothing about the people of that nation."

Finn huffed. "It never occurred to me that you might need a legal system. I guess I imagined Haven as a paradise, free from the problems of our past."

"We're still human beings, Finn, and still flawed," Pen said. "Haven's citizens aren't immune to lapses of judgement, or acts driven by anger and passion. But, so far, the level of crime that we've had to contend with has been minor." She gestured to the crowds waving at them. "Now we have a million more people to consider, and a great many of them are very troubled individuals. It would be naïve to think that Zavetgrad can just become a utopia, where no-one acts against their neighbor."

Finn nodded and Soren Driscoll instantly came to mind. His old adversary might have redeemed himself by becoming a soldier of Haven and fighting for freedom, but Soren was exactly the kind of troubled individual that Pen had been talking about, and he wasn't the only one. Once the dust settled, and the celebrations ended, life would have to go on. That would mean restarting the factories and farms and power stations, so that Zavetgrad's infrastructure didn't collapse. Finn knew there would be tensions. Not everyone would want to go back to work, doing the same job that they'd slaved at for a decades or more, even if the conditions were vastly improved. There would be unrest, and there would need to be a way to manage it, but those were problems for the future, Finn told himself. And they were problems that he was more than happy to allow Pen and her staff to deal with. For his part, he was done with conflict. Whatever came next for Finn Brasa, he didn't want to fight anymore.

"You should execute them and be done with it," Elara said.

Her sudden interjection and ice-cold analysis shocked both Finn and Pen, and both simply looked at her, wide eyed.

"It doesn't matter that these prefects suddenly developed a conscience, they're guilty," Elara continued, since her shocking statement had gone unchallenged. "You can convene a court and hear their cases, but it won't change what they did, or who they are. Granting them mercy will only enrage the people who suffered abuse at their hands." Elara then turned to Pen and the two women stared at each other with their equally intense green eyes. "Justice has to be done, and be seen to be done. Otherwise, petty crime will be the least of your troubles."

"That sort of justice is how the Authority did things," Pen answered, calmly. "I have a different point of view."

"That's because you never lived here," Elara said. She was angry but it was contained. "If you had done, then you wouldn't, not for one second, consider letting these monsters live."

Pen thought this over and appeared to acknowledge Elara's point, but just like her dogged genetic daughter, she was not easily swayed. "Perhaps that's why it needs to be Haven who oversees the transition," she countered. "Your anger is still too raw."

"My anger is why I'm still alive," Elara said.

"But you don't need it now," Pen cut it. "You've won, Elara. The Authority is gone, never to return. Now, it's time to begin healing."

Elara shook her head. "It was a mistake to let the prefects leave. You might be all about forgiveness, but they're not. They're golds. They'll always consider themselves better than us, and they won't forget that we took this city from them."

"Maybe you're right," Pen admitted. "But first they'll have to survive outside the wall, and that will occupy all of their energies for many years to come."

"If they survive, they'll want revenge," Elara said.

"Or maybe they'll want to come home," Pen countered. "Either way, it will be their choice." Pen leaned forward, as if reducing the physical distance between her and Elara might also narrow the gaps in their ideologies. "Choice is what the Authority stole from you, and countless others like you, over more than two-hundred and sixty years. I'm not the Authority, Elara. I want people to make their own choices, for better or worse."

"I think you're wrong," Elara said, unmoved.

"For all our sakes, I hope I'm not," Pen answered, smiling. "But these are problems for another time. Right now, we need to celebrate your astonishing achievement."

While they had been talking, Pen's ground car and its motorcade had driven into the Authority central square, and was pulling up in front of the former mayor's buildings. A raised platform had been set up, ready for them to address the thousands of people who had squeezed into the square to see them. It reminded Finn of a trial day and an uneasiness crept through him, like a chill on a cold winter night.

"Is this really necessary?" he said.

"Ever the reluctant hero," Pen replied, still smiling. "I appreciate that you may not relish the spotlight, but the people need an outlet for their joy, and you are its focal point. It won't always be so, at least not like this."

Finn sighed then glanced at Elara, who looked even more reluctant to exit the ground car than he did.

"Then I guess we should get this over with," he said. "Then maybe I can have a shower and a pint."

"Hopefully, not at the same time," Pen said, still trying her best to keep the mood light, despite Elara's scathing response to the principal's acts of benevolence toward the authoritarian golds.

The door was thrown open and Finn saw Lieutenant Thornfield, newly raised to Colonel, standing outside. General Riley had given Thornfield the task of guarding the principal, during the special prefecture's attack on Haven, and the man remained dutifully by Pen's side.

Finn stepped out of the car and was almost blown back into his seat by an explosion of noise that suddenly erupted all around the central square. It felt like being hit by a strong gust of wind. Elara stepped out next, with Scraps on her shoulder, and the noise grew to a near deafening level. It was even louder than the din that had assaulted them inside the space capsule as friction with the atmosphere threatened to shake the pod to pieces.

"Colonel," Finn shouted, nodding to the officer.

"Major," Thornfield replied, still using the rank that Riley had given to Finn. "It's good to see you again."

"You too, Colonel," Finn said, and the two men shook hands.

Colonel Thornfield then turned to Elara and nodded. The officer considered also offering her his hand, but hesitated then finally chose caution. Finn understood the man's reticence. To Thornfield, Elara was still The Shadow, and to even be in her presence would have felt like standing next to an unexploded bomb.

Hundreds of fireworks streaked into the sky, launched from the rooftops of the surrounding buildings, then exploded in a chaotic melee of crackling sparks. There was red, silver, purple, orange, blue, white, rusty brown and green. Every sector was represented, apart from one. Gold was absent, and not by mistake. For almost three centuries, gold had ranked above all colors, and had been worn by a privileged few. Not any longer.

Finn followed Pen and Colonel Thornfield onto the podium that had been set out for them. Up on the platform, without ground cars or the mass of bodies in the crowd to shield him from the sound, the cheers were even louder. Pen and the Colonel stayed back, careful to ensure that Finn and Elara remained in the spotlight. Pen did not wave to the crowd, or try to use the occasion to grandstand and increase her own fame and public profile. She could not have been more different to the regents who had come before her, and whether Finn entirely agreed with her philosophies or not, he was glad of this at least.

Suddenly exposed to the full energy of the gathering, Finn

felt like he should do something other than simply stand in awe of the occasion, so he chose to nervously raise a fist and shake it, triumphantly. The gesture resulted in a thunderous ovation that shook the wooden boards beneath his feet to the point where he feared the podium might collapse from under them. Elara pumped her fist too, and so did Scraps – the little robot was reveling in the occasion – and a chant of "Metal and Blood" started up from somewhere in the middle of the crowd. It caught on quickly and before long the words were resonating with such power that Finn wondered if it might even have been possible to hear it across the Davis Strait in Haven.

It was while the chant was building that Finn noticed the golds, because they were the only people not singing. Still dressed in their everyday finery, the privileged former members of the Authority were out on the street like the workers, but cordoned off into a separate area that was guarded by a line of foremen. At first, Finn thought that the robots were there to make sure the golds didn't scurry off back to their luxury condos, until he realized the machines were actually lined up for their protection. Surrounded on all sides by workers from Stonehaven and Volthaven, the golds were being subjected to a barrage of verbal abuse, plus the odd lump of moldy algae bread.

It could be worse... Finn thought, grateful that the mob hadn't chosen to push through the line of foremen and tear the golds to pieces with their bare hands.

"Would you like to say a few words?" Pen asked, directing Finn to a lectern that had a microphone set up ready.

"I think this is more your arena than mine," Finn said. He

looked at Elara, not wanting to speak for her, but she vigorously shook her head.

"They're all yours, principal," Elara said.

Pen nodded then approached the lectern and raised her hands. The chant died down, and Finn was impressed with how quickly Pen had managed to control the crowd. It was like they already knew and trusted her.

"People of Zavetgrad, this is an historic occasion," Pen began, and her voice boomed through speakers all around the square. "It has been a long and hard road, but I never doubted for one second that this day would come. Your fighting spirit and desire for change and freedom was always within you. All that was needed to release it was a spark."

Pen gestured to Finn and Elara and thousands of eyes fell upon them, expectantly.

"And here they stand," Pen continued. "You know them as the Heroes of Metalhaven, but Finn Brasa and Elara Cage are so much more than that. Thanks to their courage, Nimbus has been destroyed, and the Authority has fallen."

The crowd roared, and the noise of thousands of people shouting and stomping their feet shook the frozen ground like an earthquake. Finn remembered how much of Zavetgrad was built above an underground lake and river system, and he half expected the city to be swallowed up in a giant sink hole.

"Thanks to Finn and Elara, and to your own courage, Zavetgrad is now free, and able to embark on a new chapter," Pen continued, raising her voice almost to a shout to be heard over the tumult of the crowd. "I won't lie to you and say that this transition will be easy, but it will be nothing compared to the suffering you have all endured for so long. Together, we can build a new Zavetgrad, a new city, where all of us, not just a privileged few, will reap the rewards of our labors." Pen paused then smiled broadly and held up her hands again. "But the future does not begin today. Today, and for however long the recovery centers stay full of ale, we celebrate!" There was an enormous cheer. "We celebrate our freedom. And we celebrate those who have brought it to us!"

Pen stepped back then turned to Finn and Elara and began to applaud. The cry of "Metal and Blood" began again, but this time it was drowned out by the symphonic sound of thousands of voices raised up in song. The tune was vaguely familiar, then Finn spotted the chorus of singers on the far left of the square. It was a body of Seahaven workers, easily distinguished by their waxy blue overalls. More impressive than the shanty itself was the fact that every worker in the choir already had a pint of ale in his or her hand, which only served to make Finn feel thirstier than he already was.

"Let's find a bar," Elara said, ushering Finn toward the steps. "I think this party can continue without us."

"That's the best idea I've heard in a long time," Finn said, hustling away while continuing to smile and pump his fist into the air.

They climbed off the podium then hurried back toward their ground car, past a long line of workers, who shouted and reached out to them, as if they were old-fashioned movie stars from before the collapse of civilization. Half-spilled pints of ale were shoved at him, but Finn didn't care about getting beer splashed onto his armor, and he gratefully downed whatever alcoholic liquids managed to make their way into his hands.

Close to the ground car, Finn spotted Pritchard, his old valet, in the crowd, and he tapped Elara on the shoulder, before working his way toward the man. Then, to his surprise, he saw that Cora, the Spacehaven worker from his trial who had escaped to Haven, was standing beside him.

"So, they finally let you out without a guard?" Finn said, shouting almost at the top of his lungs.

"Yes, though I still have a long way to go to earn everyone's trust," Pritchard called back. The man was wearing Spacehaven white, as was Cora, adopting her old color while back in the city. "I'm glad you made it back in one piece," his old valet added.

"That makes two of us," Finn said, grabbing Pritchard's shoulder and squeezing it.

"Cora is helping me to adjust," Pritchard added, turning to the woman by his side. The expression on his face changed, and it was a look Finn recognized. It was the same look he got whenever Elara walked into the room. "She has been most helpful."

"I'll bet she has!" Finn said, shaking Pritchard more vigorously.

Cora and Pritchard both looked away and the skin on their faces flushed with color, despite the temperature in Zavetgrad holding at a chilly seventeen Fahrenheit, or minus eight on the Celsius scale.

"Would you look at that," Elara said, stealing Finn's attention away from the bashful new couple. "Talk about new beginnings..."

Finn saw an area of the crowd that had been designated for children from the workhouse. It was far less crowded and there were braziers set up to provide warmth, but while it gladdened Finn's heart simply to see the children safe and smiling, they were not alone. With them were hundreds of women from the birthing center, the pink sashes on their overalls clearly setting them apart from every other worker in the city.

"Families reunited?" Finn said, noticing that the women and the children had organized themselves into little cluster groups.

"Not families, not yet at least," Elara said. "They're strangers to one another. But in time, hopefully that will change."

"Sir, do you have a moment?"

It was Colonel Thornfield. With the constant noise from the crowd, Finn hadn't heard the man come up behind him.

"I'm hardly the expert on military protocol, but doesn't a colonel outrank a major?" Finn asked.

"It does, yes." Thornfield replied, looking embarrassed. "But it doesn't seem appropriate for you to call me, 'sir', not after everything you've done."

"Then how about you just call me Finn?"

"Yes, sir," Thornfield replied, and Elara laughed. It was like Pritchard all over again.

"What is it that you wanted, Colonel?" Finn said, trying to jog the man's memory.

"Yes, right..." Thornfield said, ushering Finn further along the line and to another sectioned off part of the crowd. "They said they'd only respond to you, sir," the officer continued, pointing to the young men and women, waiting patiently, with expectant looks on their faces.

"Ah, I see," Finn said. The group of people that Thornfield had led him to were the servants from Elysium. They were all wearing Seahaven overalls. "Yes, I think I can handle this," he said, though he wished he didn't have to.

"Regent Hope..." a woman said, acknowledging Finn whilst also curtseying.

It was the same woman whom Finn had convinced to orchestrate the evacuation from Elysium. Finn had grudgingly adopted the title, Regent Hope, in order to secure her cooperation.

"We did what you asked, my regent," the woman continued, "and now we await your command."

"I told you that you're free," Finn said, taking the woman's hands and standing her up, so that she was no longer bowed before him, like a faithful serf. "You can do whatever you want now. Be whomever you want."

The woman appeared confused. "We want to serve you..."

"No-one is a servant anymore," Finn said. "In this city, you're free, do you understand?"

The woman frowned, clearly not understanding. Finn wasn't surprised. The concept was utterly alien to her, and the people she had helped to rescue.

"Look, how about this," Finn said, trying another approach. "You were all trained and educated to a degree far beyond that of most workers in this city. Zavetgrad will need people to help rebuild its infrastructure, and manage its departments. If you want to serve, then serve Zavetgrad itself."

"And will that please you, Regent Hope?" the woman asked.

Finn shrugged. "It would please me to see you all happy."

"Then if it pleases you, Regent Hope, we shall serve Zavetgrad!" the woman said, before smiling and curtseying again. It wasn't exactly what Finn had meant, but it was a start.

"Your car is ready," Colonel Thornfield said. "Principal Everhart has set aside some quarters for you, inside what was the primary prefect hub close to Metalhaven Reclamation Yard seven. It used to belong to the sector's Head Prefect, a man called Captain Viktor Roth." Thornfield shrugged. "She said you would find that amusing."

Finn laughed. "I do, thank you, Colonel."

The car pulled up alongside them, and with a final wave and fist pump, Finn and Elara slid into the vehicle. The door was closed behind them, but the hefty slab of metal barely did anything to dull the sound of the crowd, which, fueled by hundreds of barrels of ale, and a huge choir of Seahaven voices, had gone into full party mode.

"It doesn't seem right that they still see me as a regent," Finn said. The Elysium servants were still weighing heavy on his mind. "It feels dirty somehow."

"You're being what they need you to be, at least for now," Elara said, unconcerned. "It's a noble act." She nudged him with her shoulder. "You're a noble man, Finn, more so than any hereditary aristocrat that has tried to lay claim to that title in Zavetgrad's fucked-up history."

Finn grinned at Elara. "If I'm a noble, like the princes from ancient stories, then don't I get to pick my bride from anyone in the kingdom?"

Elara laughed then kissed him. "We've already had our fairytale ending," she said, wiping the wetness off his lips with her thumb. "You don't get another."

"Where to, sir?" the driver of the car asked.

Finn rested back in the seat and smiled. "Metalhaven, Reclamation Yard seven," Finn said. "Take us home."

27
FAMILY

Finn and Elara huddled together on top of the gene bank, close to Reclamation Yard four, where the Metals still operated their HQ. It had been twenty-four crazy hours since the celebration in the Authority central square had begun, and still some workers were out partying. For their part, Finn and Elara had slept for most of that time. For Finn, it had been a restful sleep, the first he'd experienced in a long time.

"It still doesn't look any different," Elara said, as they gazed out across the city. The sun was setting, bathing everything in a warm orange glow that belied the freezing temperatures. "But it feels different." She rested her head on his shoulder. "Do you know what I mean?"

"I feel it too," Finn said, and he did.

When he'd been a worker, Finn had always felt tense, like a stretched rubber band. All it would take was to look at a prefect the wrong way, and you could end up in a cell, or beaten and bloodied in the snow. There was never any release from that tension, even in the relative privacy of their pokey tenement block rooms. The menace of the Authority pervaded every aspect of their lives, from dawn till dusk, and now it was gone.

Finn quickly checked on Scraps, and found him soaking up the last of the sun's rays with his solar panels, while perched on the wall overlooking Yard four. For the first time in centuries, it stood unused.

"I'm sorry to interrupt…"

Finn glanced to his rear and saw Trip. He was with Xia, and Finn noticed that her right forearm was cast in plaster. There were other cuts and bruises evident on her face and neck, and Finn imagined that there were many more injuries that he couldn't see. He didn't know what Xia had been through, but after seeing her fight, he was pretty sure that she'd given the Authority's forces hell.

"It's okay, Trip, what do you need?" Finn asked. Then he frowned. "And where's Briggs. You three usually come as trio."

"Ah, well…" Trip said, and the tone of his voice and sudden sagging of his shoulder told Finn everything, without the man needing to say another word. "I'm afraid he didn't make it."

"Fought well," Xia said. She stood tall, but her lips were quivering. "Made us proud."

"I don't doubt it," Finn said.

"I just wanted to see you, and to say thank you in person, before we head out," Trip continued.

"Where are you going?" Finn asked.

"Oh, not too far," Trip said, sensing Finn's concern. "Pen, the principal lady from Haven, has put us in charge of a sector. We leave tonight so we can get set up."

"That's great news, Trip, I have full confidence in your abilities to make that sector the best in the city," Finn said, genuinely happy for the pair. "Which sector is it?"

Trip grinned a little sheepishly. "Makehaven…"

"Makehaven?" Finn laughed. "They put you in charge of producing ale?"

"Not just ale!" Trip protested, and Xia choked down a laugh. "But yes, ale will be pretty high on my list of priorities. The city has to drink, after all!"

"Just so long as you don't drink it all first," Finn said. He took Trip's hand and shook it warmly.

Finn considered giving Xia a hug, but like Thornfield with Elara, the gritty rebel fighter exuded a dangerous aura, and he feared getting too close. Instead, the two simply nodded at each other in a gruff, soldierly way.

As Trip and Xia left, Finn saw Pen and Colonel Thornfield arriving. Pen was again wrapped up in the enormous greatcoat that could have kept two people warm, yet still the principal was managing to shiver from the cold.

"Has it sunk in yet?" Pen said, greeting them both with a warm smile – the only part of her that was warm. "What you've achieved, I mean."

Finn snorted a laugh and shook his head. "Not even remotely."

"Well, there's no rush," Pen said. She moved to Finn's side and looked out across the city. Scraps saw her, then folded up his solar panels and ran over, climbing up the principal's leg and finally planting himself on her shoulder.

"Hi Pen-Pen!" Scraps said, waving at her.

"Hello Scraps, how are you?" Pen said, cheerfully.

"Okay-kay!" Scraps replied. "Nice to be home."

"I'm sure it is," Pen said. "And as I now understand it, we have you to thank for everything. I fear that we may need a second parade, solely in your honor."

Scraps giggled, then quickly became sad. "Not just me. Chiefy too."

"Yes, I'm so sorry about your friend," Pen said, taking a hold of Scraps' hand. "So much loss…"

"It okay!" Scraps replied, suddenly perky again. "Scraps remembers." The little robot tapped his head. "Scraps remembers everything, and everyone."

"What about you, Pen?" Finn asked. "Is Zavetgrad now your home too?"

"I like to think of home as being the place where I can do the most good," Pen replied, somewhat cryptically. "For now, Zavetgrad is home, but the process of reconciliation will not be easy. For some, it will not be possible at all. But we must try to be better than those that came before us. The process of healing starts now, and it will take decades, and generations."

Suddenly, Finn could hear Ivan Volkov in his head, warning him of a bleak and uncertain future.

The number of genetically viable babies born has been reducing year-on-year since the city was founded. Ivan had told him. *In ten years, there will be no-one with a Genetic Rating of five. In twenty-five, the highest will be a Genetic Rating of three. In fifty years, everyone will be sterile, and no medical intervention will work.*

"We may not have that long…" Finn said, ominously.

Finn recounted what Ivan had told him and Elara inside the space capsule that had ferried them to Nimbus. The principal listened attentively, not interrupting.

"Our scientists have seen this data," Pen said. The fact she was not surprised by what Finn had revealed somehow gave him comfort. "But it's a pessimistic view of the future, that doesn't take into account humanity's incredible capacity for healing. We're far stronger than weasels like Ivan Volkov believed."

Finn laughed. "What the hell is a weasel?"

Pen frowned and waved off the question, choosing instead to focus on more important matters. "Haven has been working on the 'survival problem' for decades, and now we have the entire resources of this city at our disposal," she continued." She paused and spent a moment to soak in the view of the sunset, as glorious as any sunset a human being had ever seen. "No, this city – this planet – won't die. I won't let it."

She breathed in a lungful of the icy air then turned to Finn and Elara. There was a mischievous twinkle in her eye, and it made Finn feel uncomfortable.

"Speaking of the future, as two bona-fide double fives, we'll need your help to begin the process of repopulating the city," Pen said.

"Fuck that," Finn snapped, and Pen jolted back in surprise. "No-one is sticking a needle in my balls ever again."

Pen scowled at him, like a disappointed mother. "I was thinking of a more natural process of conception..." she said, nodding toward Elara, not at all subtly.

"Oh..." Finn said, embarrassed. "Right..."

"Have you thought about children?" Pen said, not holding back on asking the big questions.

He scrunched up his nose then looked skyward. For once,

the looming presence of Nimbus was missing, but he knew that there was still something up there, circling the planet.

"Funnily enough, we've both thought a lot about what our children might be like," Finn said, thinking of Adam and Eve, the Prefects Alpha and Omega.

"Really?" Pen said, with an eyebrow raise that was exactly like Elara's. "Well, I sense there's a story there for another time."

Colonel Thornfield coughed politely, and Pen glanced at the officer, who tapped his wrist, to indicate that their time was over.

"Duty calls…" she said, sighing with disappointment.

Scraps, sensing that his perch was about to walk away, jumped from the principal's shoulder and landed on Finn's instead. Pen then moved in front of Elara and took her hands into her own, without displaying any of the fear that others showed around the infamous Shadow.

"I look forward to spending more time with you, Elara," Pen said, and it was deeply heartfelt. "I know that right now all we share is DNA, but in time, I hope truly hope that we will become something more."

Elara, surprisingly, smiled. "I do too."

Pen then pulled Elara toward her and wrapped her arms around her body. Elara resisted at first, then gradually eased into the embrace, before finally the two woman were hugging each other so tightly that Finn was surprised that either of them could breathe. Finally, Pen drew back, planted a kiss onto Elara's cheek, wiped away a curious red smudge that had been left behind, before nodding to Finn, and heading off to rejoin her colonel.

A tear rolled down Elara's cheek and she brushed it away

aggressively before spinning around and facing what remained of the sunset, in the hope that Finn hadn't noticed. It crossed his mind to make a joke, as that was his go to response in awkward situations, but this time he held back. Elara needed to appreciate the moment, not have it trivialized.

"Scraps likes Pen," Scraps said. "She nice-nice!"

"Yes, she is," Finn said. He put his arm around Elara, and she reciprocated, hugging him closer.

"We did it, Finn," Elara said, whispering the words like it was a secret. "The Authority is gone. The city is free."

"I love you."

Elara turned to him, wide-eyed.

"I never got the chance to say it back," Finn said. Then he grinned. "You know, while you were trying to heroically sacrifice yourself, and before Chiefy whacked you on the head, and bundled you into the evacuation pod." He shrugged, trying to play it cool. "But I thought you should know."

"Good," Elara said, nodding vigorously as a way to hide her awkwardness. "Well, I'm glad we agree."

"Scraps too?" the little robot said, working his way between Finn and Elara so that he was perched on both of their shoulders.

"Of course, we love you too, pal!" Finn said, ruffling the robot's nonexistent hair.

"Then we family!" Scraps said, settling himself down, and playing with their hair.

"Family," Elara said, nodding.

"Family," Finn agreed.

The sun finally dipped below the horizon, but Zavetgrad's darkest days were behind it. Finn Brasa and Elara

Cage, the Heroes of Metalhaven, had broken the Authority's iron grip over Earth's last city, and heralded the dawn of a new age.

An age of Metal and Blood.

The end.

YOU MADE IT!

Thank you for reading the Metal & Blood series, I hope you enjoyed the story! Turn to the next page to learn about some of my other books, including Kindle Storyteller Award Winner, Forsaken Commander.

ALSO BY G J OGDEN

Sa'Nerra Universe

Omega Taskforce

Descendants of War

Scavenger Universe

Star Scavengers

Star Guardians

Standalone series

The Aternien Wars *(Kindle Storyteller Award Winner)*

The Contingency War

Darkspace Renegade

The Planetsider Trilogy

G J Ogden's newsletter: Click here to sign-up

ABOUT THE AUTHOR

At school, I was asked to write down the jobs I wanted to do as a "grown up". Number one was astronaut and number two was a PC games journalist. I only managed to achieve one of those goals (I'll let you guess which), but these two very different career options still neatly sum up my lifelong interests in science, space, and the unknown.

School also steered me in the direction of a science-focused education over literature and writing, which influenced my decision to study physics at Manchester University. What this degree taught me is that I didn't like studying physics and instead enjoyed writing, which is why you're reading this book! The lesson? School can't tell you who you are.

When not writing, I enjoy spending time with my family, playing Warhammer 40K, and indulging in as much Sci-Fi as possible.

Printed in Great Britain
by Amazon